The End of August

PART THREE

Rue Volley

Book design by Rue Volley
Additional graphics by Rue Volley
Interior Design by Dreams2Media
Editing by Lily Luchesi

Published by Rue Volley Books LLC
www.ruevolley.com

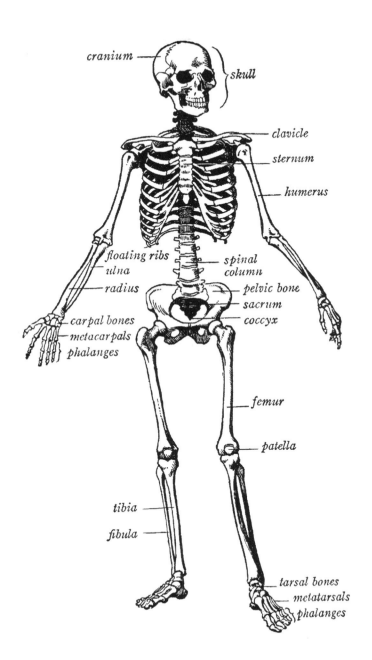

cranium

skull

clavicle

sternum

humerus

floating ribs
ulna

spinal
column

radius

pelvic bone

sacrum

coccyx

carpal bones

metacarpals

phalanges

femur

patella

tibia

fibula

tarsal bones

metatarsals

phalanges

Always For Love.

This book is written from TWO points of view. Each chapter has the character's name (**August East or Keller West**) at the beginning of it to avoid any confusion. Please pay attention to each change. Sometimes the character will have two or more chapters in a row.

CHAPTER ONE

AUGUST EAST

Keller leans into me. His legs are weak. I hold on to him, navigating a path to the overstuffed armchair, silently urging him to sit down. My gaze lowers to his arm. A small trickle of blood is all that's left behind from a life-giving IV that's been nursing him for nearly a month. He clearly tore it out in a hurry. My brow furrows. I kneel, studying his expression. Searching his eyes. He's lost some weight. But that undeniable spark remains, because he's *Keller West.* I don't believe anything, or anyone, could extinguish it.

I settle into his presence. I've missed him more than I care to explain. If the room were empty, I'd kiss his beautiful lips, hold his hand, comfort him as I should, but I'm trapped here in this stark reality that what we share isn't easily expressed in public. Although I'm sure no one would object in this room. I'm still fearful, which is new for me. I hate it.

His sunken eyes add to my guilt.

What have I done? How selfish am I? He saved me, and how did I repay him? By allowing myself to—well—I—I can't even think about it, let alone say it.

I catch Shy staring at the two of us. She rubs the side of her neck. Her uneasiness, and mine, won't be enough to erase what we've done. I part my lips. I can feel her panic from across the room. It's spreading like poison.

I'd never tell him this way but he must be told. I promise myself I will as soon as he regains his strength. I hope I'm not making excuses, but telling him I—that Shy—that we—well, I don't think telling him now is the right time. Not while he's swaying on his feet from a months-long coma—not to mention, Maggie is lying face down in the room. Dead.

She's dead, isn't she?

The entire room flinches in unison when a ghostly moan breaks through the stunned silence. I rise as the pale fingers flex. A ring-heavy hand slams on top of the table. Vincent lifts a leg and screams.

"Jesus, Mary and Joseph!" Evie exclaims while crossing herself. I never took her for someone who believed in all of that, but maybe it explains why she's so obsessed with ghosts.

2

A raspy voice draws my attention, "That was unpleasant." Maggie grips the side of the table, regaining her composure. She tilts her head to the right and cracks her neck. It seems to ease some of her discomfort. She tilts it to the left and then rolls her shoulders. More bones seem to align.

The room is speechless. Keller stands, using the armrest as a support to stabilize his weakened legs. He takes a few steps toward her and Maggie's eyes spark with recognition.

My expression switches from concern to confusion. She steps around the table and places a hand to the side of his arm, offering a reassuring nod.

"Welcome back." Her eyes spark with joy.

I narrow my eyes, exchanging a curious look with Shy, who is as confused as the rest of us.

"Maggie?" Evie asks, holding her mic up with a trembling hand. Even she, the queen of the macabre, is shaken by what we all witnessed.

Maggie steps to the side and offers a gentle grin.

"Hello, Evie—oh!" she acknowledges all of us. "It seems we have a team assembled here." She scans the room and shakes her head before trying to adjust the messy ball of hair atop her head. "I apologize for the state of things. It's never this disheveled." Her eyes scan the room.

"Um—what the hell is going on?!" the color drains from Vincent's face.

"Mmm, well. It's difficult and not all at the same time."

"I'm ready." Evie steadies the mic. I have to hand it to her. She's recovered expeditiously.

"Oh, my sweet girl. This isn't something the world should know—not just yet."

Evie scowls, lowering the mic, before biting her pouty lip. She turns off the recorder.

"But, I promise, you'll have exclusive rights to all of it as soon as all of it is done."

"All of what? And done? What's done?" Vincent lifts his arms and lets them fall at his sides.

Maggie tilts her head with a grin, reaching in to take Vincent's hand. He's reluctant to move, but she pulls him along, adjusting the chair by the table and insisting he sit down. She taps his shoulder as his chest continues to rise and fall.

"As you know, I'm a psychic—to some, this seems to be a mere parlor trick, but it isn't. And on this night, it's proven much more important than I could've ever imagined. My place here—in Whynot —has always been important. Regardless of the year, or time, or situation. I'm bound to this place as much as it's bound to me." Maggie's gaze settles on Keller, then me, like she's including us. Her expression softens.

"You—you were dead." Vincent stutters while pointing at the floor where her body lay when we entered the room.

4

"I'm sure it seemed that way, but truth be told, I had to go to the edge of all things to retrieve something of extreme importance."

"What?" Evie asks.

Maggie's eyes spark with success. "Why, your friend, Keller West."

Vincent laughs, but it soon dies out when Maggie flashes him a look.

"He was in a coma." Vincent fidgets on the edge of the chair, seemingly ready to run at a moment's notice.

"Yes, he was, but I was able to contact him in between."

"In between what?" Evie asks.

Maggie lets out a sigh, straightening her things. Obviously, she doesn't like a mess.

"In between what?" I repeat, hoping she'll answer.

She pauses while staring at the card on the table. She lifts it, flipping it over in her hand.

"Life and death."

"Come on!" Vincent rises, ready to leave. I think he's had enough.

Keller speaks up, "No—it's true. She did. Maggie is the reason I'm here. She showed me the way back to Whynot—to all of you. I don't think I would've woken up without her help."

5

His bright blue eyes pierce me. I'm filled with an uneasy guilt that's eating away at everything.

"So, you saw her in your—whatever you call it?" Vincent asks.

Keller nods, "It was—I don't know, like an endless dream, but so real. I could smell, taste—" he glances at me, "feel. It was so real but the whole time I knew something was off—wrong, but Maggie, she found me and I listened to her, or I wouldn't be here."

Vincent's mouth sits agape. He wants to discredit him, but how can we when Keller is sitting right here in front of us? It's nothing short of a miracle.

"Well—I'm so glad," Shy offers while moving in and wrapping her arms around his waist. She closes her eyes and melts into him. Her show of affection nearly angers me. It should be me standing in her place, but maybe she's doing the three of us a favor. It's not like I can tell him what's happened while he was fighting for his life.

I'm such an idiot.

Selfish. Ridiculous. Weak.

I placed my needs over his after he *saved* my life. I know he'll never want to speak to me again once he knows the truth, and it's only a matter of time. The truth always finds a way. Always.

I look up and catch Maggie staring at me. Her

6

expression is peculiar, like she's trying to see through my façade. It forces my stomach to churn.

"You have such beautiful eyes. One green, one hazel. So unique. Unforgettable, really."

"I don't know if my eyes are really that important." My nerves and agitation get the better of me as Shy continues to comfort Keller.

"Do you dream?" she asks.

I'm immediately drawn back to Maggie, "Sometimes."

"Of flame and ash?"

My throat feels dry so I reach up to rub it. "I think Keller should get checked out, don't you think?"

Shy backs away with a nod. "Yes, you should get checked out, Keller. You probably shouldn't be walking around like this."

"Are you kidding me? I feel better than I've ever felt in my life."

"You just—you were in a coma, Keller," Vincent clarifies.

"I know, but trust me, I'm good." He flexes his once injured hand. "Better than good. Great."

Maggie grins. "That's so good to hear because we have a lot to do."

"What?" Evie asks.

A silence settles in the room as Maggie speaks, "Something dark has come to Whynot, something

7

with evil intent, something that wants to destroy everything we hold dear, and it'll be up to us to send it back to where it came from—all of us."

We all share looks as we gather in a loose circle. The team properly assembled for what seems to be the first time. But not the last.

CHAPTER TWO

KELLER WEST

I sit on the step, gathering my thoughts and trying to make sense of things, but I'm not sure I really can. Flashes of memory flutter across my mind's eye.

Laughter.

His face.

His lips against mine.

A football in my hand.

The smell of food on the table.

My grandmother's voice.

Christmas morning.

I blink it away as a familiar warmth settles against my side. East has taken a seat next to me, leaning into my shoulder. I reach down and take his hand, but it's short-lived as a voice cuts through.

"East? East!"

"Mom?" East acknowledges her.

"My darling, where have you been? I've been—" Her head cocks as she realizes who's standing with me. "Keller?" she asks with a spreading recognition. "Oh!" She rushes in and gives him a hug. She knows how devastated I've been. "I—what, how did you get here?" She backs away, looking him over.

Maggie intervenes, "Mrs. Porter."

Mom corrects her strange mistake, "It's Mrs. East—but you can call me Rosetta."

"I apologize. Old habits," Maggie admits.

I frown at her rebuttal.

"What's happened here?"

Maggie half grins. "A miracle, it seems."

No one corrects her, but his mom is visibly confused.

Rosetta approaches me with care. "You should be at the hospital, and someone needs to contact your parents at once."

"Of course," Maggie offers, "I'll call Marcy, she'll be thrilled to know Keller is going to be just fine."

East steps away and his mom follows, placing a hand on his arm. "What are you all doing here?" she asks.

East lets out a sigh. "It's a long story."

"I have time," she admits with the tilt of her head.

"East?" I call out as they both turn to face me. "Mrs. East, can I talk to him, please?"

She nods, allowing him to rejoin me. I lead him to the edge of the porch, far enough away to allow me to speak without fear of someone listening to me.

East won't look at me, so I lean in, hoping his eyes will meet mine; finally they do. I get lost staring at his beautiful face—those lips. The memory of being with him in that house still lingers so closely. I almost expect for him to laugh, take my hand, and lead me back to his home as the train whistle cries out in the distance, but that's not the truth of who we are. To be honest, I'm not sure what happened yet. All I know is I love him and I want him to know in whatever way I can.

"I'm okay," I whisper.

"Keller."

I interrupt him, while reaching in and taking his hand, "I am."

"You were in the hospital—in a coma," he utters.

"So, you tell me."

"You were. Your mom told me."

"Well, what matters is I'm here now. I'm awake—probably for the first time in my life."

His expression changes. I can't tell if he's happy I've said it, or if he wishes I hadn't. Either way, I had to let him know.

"You need to get checked out," he orders.

It's not the reaction I hoped for, but I don't know

11

what I expected. I've been gone for a month and who knows what happened in that time. Maybe he doesn't feel the same way about me. Maybe he—oh my God, did he meet someone? Is he—my emotions get the better of me.

"Are you dating someone else?" I ask, unable to keep it to myself.

"What?" His entire demeanor changes. He's uneasy. "Wh—why would you ask me that? What are you saying?"

My eyes narrow. He's visibly shaken. It makes me feel like he's hiding something, but I don't want to accuse him of anything.

"Hey—I'm sorry, I just, I—well, I lo—"

He steps back, letting my hand float away from his. I can't say it now. I know I love him. I feel it more than I've felt anything else in my life, but something's happened. Something's changed. I can tell by his reaction. I don't know what it is, but my heart drops into the pit of my stomach. I could easily throw up right now, but I won't. I'll hold my shit together. I refuse to be weak.

"I have to go, but we'll talk, okay?" He seems to have suppressed his emotions.

Every hope I have sinks to the bottom of the ocean as he turns away. I know that tone. I understand his words. I've been there too many times to count as girls came and went. As I let Shy come and go. He's letting me down easy, isn't he?

No—is he?

How could he?

What happened?

My gaze shifts and I catch Shy looking at me.

What has she done?

CHAPTER THREE

AUGHST EAST

W hat?" Mom's eyes narrow as we all sit in the living room after spilling what we can about what happened. Keller is no longer with us and neither is Shy. She stayed with him and I don't blame her. He needs someone other than a bunch of teenagers to tell him he's okay.

"Wait—so Maggie was dead?" she asks.

Vincent shakes his head. "On the floor, so we thought, but she came back like Jesus."

Evie bumps him from the side. Mom hides a grin. She isn't religious, which might seem strange to some, considering her profession.

"Vincent—rude," Evie whispers.

Mom offers a gentle nod, "I'm not offended."

"Well, she was laying the floor all—" Vincent distorts his face and hands.

Evie decides she's had enough and slaps his arm.

"Ow—Evie, knock it off."

"Stop." She clears her throat then turns her attention back on my mom. "There is something here."

A look of confusion spreads across Mom's face, "Here? In the town?"

"In this house," Evie clarifies.

Mom places her hands on her knees and tries to remain objective. "*Something* as in what exactly?"

"Paranormal." I decide to join forces with Evie.

Her eyebrow cocks as her gaze settles on me, "August Elliott East—what are you claiming?"

"I know it sounds strange, but I—I've seen things."

"My love—" I know what she wants to say, but she stops short. It's hard for me to claim anything when I have vision-inducing seizures, not to mention lingering trauma, but I can feel this thing growing inside of me. This uneasiness. Doubt—maybe even fear. I know something is wrong.

"I know—they know, Mom." I wave a hand. "I told them I have seizures—but it isn't that."

She adjusts on the chair. I think she may be surprised I shared something so private, but she needs to know I'm serious.

"Okay—listen. A lot has happened here in a short amount of time. We had a terrible scare at the nuclear plant, and then, well, your friend, Keller, was seriously injured."

15

"It isn't that," I interject.

"East, you've been through so much—I didn't even mention the fire."

I swallow hard. I wasn't planning on talking about what happened back home.

My spine straightens. "They know there was a fire."

"But they don't know everything," she adds, gently, but it's painful just the same.

Evie defends me, "We know about the town and how it burned almost everything to the ground."

Then Mom provides the final blow. "The fire began in our home—in Easts' room—and, well, all of his friends died because of that fire. Every single one of them."

Her words tear through me like the edge of a razorblade. I understand why she felt the need to say it, but it doesn't change the fact that it hurts me.

It will always hurt me.

Death isn't something I fear, but losing the people I love is. And I lost them all.

Evie cannot add anything as she glances over at me.

"I don't remember—you know that," I mutter.

Mom is teary-eyed, but she clearly believed she had to share the truth. I almost wish she hadn't.

Vincent stands up and shares a look with Evie. "We—I think we should probably go home."

16

"Yeah." I focus on my hands.

"But we'll see you on Monday at school, okay?" he states, like nothing's happened.

I nod. "Yeah, Monday."

"I'll bring cookies," Evie baits me. But cookies won't be enough.

I'm broken-hearted. Just when I felt like there might be a moment of clarity, I'm left empty and embarrassed, like this whole thing might've been my fault, from beginning to end. The only thing I can't explain away is Keller's claim that Maggie helped him wake up, but he was in a coma and Maggie is the town's psychic. Her business would do well to have something like this make its rounds through gossip.

I shake my head as they head toward the door. Mom follows, I don't. I'm stuck in place, wondering why I allowed this to happen. I like all of them—my *new* friends. I care about them more than I expected to. I let myself get attached when I probably shouldn't have. But what does it matter? We'll probably move to Arizona. To a place where the sun never stops shining. There would be little rain, and few storm clouds in the sky. No temperamental seas. The pine trees would be gone. There would be nothing I like, but perhaps I should be in exile. I could hide away and get lost in my books, movies, and music once again and stop including others in my detached bouts with reality.

And Keller West? He's a pipe dream. Something I could never truly have—not in this place—not here—maybe not anywhere. This town may be accepting of Delilah and her wife, but they wouldn't be so happy about their star quarterback giving up on his chosen path while he wastes away with someone like me.

A boy who isn't well. A boy who would rather dream up elaborate stories about ghosts and all things paranormal rather than face the truth.

I may be broken, and until I'm put back together, I shouldn't drag anyone down with me, no matter how much I may want to love them.

No matter how heartbroken I will be.

"East."

I lift my chin to see Mom standing in the doorway. Her arms are loose, hands clasped. She knows what she's done, but maybe she did me a favor. I clearly couldn't do it myself.

"I'm going to bed."

"Honey," she reaches out as I pass her by, but I can't talk about this right now.

I pause, not looking back. "And maybe we should homeschool," I add, before walking away. I reach the stairs before the first warm tear rolls down my cheek, but I angrily wipe it away.

CHAPTER FOUR

KELLER WEST

I push away the light shining in my eyes. "I'm fine," I claim, because physically I feel better than I have in forever, but mentally I'm a mess. My thoughts are scattered here and there as I try to effectively catalog the memories—both here and those that happened while I was asleep.

"Tell me what happened," Mom demands.

The doctor stands up straight, leaving me on the side of the examination table, feet dangling and arms crossed.

"He appears to be fine."

"Fine?" She cups my face. "He was just in a coma for nearly a month and now he's magically fine?"

"Marcy," Maggie speaks up from the examination table across from mine.

Mom glances in her direction, but they don't speak.

Dad pipes in, "Can he play?" brow raised in anticipation.

I grit my teeth.

Why is he here? He doesn't need to be in the room. He doesn't deserve to be. He left—not us. He took off when mom needed him. He did that—not us.

I laugh, Dad's eyes pierce me. "What?"

I shake my head while gripping the edge of the table. "Ask me."

"Ask you what, Keller?"

"Ask me if I want to play—go ahead, Dad, ask me. Have you ever thought about that? Have you ever once thought about anything other than what **you** want in your entire life?"

"Keller," Mom whispers while touching my arm.

"No, Mom—let's do this here, where if he wants to hit me, I can at least get some medical help."

"Keller, stop." Dad's muscles flex in his jaw.

I don't care. I don't care about him, or football, or any of it.

"What are you doing here anyway, Dad? Don't you have a girlfriend who's like five years older than me?" the venom spews.

"Son, I know you're upset. This whole thing must be traumatizing."

I chuckle. "Traumatizing?" I glance at Mom. "Are you teaching him new words now?"

20

Dad clears his throat. "I'm home now. I know I messed up, but I'm going to make it all right—every bit, I promise."

I look down, lightheaded and nauseous. Finally, I jump down and throw up in the trash can. I grip the edges of it and then take a sluggish breath, feeling a cold sweat covering my skin like the beginning of a flu.

I can feel a hand on my back. Mom's come to console me.

The doctor happily interrupts the family drama. "I'd like to run a few tests."

"Yes—yes, of course." Mom steps away.

I turn to face her. Dad places his arm around her shoulder. I roll my eyes.

What the hell is going on?

"Is it possible that I woke up in the wrong timeline?" I'm worrying.

The doctor seems confused. "I'm sorry?"

"Nothing." I resign myself to what seems to be my new reality, where my dad has weaseled his way back into our home, and August East no longer feels the same way I do.

I think I may've died and gone to Hell.

CHAPTER FIVE

AUGUST EAST

I sit by the window in my bedroom and toss a small blue rubber ball against the glass, again and again it comes right back to my hand without veering off course. I wish I could be so stable—so predictable. So mundane. But here I am, once again thinking about why I put myself out there.

I'm a fool to think I'll ever have anything I want.

I'm not the boy who gets to do it all over again. I went to Whynot High hoping I'd meet new friends, and, surprisingly, I did. Why anyone finds me worth befriending is a mystery, but I secretly hoped they would. And now I'm wondering why I did it to myself. Why I held out hope.

Why?

And there's Keller.

Sweet Keller West.

A boy who has everything going for him. A boy who has a full ride to any college he chooses. Here, he's a star. The brightest of stars in the sky, and what am I but a black hole, devouring all things bright—all things good—and robbing them of their beauty.

I knew when we came here that I could simply stay in this house and my mom would be happy to homeschool me. I could've done that—could've, but I'm selfish.

The ball moves past my hand. I close my eyes while sighing. It hits the floor and rolls across the floorboards. I reluctantly get up to retrieve it as it changes course and rolls to the left. I lean down, but it moves faster until finally it disappears under my bed.

I kneel, annoyed that it's forcing me to chase it. I'm sure the floor is uneven. The house is old and things warp with time.

I spread out on my stomach, reaching under the bed as far as my hand will feel the ball at my fingertips. I grunt, moving my body under the bed and finally retrieve it, but as I do, I notice something caught under the box spring. I roll the ball to the other side, setting it free as I flip onto the back and shimmy my way under, gently pulling on what appears to be a locket. I push my way out from under the bed and sit up, opening my hand to see what I've found. In it lies a brushed silver necklace holding a small flat charm

23

with a rose etched into the face. I struggle to open it, but it's no use. The locket is sealed shut with rust. My lips purse and I rise, letting it dangle from my fingers in front of my face. The locket twists and turns, but finally comes to a stop.

"What are you?" I ask.

The chain is fairly long. I slip it over my head and put it under my shirt before I even think about it. Like it's something I should treasure when I've never seen it before. But, oddly enough, it calms me down. I know it's in my head, but I don't mind. I'll take it.

A knock comes to my door that's sitting half open. I turn, placing my hand against my chest as if I'm protecting it.

"Son."

Dad's come to see me. It's unusual. I love him but we don't have talks—not like Mom and I do. It's just never been that way for us.

"Hey, Dad."

"Mind if I come in?" he asks.

I hesitate but abandon the thought of telling him I'd rather be alone. Instead, I silently allow him with a nod.

He enters the room, eyes moving over everything. His focus lands on the window for a moment, and then he blinks out of it.

"So, it's been something else lately, huh?"

I chuckle, unable to hide my sarcasm. "A little."

"I wanted to let you know that I'm here for you, you know, if you need to talk about anything."

I take a seat on the edge of the bed and he stands, placing a hand on his hip and then removing it. This is awkward for him. I can tell he's uneasy. Mom's always been the one who's talked to me about everything. The fire, my friends, seizures, nightmares, the move. All of it. Sometimes it felt like it was just me and her because of the long hours my dad had to work. I don't blame him, and I don't have any anger. He works hard. He always has.

"I know, Dad." I offer him some peace of mind.

He walks over to the window and stares out at the town, "I know it's been hard. All of it," he clears his throat to the side of his hand, "that fire, well, son—it was your fault."

My stomach drops, I fidget with my hands, "What?" I ask, knowing he couldn't have said what I think he said.

Your fault...

"It was." He keeps his back to me as he lifts a finger and starts drawing on the glass. "You did that. You ruined our lives. You started that fire because you always had a sick fascination with it. I told your mom that you should be locked away—in one of those places," he snaps his fingers, "you know, for the criminally insane. But no—you are her baby boy. Sometimes I think she loves you more, August—more than me."

He turns and his eyes are hollowed out, leaving behind two bloody eye sockets.

I gasp, sitting straight up in my bed, fighting to focus in the darkened room. I drop back on the pillow, laughing to myself. It was a dream. That's all it was.

I reach up, tapping my chest, and feel something hard under my shirt. I reach in and pull out the locket, letting it dangle in front of my face once again.

"Did you do that?" I ask it, knowing it's a silly question.

I nearly jump out of my skin when the phone rings and it stops after the first ring. Mom must've grabbed it. I slip onto my side and stare out the window, thinking of someone I shouldn't. Thinking of him.

The boy with raven-black hair and bright blue eyes.

I dig at the locket's edge, but it still won't budge, so I close my eyes and allow myself to drift off to dreamless sleep.

CHAPTER SIX

KELLER WEST

I'm good." I roll my shoulder as Dad tries helping me out of the car. I don't need his help, not now or ever, and I want him to know it.

I push past him and make my way toward the door. Moms rushes in to unlock it before me so I can get inside. She said little on the drive home. There was talk of dinner, the new movies that arrived at the video store, and my Dad smiled when we passed the football field.

I hate him. I can't help it. I wish I could bury this feeling deep inside, but I can't and I fear it'll only get worse now that he's here.

I pause for one moment and catch a glimpse of East's house up on that hill. The memories of being there with him in another timeline still consume me. I can feel him. Smell him. Taste him. I don't know if

I'll ever be able to move past how I feel about August East. He's changed me. I'm awake now and I can't go back to sleep.

"Keller."

I close my eyes. My dad's voice immediately ruins everything. "What now?" I ask.

My mom steps in but Dad holds up a hand. "No—go get dinner started. This has to be done, Marcy."

Her eyes dim, she steps away, allowing him to once again rule over her like an obedient dog. My heart sinks. "Mom, you can stay—don't think you have to—"

She shakes her head and I stop. I don't want to make things any worse than they have to be on her. They used to fight every single day. I didn't miss it when he left us. She turns away, doing as he asks, leaving the two of us alone in the living room. I spot one of my games on the floor and lean over to pick it up. I lose my balance and Dad swoops in to help balance me by placing his hand under my arm. I jerk it away and his expression hardens.

"Keller, it doesn't have to be like this."

I chuckle. "Like what? Like you didn't leave?"

He lets out a sigh instead of getting angry. I wasn't expecting it, so it lowers my guard.

"I know I hurt you—the girls, your mother. Do you not know that?" he asks.

"I'm surprised you do know."

He nods. "Listen, I get it and I probably deserve it."

"Probably?" My eyebrow cocks.

He lifts a hand. "No—I do. I deserve it. What I did, well, it wasn't right. I don't know what the hell I was thinking—or if I was thinking at all." He rubs the side of his neck. The light slides along his wedding band. My jaw clenches.

"You cheated on her."

His eyes narrow. "I know what I did."

"Do you? Do you really know what you did to her—to us—Dad? You broke her heart, and she cried so much—which you didn't deserve—but she was heartbroken. And Jaime and Jenna, they cried too, but you know who didn't cry, Dad? Me. I didn't cry one damn tear for you. Not one, because you would not get that from me."

He places his hands on his hips and resigns to allow me to vent. I'm stunned he hasn't yelled at me yet, or told me to shut up, or go to my room. But he's refusing to fight me. The one time I really want it to happen. But no, he's failed me again.

"I'm proud of you, son."

I scoff, "Proud? Of not crying? Of course, not. Boys don't cry, right, Dad?"

"Not about crying, Keller—about everything you've done. How you stepped up when I didn't."

29

His words infuriate me. "What?"

"Yes—I know I messed up—but I did and I don't know how I can ever make it up to you, but I'll try."

I shake my head. "I don't want you to make anything up to me." I jab a stiff finger toward the kitchen. "You need to make it up to her."

He pauses. I might've finally pushed enough buttons to make him show me he hasn't changed one bit. I know that asshole is in there. The one who broke Mom's heart and abandoned his kids. The one who moved a whole state away and started sleeping with a girl years younger than he is. The one who blackened my eye.

"I promise I will."

I move in closer to him and lower my voice, "You may have Mom fooled, but I know who you are."

We let the silence sit between us. The only interruption is the light humming coming from the kitchen.

Mom's humming.

She never hums unless she's happy.

I look down at my throwing hand and trace the scar on my palm.

Is she happy? Is this what she wants? Has she forgiven him for everything he's done?

The humming continues. Dad grins.

"I love it when she does that," he admits.

I move closer to the kitchen and listen to her

continue. I feel the tears in my eyes. Is this up to me if it makes her happy? If she wants to forgive Dad and allow him to come home, then who am I to keep trying to stop it?

"I asked if we could have chili cheese dogs."

I turn to face him, sucking up my emotions because I refuse to let him see me upset.

"You don't like them."

"No, but you do."

I'm left speechless.

He isn't selfless, is he? He never cared about what we liked before, so why now?

"We have a little time before it's ready. Maybe you should go get a shower and whatever else you do in that messy room of yours."

I blink through his lightheaded joke.

"Go ahead, Keller. We'll let you know when it's ready."

I turn away, unable to clap back at him. I want to. I want to make him as uncomfortable as I can, but he's making it nearly impossible with all this bullshit selflessness.

I move down the hallway, nearly tripping as my feet refuse to move as swiftly as I'd like. But I reach my door and move inside, closing it behind me. Finally—peace. I rest my shoulders against the hardwood and focus on East's house through the window. The

31

sun is setting, and the light is shining right on his bed-room window. For one moment, I think I see a figure move behind the glass, but it's wishful thinking. Even if he was there, it wouldn't be for me.

CHAPTER SEVEN

AUGUST EAST

I linger in bed, stretching my arms with a joyful yawn. I love those few seconds of bliss when you first wake up. It's when everything is right. Nothing's gone wrong in the world, and, more importantly, you've done no wrong.

I slip from the side of the bed and feel a ball beneath my feet. I twist my foot and stare at it as all the memories flood back in. I reach up and feel the locket lingering beneath the material of the t-shirt. I let out a defeated sigh.

"Great," I mutter before running my fingers through my unruly hair. I pause, biting at the edge of my lip and then make a decision while shuffling into the bathroom.

I stare at myself in the mirror.

Who am I? How could I be this reckless with

something I treasured so much? Keller meant the world to me, and I discarded him like trash. I allowed myself to take comfort in Shy's weakness and my own. My gut aches. The guilt will tear me apart if I let it. I have to tell him—sooner, not later. He has to know what's happened. I can't simply walk away from him and leave him wondering. It isn't fair. None of it is fair.

I open the cabinet and stare at the razor. Someday I'll need to shave. Right now, I don't. But I'm sure it'll happen soon enough. My dad gave me this, thinking I'd be using it by now.

I reach in and grab it, carefully loosening the head to release the sharpened piece of steel. It slips out and into the palm of my hand. I spend too much time staring at it. It's strange that something this small could be so destructive. I won't lie, admitting that I never struggled with the thought of using it to end things. I don't see how I couldn't after what happened in my hometown. I spent months struggling with guilt that nearly overwhelmed me. Anyone would. Anyone with a heart.

Again, I place my hand against my heart. I'm not so sure I have one. If I did, then I would've stopped Shy that night and told her to go home. I would've refused to let her—to let me—I would've thought about him. I should've thought about him, but I didn't. I was selfish.

34

I wipe away a tear. Then straighten my shoulders, staring at my reflection in the mirror. It doesn't take but a moment before I grab the first loose curl and hack away at it. It drops to the floor and then I grab a second and third. Soon I'm standing in a small pile of what was once a mane that I sported.

I drop the razor in the sink and it slides circular, then stops short of the open drain. I rush my fingers through what's left and shake out my head, rising to see that I've done a better job than expected. I still have some length left on the top, but the sides are shorter, as well as the back. I don't hate it but it's the release I needed.

My old therapist calls it *stress cutting*. I have to agree with him. It definitely relieves the stress. Better that it's my hair and not my upper arm. I turn to glance at it, lifting my sleeve. The scars remain. Straight and true. Whiter than my already pale skin. I don't regret doing it. It was necessary at the time. I'd rather it be that than my mom burying me.

I couldn't do that to her and I kept that in my mind every single time I carefully cut across my skin. Deep enough to feel it—not deep enough to cause serious harm.

But those days are behind me now. I know it as I stare at my reflection and accept my new hair for what it is. I consider it a punishment of sorts—or maybe

35

I'm shedding my skin—evolving. Like a snake or a butterfly.

"East!" I hear Mom call from beyond the room. "Breakfast!"

"Coming!" I reply before giving my head one last shake over the sink. I leave my hair behind; I just wish I could leave my heart.

CHAPTER EIGHT

KELLER WEST

I stand in the doorway, watching my family eat breakfast at the table. Mom has moved out of her regular spot, and Dad has taken her place. I grimace, knowing I have to join them. I straighten my shoulders, wanting to appear as normal as possible.

I need to go back to school today. It may take some convincing, so I should be nice to everyone—even though my stomach is twisted in knots.

"Honey, come sit down." Mom ushers me over with the wave of her hand.

I push off the door jam and reluctantly make my way over to a chair closest to her without making eye contact with my dad. I'm afraid I need food to calm me down before I speak to him again, but he can't help himself.

"How's your hand?"

I thumb at the center of my palm, massaging the tightened spot that feels achy. But then lie.

"Good." I let a fake smile tug at the corner of my lip.

"That's great to hear." He scrapes his fork across the plate and my eye twitches. Mom gently bumps my knee with hers, so I'm forced to look.

"I made waffles and bacon—your favorite." She loads my plate like I'm five years old again. I can't fault her for trying. I know this is as uncomfortable for her as it is for me. I was away for the last month, while life went on without me.

Jenna and Jaime enter the room in a whirlwind of chatter, taking their seats and grabbing what they can to eat. Jaime butters her waffle while Jenna takes a bite of her bacon mid-sentence.

"He did not," she protests.

"Did so—everyone's talking." Jenna nods before shoving a chunk of waffle in her mouth and washes it down with some orange juice.

"Everyone who?" Jaime's eyes light up with suspicion.

"I don't know—everyone."

Jaime snorts, shaking her head.

Mom interjects, "Gossip is a bad habit."

Dad nods while placing his elbows on the table and interlocking his fingers. Elbows on the table is a

38

pet peeve of mine—it used to be his, too. He knocked mine off a few times when I was growing up. I guess he can do whatever he wants while telling other people they can't.

Annoying. I take a bite before I blurt out something stupid to piss him off.

"Your mom's right."

I nearly choke on my food and have to clear my throat to the side of my hand.

He's the one to talk about gossip. Everyone knows his business and how he ran off with some girl much younger than he is. He left us all here to deal with it.

"You, okay?" he asks.

I finger at my throat. "Wrong pipe." I cough through the words.

"Take a drink," he adds.

I was already reaching for the glass. I'm tempted to tell him I can think for myself, but I catch Mom looking at me. I abandon the thought for her sake.

I drink nearly the entire glass of milk before placing it back on the table and staring at the food on my plate. My appetite is gone, but they'll think something's wrong if I don't force myself to eat, so I take another bite.

I swallow, then ask out of spite, "Who?"

Jaime bites her lip and then shares her information. "August East—I heard he's, well, he likes girls and boys."

My dad chuckles. I hate him. He's never been accepting of anyone that doesn't fit the mold.

Jenna rolls her eyes. "I don't believe it, but who cares?"

"Right," I add before I can stop myself.

Dad spends a few seconds staring in my direction before leaning back in his chair and drumming the table with his stubby fingers. My hands look like Mom's. I'm grateful.

"That's all we need," he grumbles.

Mom interrupts by grabbing the plate of half empty bacon. "I have more. We need to eat it up! We have so much freshside in the freezer now, thanks to that cow you bought, honey."

Honey.

I hate him. She doesn't owe him a damn thing. None of us do. I wish I could toss him out the front door, but he's seemed to settle right back in like a tick.

"You didn't have much, Marcy."

I sigh through his jab. We had little meat because she was busy busting her ass to provide for us, and I gave every dime I made at the theater toward more groceries and some bills. The money he sent paid the mortgage, and that's it. Nothing else, but he didn't give a shit, did he?

I watch her stop in front of the stove, thinking it over like I would before she places some more bacon on the plate and returns. She places it on the table and takes her place next to him like an obedient pet.

"I called your coach."

I narrow my eyes. "Why?" I ask.

"To let him know you'll be coming back—I mean, if you're ready."

I rub the side of my neck. "Yeah, I'm ready."

"Good!" He slaps the table and the cutlery jingles. Mom flinches. I have to keep my mouth shut. I can do this. I know I can. She's the one that'll have to listen to his bullshit if I make him mad, so I won't.

I feel sick to my stomach as I allow him to dominate all of us—well, not the girls, they don't care. But Mom and I are both sporting the same stressed expression. It makes me wonder how he got back into the house with her. I assume he bullied her and made it seem like if she didn't, then it would be her fault me and my sisters wouldn't have a stable home. But he's provided no stability. What wonderful memories I have of him are delusional. I never noticed his aggressive nature until I got a little older, but once I knew, nothing would ever be the same.

I push my chair out and stand, feeling a little lightheaded, but I hide it well. "I'm going to get to school."

Dad reaches in his pocket and tosses a set of keys at me, I catch them—barely. He laughs, "You better sharpen those reflexes."

I stare at the keys with confusion spreading across my brow.

"Take the truck to school."

"I can walk."

"Keller, take it."

"I don't have to—"

Mom places her hand on my arm and I stop pushing back. "Okay, thanks."

She relaxes and so does he.

I head for the door and he calls out behind me, "Say hi to your coach for me!"

"I will." Like it matters.

I step out and feel the fresh air on my skin. My jaw aches. I didn't realize how much I was grinding my teeth.

"Hey."

I look up and see Shy walking toward me. She's dressed in all baby blue today. High-waisted jeans and a top to match that ties in a knot on her right hip. She has a yellow bandana wrapped in her hair and brings a powerful scent of strawberry with her. I catch the light slipping across her shiny lips. She's wearing gloss. I remember how sticky it was when she kissed me. I wish I had one of those clear containers with the ball rollers, but I wouldn't be able to use it, anyway.

I paid little attention when I slipped on a white t-shirt and my faded jeans. I used to worry about what

I looked like when I was getting ready for school, but now it seems low on my list of concerns.

Shy stops, leaving a couple of feet between us.

"Want a ride?" I ask while wiggling the keys.

She narrows her eyes. "Doesn't your mom need the car for work?"

"Dad gave me the keys to his truck."

"He did not."

"He did."

"Wow." She shifts her weight on her platform white tennis shoes. Few people can pull them off, but she does.

I open the passenger door for her and she slips inside. I make my way to the other side and my vision blurs for a brief second. I shake it off. I know it'll be a while before I feel normal again, but I'm going to power through it. I'd rather be dizzy at school than listen to my dad run his mouth at home.

I slip the keys into the ignition and the engine purrs. He's always taken better care of this truck than he ever did any of us. I lean back in the seat, gripping the wheel.

"How are you feeling?" she asks.

I glance over at her, shaking off the feelings of nausea, "Good—I mean, it comes and goes, but I'll be fine."

"What comes and goes?"

"I just get sick to my stomach and a little lightheaded."

"Keller," she places a hand on my arm, forcing me to look into her bright eyes, "maybe you should take some time before you try to do this."

I shake my head, looking straight ahead. I feel her hand fall away. "I can't be in there."

"Okay, I get it, but you have to be honest about how you feel and if you can't do this, you can't."

I chuckle under my breath while backing out of the driveway. Normally, I'd think about hitting the mailbox, but I'm at his mercy. Well—Mom is.

I pause, pushing the gearshift into drive. It takes a moment, but I get it. "I just don't want Mom to put up with his shit."

"I get that but you also need to be healthy."

I push on the gas, drawing us both back into the seat. His gas pedal is touchy—it always was. He taught me how to drive in this thing, then promised it would one day be mine, but we all know how that turned out.

I soon find myself driving past The Mill House. I can't help but glance over. My eyes find his window, and for a split-second, I think I see a silhouette in the window.

"He isn't coming."

My brow furrows. "Who?"

She half-laughs. I know I'm being ridiculous. "East. He's going to homeschool."

"How—I mean, who told you that?"

She adjusts against the seat. I notice she's uncomfortable and I don't know why.

"I called to check on him and his mom told me."

"Is he okay?"

She leans against the door, staring out the window, "Probably not—I mean," she looks at me, "who is in this town?"

"I mean, is he sick with his seizures and stuff?"

"She didn't say that."

I park in an open space in the school parking lot and we both get pushed forward a couple of inches, then back. She chuckles, "I can't tell if it's the truck or your driving."

"Both," I admit before turning to face her.

"You look tired, Keller."

I look down at the scar on my hand and flex my fingers. "I guess I'm not really wanting to sleep after being in bed for a month."

She offers a guarded grin, which isn't like her. I'm not sure why things feel so different between us, but they do. Maybe it's because I can't stop thinking about him and how he seems to not care the way he did before. I miss being his only focus. I didn't appreciate it until it was no longer there. But it's left a gaping hole in my heart I can't fill with football and faking my happiness at home.

"Just be easy on yourself, okay?"

I tilt my head. "Does that sound like me?"

She giggles while staring down into her lap, "No, it's not the Keller West I knew."

I lean in. "Hey, I'm here."

She blows out her cheeks and for a moment I think she wants to tell me something, but we both flinch when a loud thud comes from behind. I twist in the seat and see Ty humping the air in the truck bed. God, he's obnoxious, but I'm stuck with him until I leave this town, and there's only one way to do that.

"I hate him so much," Shy mutters.

I nod. "You're not alone."

Her expression changes as she straightens her spine. "I'm going back to cheer."

"Yeah?"

Ty slaps the back window and Shy rolls her eyes. "Yes. Because I miss it."

"I understand. It's what you know."

She tugs at her earlobe, "Yeah, I guess we can't escape it, huh?"

I glance at Ty, who's now yelling at the sky and beating his chest like a beast. "I don't think we can."

"Well, I guess we should go in and endure it."

I nod as she slips out of the truck and I'm keen to

follow. I don't want her to have to deal with Ty Miller any longer than she has to.

He's already up in her ear as she leans away. I step around the back end of the truck.

"Bro." I hate that word.

Hate it.

"Bro!" Ty exclaims while Shy escapes.

He approaches me with a huge smile, showing off his white teeth. He doesn't deserve the teeth he has. All straight and perfect. He is a good-looking guy, but I've never once thought about him at all unless a linebacker is barreling toward me. I guess I use him, and I don't feel bad about it. If anyone deserves to be used, it's him.

"Lookin' kinda thin, man! Are you not eating?"

I straighten out of habit, taking away some of his height. "I ate like a pig this morning."

"Good! We got games comin' up and you need to be in kick ass shape."

"I am, just need to get back out there and throw a few balls."

"Yeah!" He slaps me on the arm and I have to stabilize myself because it nearly moves me. "Oh—" He spots two cheerleaders making their way toward the front doors and starts jogging backward while pointing at me, "The King has returned!"

"Yeah, the King," I parrot him, even though I don't feel like one.

I reach out and hold on to the side of the truck bed as the dizziness fades. I really wish it would go away, but I also know I probably should've stayed home this week—or maybe even more.

But I'd rather be anywhere than with my dad.

CHAPTER NINE

AUGUST EAST

I watch a truck go by and lean in, realizing Shy is in the passenger seat, but worse than that, Keller is looking up at my house, into my window. I back away, feeling a knot forming in the pit of my stomach.

What the hell are they doing driving around together? My paranoia rises. I imagine her telling him what we did, right here in my kitchen. I rush to the bathroom and throw up but there's hardly anything there but bile. I've eaten little since the day Keller woke up.

"Love?"

I hear my mom calling out to me, so I hurriedly swish some water in my mouth and look at myself in the mirror. I'm paler than usual. I look weak, because I am.

I step out of the bathroom and fake a grin. "Yeah?"

She's standing in my room, staring at the posters on the walls. Her attention is drawn back to me.

"Are you okay?"

I nod, but I'm not. "Sure."

"East." She tilts her head.

I know lying to her is silly. I've never done it before. "I was nauseous." I glance behind me.

"You should eat."

"Nothing sounds good."

"Let's make some tea." She moves toward the door without confirming that I want any, but she's not asking.

I'm stuck in place, but she pulls me out. "August—come."

I nod, allowing her to lead, but I pause, like my legs are suddenly heavier.

"East?"

I turn to face the painting. Charles Porter stares down at me. The weight of his expression nearly sucks the air out of the space. I hear whispers rising from all around me. My ears begin to ring and my eyes widen. I watch as his head turns and he's now looking at my mom. I shake my head and look at her, but she seems oblivious to the change in the painting.

"East? East."

I part my lips, glancing back up at the painting and it's returned to normal, but with one thing missing.

50

The child is now gone.

I narrow my eyes and lean in, but the child in white is no longer there. I feel a hand on my arm just as the ringing in my ears reaches a fevered pitch. Then, like magic, it stops and I blink through it.

"Are you okay?" she asks and I look back at the painting, which now appears to be completely normal because the child has returned.

My throat feels dry so I clear it to the side of my hand, "Yeah—I think I need that tea and something to eat is all."

"Of course."

As we're descending the stairs, the doorbell rings and I pause as my dad steps in and opens the door. It takes a moment for my eyes to adjust to the bright light streaming in from the outside world. Being in this house can sometimes feel like there's a perpetual storm going on beyond the walls.

A small frame comes into focus and I realize it's Evie Rice. I let out a sigh. I hope she isn't here to demand another walk-through so she can try to capture a ghost on her tape recorder.

"Sure, come inside," my dad cheerfully invites her in.

Her gaze lands on me faster than I expect. She's obsessed with this house, so I don't think I'm the reason she's come back here.

"Hey," she offers with a weak wave of her hand.

"Hey," I reply as my mom lingers, but Dad takes her hand.

"Let's go make that tea," he pulls her along with him and out of sight. I appreciate the privacy, but I'm still confused about what Evie wants from me.

She reaches into her pocket and removes her hand. I narrow my eyes, not sure what she's doing.

"I have something for you."

"What is it?"

"Gothic Quacker."

Confusion spreads across my face as she lifts my hand and places this little rubber duck in the palm of my hand. I lift it up and stare at the black duck with white eyes, a red bill and markings on it, making it look like you can see its rib cage and backbone. She's obviously painted it, but it's cute.

"Gothic Quacker?"

"Yes, that's his name. Gothic Quacker. He's been with me for years and I always have him on my nightstand. I got him from my mom when I was—well, I was depressed, and he always made me feel better."

I shake my head. "I can't take him, Evie." I hold him out to her and she steps back.

"Nope, you need him, not me."

I pull him in closer to me and smile. I pet his head and catch her watching me, so I straighten up and give her an approving nod. "Thank you."

"No problem, I figured he did his job and now he can help you. He's a great little duck."

I smile, she tilts her head. "What?"

I pick a piece of lint from my shirt, "I don't know—I guess I never pegged you for a softy."

"Shut up, I'm not."

"Right." I'm not convinced. She moves past me and stares up at the ceiling.

I take a scant breath, tucking the gift away in my pocket. Oddly, I feel better with him than I did without. Maybe there's something to this rubber duck—or maybe Evie is an amazing friend.

She turns back to face me. "Are you not coming back to school?"

My jaw tightens, "I, well, I thought maybe I should homeschool, since you know. The fire and all."

She waves a hand. I look at her dress. She's reminding me of Wednesday Addams today, complete with a pair of black Mary Jane shoes and half rolled socks.

"It did no damage besides the smoke. I guess it was smaller than it seemed."

"But the room was full of flames."

She stops to stare at me. "East, there was zero damage, minus a charred mark on the wall and smoke—honestly, I don't think anyone hated getting out early that day."

"So, wait, the room is okay, then?"

"Yes, like I said, it's just a charred mark on the wall from an old outlet, like our counselor said."

I narrow my eyes. "I—it's not how I remember it."

Evie thoughtfully looks me over, "Didn't you say she hypnotized you?"

"Yeah."

"Well..." She doesn't explain.

"It seemed so real."

"How many dreams have you had that seemed that way? I'd guess being hypnotized is the same way."

I look down. "I have, but it's just—I swear the entire room was on fire."

"Well, it wasn't. They're fixing the wall and probably fumigating it for the smoke, but other than that, the school's fine. Except for Mr. Rider, who's signed on to check every outlet and socket. But he knows what he's doing and I'm sure he appreciates the extra money."

"Do you want something to drink?" I ask, while fingering at the miniature rubber duck in my pocket. I forgot to ask, but she's made so many things better in such a short amount of time.

"Yes! Thank you."

I grin, so does she.

"Thank you." I owe her now.

"No problem. Besides, I thought someone should

tell you so you can come back to school—because you will be, right?"

I pause, biting at the edge of my lip. "I told my mom maybe we should just homeschool."

"What? Why?" she asks.

"Because of everything that's happened."

She leans in. "I told you the school is fine."

"But Keller isn't."

She pauses. "Oh. That's not something I can fix. That's up to you and him, but he's back."

I perk up. "At school?"

"Yes, he came back today."

I narrow my eyes, "Why are you not in school?"

She places her hand on her hip. "I got a pass to come see you."

"And here I thought you were being a rebel."

She laughs. "Most days, but I asked because I thought you could use some company and Gothic Quacker."

I chuckle. "Did you name him?"

She rolls her eyes. "What do you think?"

"I'd say yes."

"You would be correct."

I reach in and take her hand. "I appreciate it—all of it."

She clears her throat. I don't think she's used to being this close to someone and having a genuine friend.

"It's fine—"

We stand in awkward silence and I let go of her hand. She folds her arms over her chest.

"Tea's this way. I can smell it. Mom makes the best."

"I can stay then?"

I half-grin. "Yes, and you can see the library, if you want."

Her eyes brighten. "I'd love that!"

It seems fair to offer; in fact, I'll even take her in the atrium if she wants so she can see the poisonous garden, but I have a feeling she'll be happy to hang out upstairs.

CHAPTER
TEN

KELLER WEST

I stare out the classroom window with my chin in hand. I've tried my best to pay attention to what my teachers have been saying today, but my thoughts continue to wander. Flashes of memory consume my mind's eye.

I've been remembering more and more about the accident. The way I felt, how painful it was to not only cut my hand, but the crushing weight of the door. I thought it was lost to me, but it isn't. It lingers like a ghost—just like August East.

My memory of him is a mish-mash of the past and the present now. I can feel him against me. A moment I don't think I had. I must have willed that life I never had into existence, and then there's Maggie Mischief, who claims she retrieved me. I don't know, maybe she did. Is it so crazy to think she reached into my mind and helped me come back? I think there have been stranger things happening in this world. I know Evie would agree.

I think about Evie, Vincent—even Shy. I haven't crossed paths with Evie or her brother all day, and Shy has been busy talking with her old squad.

But I miss them. I make a promise to myself that if I see them at lunch, I'll sit with them again. I want to. I don't think anyone else in this town can understand me better, and honestly, I feel more relaxed when I'm around them—like I don't have to watch my words, or how I feel.

It was a freedom I miss. Especially now that Dad moved back home.

I know my sisters and mom are used to it, but I'm not and I can't say that I'll ever be, because deep down I don't want to.

I flinch when I hear my name called.

"Keller?"

I look up to see Delilah, our school's counselor, standing next to my teacher. She's really a shrink. We all know that, but she plays a milder version of that here at Whynot High.

I sat down and talked to her once when the news spread that my dad left town and was gone longer than anyone expected. I guess I never thought about everyone knowing the truth because no one picked on me. That's not how it works when you're the quarter-back on the football team with championships under your belt. I'm shielded with that armor.

"Yeah?" I ask, adjusting myself in the uncomfort-able wooden chair.

"Could I have a word with you—in private?" she asks.

I stand, leaving my books behind.

"You can bring your things," she adds, so I re-trieve them, volleying a couple of stares on my way back. Again, no one says a word, but I know rumors will spread.

I step out into the hallway and Delilah closes the door behind her. I refer to her as Delilah because she's always insisted that all kids do. I think it's her way of making us feel comfortable. I mean, I would guess that's her reasoning.

She closes the door behind her and gives me a hurried once-over. I draw my books into my chest. I don't know exactly what she wants, but she's here for a reason.

"How are you?" she asks.

I know she means it. She's never seemed like the person who talks to anyone because she's told she has to.

"Good," I offer my partial lie.

She tilts her head. "Really?"

I part my lips, pausing as a hall monitor with a bold sash draped across his chest passes us by. Once he's moved out of earshot, I decide to be honest, because hiding something from her is probably a bad idea.

"Kinda."

She nods, reaching in to touch my arm. It unexpectedly draws some emotions. My eyes glass over. It angers me. I'm not one to cry about anything. My dad taught me it was a show of weakness and his constant reminders ground it into my head. I hate that I let him dull that part of me. But it's all I knew when I was growing up.

Be strong! he'd demand. *Winners are not weak!*

Delilah eyes the hallway, then the door behind us.

"Want to take a walk?" she asks.

I nod. Getting away from my peers is probably the best option before I go and do something stupid like cry.

We move away from the classroom and down the hall. I feel my muscles easing with each step. I glance over at Delilah, who isn't staring at me. She'd be good at her job and I'm not sure this place deserves her. But she's happy here because of her wife. She could carve out a bit of happiness in this world, and I envy her. Ironically, two women being together has always been accepted much easier than two guys. One seems the same as the other, but you wouldn't know it.

We reach the door and she opens it, allowing some fresh air to spill into the space. I hold still until she speaks up, "Let's take a walk."

I narrow my eyes, glancing behind me down the empty hallway lined with lockers. "You don't want to talk in your office?"

She shakes her head, "Mr. Rider is fixing the outlets and they have to get rid of the smoke-smell."

"Oh, right—the fire."

I feel her hand on my arm once again. It brings me back. "Yes. Have you spoken with East?"

My stomach flips. I imagine the blood rushing from my face. Knowing he's still in this town is one thing. Having someone speak his name and want to talk about him is another.

"Was I supposed to?"

I quickly realize that my response might've seemed rude, or maybe defensive, but Delilah is a professional, and I don't sway her one bit.

"Only if you want."

I follow her down the steps and around the side of the building. Some students eat out here in the yard. It's peaceful, with a few trees that change from orange to red in the Fall. That time has come again. It's my favorite of all the seasons.

Football games.

Hot chocolate.

Chillier weather.

Halloween.

I have zero complaints. It reminds me of who I am as we move through the sports season.

Delilah sits down at one of the four picnic tables. I join her while straddling the bench. Her expression has remained calm, but I know she's going to dig deeper into everything that's happened. I want to spill it all, tell the truth, and move forward, but doing that reveals a secret I'm not sure I'm ready to share.

Even though she, of all people, would be safe.

It isn't that. It's my relentless fear of acting on it. I've already shown too much in front of Evie and Shy—probably Vincent, too. But they're all different. And Brian, well, he'd rather die than share what we've done. He wants a normal life, and it seems like he's carved one out the best he could.

But I struggle every single day as I move through the halls of this school, wearing this costume. Playing the part. I'm a fraud.

"You know you can tell me anything, Keller."

I nod, because I know it's true.

"So, now that we're alone, how are you, really?"

I glance to the side, seeing the long row of windows that connect a hallway from one side of the school to the other.

"No one is going to question why I'm talking to you after all you've been through."

62

"I guess not." I run my fingers through my hair. It's grown even more and I know it's only a matter of time before Dad forces me to go to the barbershop.

I hate the thought of it.

"So, this is a safe space." She moves her hands in a circular motion.

I let out a sigh. "I know, and I'm sorry it's so hard for me to talk about how I feel."

She leans in with a grin, "This is my job, right?"

"Right."

"And I'll offer whatever help I can, but it's easier when you tell me something—anything would do."

I chuckle. She's easy to talk to. She was the same way when Dad left, and I had a few meetings with her. I prefer to call them that instead of *sessions*. That word makes me feel like I'm broken. I might be, but not enough to need a shrink.

"Okay, well, Dad's home."

She adjusts on the bench and places her hands on her lap. "That's tricky."

I laugh. "A little bit."

"Are you talking to him?"

"While thinking about how to bury him some-place? Sure."

It's a morbid joke, but I wouldn't mind if he up and disappeared from our lives for good.

"Keller."

63

"I'm kidding."

"I know." She smiles. I appreciate the fact that she isn't calling the police.

"I get why you're upset—you have every right to your feelings and not want him around."

I roll my eyes. "Mom acts like I should just accept it."

Delilah pauses, studying the leaves on the tree as a light breeze rushes through the courtyard. My eyes follow. But she brings me back when she speaks again.

"Your mom is in a difficult position. This is someone she loves, regardless of what he's done or how he's hurt her. He is all she's known and they have children together, which complicates everything. I'm not saying anything negative about you or your sisters, but having kids binds people together in a way that no one understands. Not to mention the financial aspect. I'm sure she's struggled."

The muscles in my jaw tighten. "I worked all the hours I could at the theater to help fill the fridge."

She leans forward. "Of course you did! You love your family and I know you'd do anything for them. Your mom loves you, Keller. She is proud of you, and I know she doesn't want you to be upset."

"I—it was a lot to come home to him."

"I bet it was."

"I hate him."

She nods. "I know you do."

Our eyes meet. "I don't know how to stop."

"No one says you have to, but I will tell you something. I grew up with a terrible father. The worst, actually. He was aggressive and mean. I think he liked to take his frustrations out on us. I never felt good enough for him—not one day of my life, until he was lying in a hospital bed, dying, and then suddenly that monster in my closet wasn't so scary anymore and I felt some relief—but I also felt something else…"

I narrow my eyes. "What?"

"Pity. I pitied him. I could see how he was filled with regret. He told me. He apologized for everything, not that it should be enough, but in that moment—for me—it had to be. Because his passing would've haunted me forever. His words would be stuck in my head and every single time I tried to accomplish anything, I would let him continue to beat me down, causing self-doubt. All of that made me hate myself. It made me hide who I truly was when I was growing up. My father never knew about how I liked women until he was dying, and when I finally told him—even though I felt like I was trying to make him suffer—he didn't. He thanked me for letting him into my life and telling him something so private because we never had that when I was growing up. All my father offered me was pressure and aggression. He told me to study, to get

A's, to beat the competition, but come to find out, it was all because he never did. He was a steelworker for the railroad and wanted more for me. But instead of telling me how proud he was, he made me feel like what I did was never enough because he thought that would make me the best."

I wipe away a tear and stare up at the trees. I know she's told me this because she wants to humanize my dad, but I don't know if he's the same type of person her father was. Both are awful in their own way.

"He didn't give a shit about us."

She shakes her head to agree with me.

"My mom was devastated—she cried every night."

"I know that had to make you angry and sad."

I lock eyes with her again. "It made me want to drive to Indiana and beat his ass into the dirt."

"Valid feelings."

I lift my hand and let it drop. "I mean, how can someone do that? How can they leave their family—their kids—and act like nothing's changed?"

"Keller, it isn't your job to figure that out or to keep paying for that decision."

I release my breath. I know she's right, but it's so hard to let it go.

"I sometimes blame myself."

She adjusts next to me, "That's a natural reaction. Kids often blame themselves when a parent leaves because it's hard to imagine you didn't do something wrong to cause it."

"Yes!"

Her expression remains calm.

"I thought about everything I did—the things I said. My dad and I don't always get along and he can be…"

She takes my hand. "I know you had a black eye."

"I pushed him."

"Still, not acceptable, and I want you to know I have resources if you need them." She offers.

I shake my head. I refuse to do that to my mom. I will never talk to anyone about my dad getting physical with me. I don't want anyone coming into our home and making things worse for my mom and sisters. I will never let that happen.

"I'm okay. I promise, and so are my mom and Jenna and Jaime. My dad and I—we just, it's complicated."

She tucks a piece of her hair behind her ear. "I just want you to know that I'm here."

"I know you are, and I appreciate it."

I hear the bell ring and I stiffen. Delilah shifts her weight on the bench and I notice the creaking of wood.

"You should get to lunch—you look like you could use some food."

I scoff. "Why does everyone think I'm thin now?"

"Because you look thinner."

I laugh. "Fair enough."

I stand and she makes me pause while taking my hand in hers. "Keller. You're perfect, just as you are."

The words rush through me, nearly buckling my knees. I sniffle, fighting off the emotions before pulling away and heading back inside.

I pause inside the door and close my eyes. I flex my hand and feel a slight tingling sensation. I don't know if it will ever be the same again, but I have to try.

CHAPTER ELEVEN

AUGUST EAST

You shouldn't have slept with her."

I choke on my tea.

Evie stares at me as I set my cup down. I'm glad my parents gave us some privacy, which I expected because they never linger, before she jumped on me.

"I—listen, it was a mistake," I half-whisper while eyeing the door leading into the hallway.

"I get that, but it's not fair."

"Evie—do you think I don't feel like a jerk?"

She cocks a brow. "I'm sure you do, but it doesn't fix it."

"And fair to who? Do you—" I lower my voice, "think I did this to Shy?"

She rolls her hand. "No—Shy doesn't do anything she doesn't want to do, so I'm just as irritated with her."

"So—unfair to who?" I ask, like the idiot that I am.

She tilts her head with the roll of her eyes. "Who do you think?"

I part my lips, ready to say it's Keller when she interrupts me, "My brother."

I stiffen. "Oh—wait, what?" I think back to how Vincent looked at Shy and my heart sinks. In my self-ishness, I forgot.

She leans forward with her tea in hand, appearing more aristocratic than I expected from her. "He's been crushing on her forever—like since birth."

"I—man." I rub the side of my neck.

"And he's a mess, and I'm sick of watching him mope around the house."

"I never meant to hurt him—or anyone."

She leans back while picking at the edge of the ta-ble. Her eyes are low, refusing to look at me.

"I promise." I add, hoping she believes me, but also trying to relieve some weight from guilt.

"And him—you know. Keller, what about him?" she asks.

I may throw up. Evie's visit seemed nice with her offering of the duck and all, but I'm thinking it was a trojan horse.

"What about Keller?"

She takes a sip of tea with one pinky standing at

attention. I'd laugh, but she'd probably toss the cup at my head.

"Shy and Keller have been together since they were babies."

I relax a little. Evie had mentioned Keller to me before, telling me she knew—but now she's come to Shy's aid. I'm not upset about it. I really don't want to talk about how I feel about him. Maybe my being with Shy has pushed those thoughts out of her head. I'd say it's best. I shouldn't cause any more problems for Keller West. It's one reason I'm avoiding him and staying here in this house. I don't mind being a coward. If I stay away long enough, he'll be free of me.

I tug at the black rubber bracelet on my wrist. It's all I have left of him. I doubt I'll ever take it off, but no one needs to know.

"Isn't she dating Brian?" I ask.

She shakes her head. "I guess—listen, I don't know."

"Did she break up with him, does he know?" My panic is clear.

Evie bites her lip, letting me suffer for a few seconds longer out of spite. "No, I think they're still dating because no one knows but us."

"Oh, good." Relief eliminates the wrinkle in my brow.

Evie glances around the room. "Brian is a lay-over."

"A what?"

Her gaze snaps back onto me, "A lay-over, like in an airport. Brian James is not her plane taking off the runway."

"Then why be with him?"

"Because she doesn't enjoy being alone."

I tilt my head. Evie is insightful. I guess being quiet in school and watching people pays off. She'll be amazing with her magazine. She seems to notice everything.

"Anyway, she'll eventually break up with him, if she hasn't already, and then she'll end up with who we all know she wants to be with."

"Who?"

She chuckles. "Keller West."

I stare into my cup and watch the tea swirl. I know it shouldn't bother me. I know I should be happy that what Evie is saying will probably come true, but my heart claims otherwise. It's actually breaking. I fill my lungs with air and decide to change the subject. "Wanna see the library?" I ask.

She jumps out of her chair with excitement.

Good, it's worked.

"Yes, please!" she exclaims.

"Follow me."

We reach the library door, ornately carved with thorny vines and roses. I step aside to allow her the honor of opening it up. I know this is something she was dying to see in the house, so bringing her here seems a fitting payment for her gift.

Evie grabs the doorknob and twists it, allowing it to creak open, finally coming to a full-stop on its hinges.

"Whoa." Her eyes are bright with wonder.

"Right?" I add to her enthusiasm, glad we've pivoted.

Evie steps inside, craning her neck to stare at the painting on the ceiling. "The Book Lover." She whispers.

"Yep, an original, I guess. The artist was a friend of Charles Porter."

"I heard about it, but seeing it is something else. This is one reason the house will never be torn down."

I stare up at it. "I agree, and were they going to do that?"

"Some people never wanted this house to stay here. I mean, they get creeped out easily, so I guess I get it, but I love it here."

She grins at me, making the energy between us much better than it had been in the kitchen. I know Evie loves her brother, and I see now how what I did was more than just a mistake. It was hurtful, and I never meant for it to happen. It's hard to explain that Shylo Martin instigated the entire thing, but, at any point, I could've said no and I didn't. It's like I wanted what Keller had—or to use Shy as a layover, like Evie called it.

Shy deserves more than that from me, but she used me, too. I wasn't alone in the kitchen that night.

I just hate that it changed everything. I want to fix it, but I don't know how. I guess the first step will happen right here with Evie Rice.

"So, most of these are first editions," I declare while staring at the rows of books resting on the shelves.

"Really? Oh, my God. I'm afraid to touch them."

"You can look—I promise my mom and dad don't mind. I don't either. I'm glad you appreciate this as much as I do."

She nods, offering a glint of hope between us. I know Evie doesn't hate me or she wouldn't be here and I wouldn't have her little rubber duck in my pocket. She didn't pay the ferryman to have access to The Mill House. I believe she was genuinely trying to make me feel better.

I watch her fingers gently run along the row, touching each spine. I get that feeling. I felt the same way when I first discovered this room. Not that the magic has worn off, but a lot has happened between then and now.

More than I like.

She pauses, staring at the books. "He was obsessed with angels and demons," she states.

"I noticed. There are more books in the shelter below the atrium."

"What?"

"Yeah, there's a complete library down there and a large table and chairs."

"Can I see it?"

I bite my lip then release it. "Sure." My hesitation sparked by my dislike for that tree.

"But I want to come back here and read everything as soon as I can—if that's okay with you?"

I grin. "Of course."

She approaches me and fidgets with her hands. I think this is the point in a conversation when normal people would hug or something, but Evie is awkward, so she reaches out and taps my shoulder like she's petting a dangerous animal.

I laugh. "Come on, I'll show you."

"Sweet."

CHAPTER TWELVE

KELLER WEST

Bro! I'm open!" Ty yells from down the field. I pull back, trying my best to hold on to the football when it slips from my hands and hits the grass. A teammate snatches it up and runs in the opposite direction. I place my hands on my hips and look down at the ground. I can't keep doing this. My hand has to strengthen or I'm screwed.

"West!"

I look up as our coach jogs toward me with a clipboard in hand. He ends up close enough to hear without yelling, "Son, what's going on?"

I shake my head. "I'm psyching myself out." It seems like a viable excuse. We all have those moments, and I've definitely been through enough to make it believable.

He leans in and grabs my face shield, giving it a light tug. "Do you need to sit it out today?"

I growl. "No, Sir."

"Are you sure?"

"Yes, Sir!"

Our coach was in the Army and he always responds better to Sir than anything else when he's questioning our abilities.

He lets go of my helmet and offers a nod of approval. There have been many times I wished our Coach was my dad instead of the one I got. He's never abusive, but he pushes us to reach beyond what we think we can do. We win because of that. We respect him.

He lifts his hand and circles his finger in the air, bringing everyone in around me.

"Listen up! What do we do when a man's down?"

"Lift him up!" we chant in unison.

"Do we leave anyone behind?!"

"No, Sir!" we yell as one.

"What are we?" Coach barks.

"Wolfpack!" everyone screams. Howls follow and beating of chests. I know my team has my back. I just have to push through this and believe in myself again.

I catch movement on the right hand side and watch as Shy joins the other cheerleaders along the sideline. She smiles at me and nods. It feels good to see her back there again. I missed her more than I knew. She takes her spot in front and begins her routine. I get caught up watching her for longer than I probably should have.

"Are we good?" Brian bumps into my side. I hold my ground, shoving my mouth guard past my lips. I give him a nod before he moves to the right of me. I narrow my eyes and he lifts his hands.

"Running back!" he calls out to me.

I narrow my eyes. His mom would flip out if she knew he was on the field again, but maybe things have changed while I was in hospital. She could've reconsidered.

I receive the handoff and take a couple of steps back. All sound falls away as the cheerleaders seem to go into slow motion. I can hear every breath, and the pounding of my feet as I pivot and dig my foot into the grass, readying myself to throw.

I see Ty and Brian, both open, both wanting me to throw to them and I decide to while rearing back and happily launching the ball into the air toward my intended target.

Brian catches the ball and runs toward the goal. He crosses the line and does a happy little dance while Ty stares at me. I don't want any shit from him, and I don't have time to decipher why I chose Brian and not him.

Brian comes running back up to me and grabs my helmet, slamming it against the front of his. He yells in my face. I spit out my guard and yell back.

Sometimes it's easier to slip back into who everyone

expects us to be instead of fighting so hard to be seen as you truly are.

I need to remind myself of this every single time August East creeps into my thoughts. Like it matters. He clearly doesn't feel the same way he did for me before everything else happened. So, for now, I'll be Keller West. Quarterback. Football star. Everyone's hero in this town.

I take a much-needed drink as Shy approaches me. I crush the cup and toss it in the can while watching my teammates run laps on the field.

"Hey," she offers a timid wave.

"What's up?" I ask, more relaxed now than I have been in a while.

"You look good out there."

"Thanks." I give her a swift once-over. "Nice to see you back in your outfit."

She looks down the length of herself and grins. "Yeah, I guess I missed it."

I tap my helmet with an open palm. "Same—I missed playing."

"Well, the team missed you. They suck without you, Keller."

I chuckle. "I doubt it, but thanks."

She bumps me. "No, I'm serious. Your backup is not that great at throwing."

My eyes skirt down the bench and I see Cory

fidgeting from the sideline. His knee is shaking up and down. "He'll get better when I'm gone."

She tilts her head. "Gone?"

I let my hand dangle with my helmet attached, "When I go to college and play."

"Oh, yeah. I meant like—you were going to stop."

I roll my eyes. "Dad would kill me."

"About that—you know I'm here if you ever want to talk, right?"

I shake my head, not holding her gaze for long. "No, yeah, I know."

"Okay, good. I just feel you've been gone forever."

A silence falls between us, so she changes the subject, "I didn't see you at lunch today."

"I went across the street and got a protein shake."

"Ahh, taking this seriously again, huh?"

I lift my helmet and put it back on. "I've never not been serious about football, Shy. You know that."

"Right," she calls out as I jog backward away from her. She runs out onto the field and grabs the strap on my helmet and tightens it up before backing away.

"Thanks."

"We don't need you hurt again, right?"

"No."

She grins, twisting her foot on the grass. "The Farm is opening up again. I'm going to go get some apples for pies later on today. Mom wants to make like a million. Wanna come?"

"Let me ask Mom."

"Okay. Just call me." She shakes her extended fingers by her ear, creating a phone receiver.

"Will do," I agree. She runs back over to the cheerleaders who are busy staring at us from the sideline. I turn to see Brian is staring at me, too.

Great.

Why isn't she asking him?

CHAPTER THIRTEEN

AUGUST EAST

E vie leans in closer to the hemlock than I'd prefer. "Be careful," I caution.

She giggles while straightening up. "I still can't believe you have these in this garden—and the Venus flytraps." She looks back at me. "A plant that eats meat—how crazy is that?"

I nod. "Really crazy. Have you seen the previews for that new movie coming out next year called *The Little Shop of Horrors*?"

She sighs, "How can I not? Vincent keeps talking about it. He actually recorded it and watches that trailer like it's the movie. He's obsessed."

"It looks fun."

She inspects her fingernails, "I guess so. I still prefer movies based on true events. Much scarier and fun."

I laugh. "Not every girl is like you, Evie."

She pauses. "How boring would it be if they were?"

"True." My eyes shift and I watch the tree. It now has a few leaves on it, which is annoying. Why it keeps pretending like it's alive is beyond me.

"So, have you used the maple?"

"What?" I ask while turning to face Evie, who's now much closer to me. It's sort of unsettling because I didn't hear her coming. I guess it's part of her spooky charm.

She points at the tree. "For pancakes."

I snort, "No—that tree looks diseased."

"Oh, come on, East! Don't be so mean." She approaches the tree, and it makes me uneasy. She steps up to it and the twisted thing towers over her small frame. I blink through the memory of the child in white who once stood there—or did they? I can't be certain now. Not with my seizures and nightmares becoming so strong and vivid.

Part of me wants to believe Maggie went into another realm and brought Keller back, but another part of me wants it to be nonsense. I sort of want everything to calm down and to make the last few years as easy as possible before I graduate. I can't find my normal. I can if I try. And some days I want that more than anything, especially now that Keller West almost died because of me.

I take a quick breath, fidgeting with my hands.

"I also like your hair. I know you didn't think I noticed, but I did. Why did you decide to cut it?" she asks.

I swallow hard. I'd forgotten all about it.

"Stress," I admit.

She reaches up and touches the tree, causing me to hiss through my teeth. If anything happens, I'll be the first to douse it with gasoline and set it on fire without a second thought.

She turns while holding her palm against the trunk. I wish she'd move away from it, but I can't explain why. It's enough that I'm being honest about my hair.

She hops down from the bench and looks me over before reaching up and messing with her hair. "I can relate. My hair was down past the middle of my back before you came here and then the day before I met you, I cut it off like this." She waves a hand.

"Well, I like it."

"And I like yours," she speaks through a grin.

It's nice to see this side of Evie Rice. I know she wants access to this house, but her friendship is growing on me. If no one else ever comes to visit, I hope I'll at least see her. I can imagine us talking for years to come and I've never really considered that before. Most things are not permanent with me.

Most.

"So, can we go to the second library now?"

I blink out of my stupor and lighten up. I hate feeling the weight of emotions. It's so much more complicated than things have to be.

I take one step toward her when I catch movement out of the corner of my eye. The roses seem to move. Evie notices it, too. She's drawn closer as I cautiously approach the section of flowers that now seem to be taking on a life of their own.

We both lean in and she yelps when an eye blinks at us from what appears to be the center of a rose, but a sudden black blur and meow effectively explains the moment when Owen rubs up against the bottom of my leg.

"Oh, Owen! You naughty kitty, you almost gave me a heart attack!" She picks him up and cuddles him against her chest. "And do you know how hard it is to scare me?" She laughs through the words. Her skin is slightly pink now, proving Owen gave her a fright.

"I thought the roses had eyes."

Evie rocks the cat in her arms. "Totally! I was scared, but ready to become famous!"

She returns her attention back to Owen as he stares at me. I reach out and he hisses, so I withdraw my hand.

"It's my garden," I clarify.

"Yes, Owen, remember you're a guest in this house."

I laugh. "I don't know if cats ever feel like guests."

She pets his head while he purrs. "True, they've always been royalty—all the way back to the Egyptians, maybe even further."

"Definitely him." I lean in and Owen growls. I straighten. "I don't think he likes me all that much."

"Nonsense. He's upset because he got lost in those roses. He probably cut himself on the thorns."

Worry spreads across my brow. "I hope not."

Evie bites her lip. "As much as I'd love to see the library in the shelter, I think I should return Owen to Maggie."

"Yeah, okay," I agree without protest.

"But," she continues, "I expect a do-over so I can see it."

"It's a deal, plus I doubt it's going anywhere."

"I'm going to go, but I'll see you tomorrow."

"Oh—what time?" I ask.

"At school, silly." She smiles.

I part my lips.

"Unless you're too scared to come back."

I rub the side of my neck. "I don't get scared."

She leans in closer. "Then prove it."

Evie moves past me and out of the garden. I'm left standing there with a smirk on my face.

"She's good."

"Who?"

I turn on my heel while clutching my chest to see Dad standing there. I have no idea where he came from.

"Dad." I chuckle through the nerves.

"I didn't mean to scare you."

"I was talking about my friend Evie," I thumb behind me.

"Where did she go?"

"We—" I glance at the roses. "Maggie's cat, Owen, was in here. Evie is taking him back to her house."

"Strange, how did a cat get in the house?"

"I don't know. Maybe he's a witch."

Dad looks at me with a strange expression, then smiles. "Was that a joke?"

I fiddle with the rubber bracelet on my wrist, "Maybe."

He approaches me while placing a hand on my shoulder. "It's good to see. You've seemed so unhappy lately, and I guess some of that is my fault."

"Dad—no. It's just, I want a home, ya know? Like we had before. And it's hard when we can't stay anywhere."

He leans in and places his hand behind my head, rubbing his hand on my hair. "That's what I want for all of us."

"I know."

He looks at my hair. "I guess you did a job on yourself."

I reach up and mess with a loose lock. "Is it bad?"

"No. I like it, now your mother may be another story. She loves your hair, as you know."

I let out a defeated sigh. "You don't have to remind me."

"She won't be mad, just maybe a little sad." He pinches his fingers together.

"I hope not because I'm sick of upsetting people."

"I think you'll make everyone happy come Halloween."

My brow furrows. "Why?"

"Because your mother is making invitations."

I shake my head, "Oh—no—please, no, not a party."

He steps away. "Good luck telling her no."

I roll my eyes and rub my face with my hands through a groan.

I guess the only positive is that means we'll still be here at the end of October. That gives me time to make some things right.

CHAPTER FOURTEEN

KELLER WEST

Standing in front of the mirror, I replace my shirt for the fourth time. I don't know why it's so hard for me to get dressed. I lean in, running my fingers through a few loose curls, and study my face.

I have lost weight. My jaw is tighter, cheeks more pronounced. It's like I've consciously decided to go on a diet. My appetite isn't back, not fully, but I'm trying. I think more than anything.

About the dreams that seemed so real.

I glance out the window toward his house. I wonder what I'd do if the light flashed from his window? Would I decipher it? Would I answer?

I'm afraid I would, but I know I shouldn't.

What's happening now is exactly where I should be. Playing football. Focusing on my future. Going out with Shy.

This isn't a date, Keller. Stop. She's seeing Brian.

I hear a giggle and catch movement out of the corner of my eye. I turn, my door's ajar. One of the girls must be spying on me—probably both because they move in a pack.

I step up as Dad pauses outside my door. I hold my breath. I don't want to talk to him. It never ends well, and I promised myself I'd do my best to keep the peace for Mom's sake.

"Son?"

I grit my teeth while cracking the door open a little wider. "Hey."

"Don't you look nice?"

I guess I do, but I wasn't fishing for a compliment. "I'm headed out to hang with Shy. She's getting some apples from The Farm."

"Mmm, date, huh? I thought the James boy was seeing her now?"

How the hell does he know anything about my friends? I push my irritation way down and shrug it off. "She is—but we're friends."

He leans in, "Watch that friend stuff. It'll get ya in trouble."

I want to punch him in the gut, but I can't.

"I should go." I step out into the hallway and close the door behind me. I catch him staring past me at my bedroom walls. He probably wants to talk about all the bands and movie posters, but I don't care. That room is mine. It's a safe space for me to live in, so I don't need him nosing around.

"I have something to show you, Keller."

I nearly sigh, but I hold back. I just want to do my time with him and move on without a fight.

I thumb behind me. "I don't want to be out too late with practice and all."

He gives me an approving nod.

Great. Be happy, you jerk. You can have the next couple of years, but then I'm gone.

He leads me down the hallway. "It'll only take a minute and I promise you'll be happy you did."

My jaw sets as I stare at his back. I could do a flying kick and knock him out if I wanted to, but I have to stop fantasizing about this shit. He doesn't deserve to take up this much space in my head.

He stops by the door leading to the garage. I'm expecting to step out and see something macho, like a punching bag. He thinks he knows karate.

He turns with a grin before swinging the door wide and allowing me to see the white Corvette with one red stripe wrapping it from the hood to the truck around the center. I stop breathing. It's a dream car of mine. I used to cut out pictures of Corvettes and save them in a scrapbook, knowing it would be a long time before I'd see one.

"Wow," I say while approaching it.

"Catch."

I turn just in time to snatch keys out of the air.

I stare at them with confusion. "What's going on?"

He steps in closer than I'd like and places a hand on my shoulder. "It's yours, Keller."

I part my lips. I could cry. I turn to stare at it as my dad pops the hood and props it open so I can see the engine. I can't help but join him as he rattles off some details about the inner workings of the car, but I'm in a state of shock.

"What's the catch?" I ask, not trusting him.

He closes the hood and leans on it while folding his arms over his chest. "Good grades and win those games."

I take a long breath and release it. I get good grades. I always have. I hate to admit that I enjoy school, but I always have. It helps me focus.

I shake my head. "I can't believe it."

"Well, believe it, and son, listen. I know I messed up," he leans in closer, "I made some horrible mistakes with you—with all of you. I was stupid and self-ish and I know this car doesn't make up for everything I've done, but I want you to know I love you and your mom and sisters. I always have, but this isn't a bribe—I want those grades to stay up."

I tear up. I needed to hear those words from him,

but I sort of feel like he's trying to buy my love and forgiveness. I don't know if I'll ever fully forgive him, but as long as Mom's happy, then I can't say anything about it. But if he ever hurts her again, I can't promise I won't hurt him the best I can.

"Thanks, Dad," I choke out instead of all the rest of my thoughts.

He straightens up, "Take her for a spin and go impress that *friend* of yours." He emphasizes the word friend, and it makes me uncomfortable. I'll never be like him. I won't cheat and sneak around behind my friends' backs. It isn't who I am.

I slip inside the car and grip the wheel as he grins at me from the other side of the windshield. I offer a nod as he presses the button to raise the garage door. I back out, careful to watch what I'm doing.

I hate how nervous I feel, but I guess this is what it's like when you really want something and want to protect it.

I glance in my rearview mirror and see The Mill House's reflection.

I guess the same thing could be said about how I feel about August East. He makes me nervous because I want to be with him and to protect it at all costs— but I think that time has come and gone now and I need to move on.

I just wish I could convince my heart.

CHAPTER FIFTEEN

AUGUST EAST

I sit on the steps and stare out onto the town. I can see his house from here and I hate it. It's always in view, like my eye is drawn to it. I can't control how I feel about Keller any more than I can stop liking boys. It's a part of me now.

I rub my eyes before flinching when the front gate slams shut. I look up to see both Evie and Vincent walking toward me. Evie was here earlier in the day, so I don't know what she wants now. Vincent, it could be anything.

"Come on." Vincent waves his hand.

"Where?"

"The Farm is open."

I shake my head. "I don't know what that is."

"It's a place where you grow stuff." He smirks.

Evie swipes at him and he ducks out of the way. "Stop being a brat."

Vincent rolls his eyes, dropping on the step next to me and bumping into my shoulder. I guess this is his way of saying we're good.

He bumps me a couple more times until I smile. "Stop."

"Missed ya at school today. Lunch wasn't the same."

"I might come back tomorrow," I glance at Evie, "I don't know yet—but the odds are looking good."

Evie rocks on her heels. She's still wearing the same dress as earlier in the day, but her hair is pushed out of her eyes with a beret.

"The Farm has the most delicious apples in the entire world."

I chuckle. "That's a big claim."

Vincent nods, "No, they do. The pies that come out of those apples are otherworldly."

I glance at him. "Using big words I see."

"Shut up, I need to practice. Your mom looks smart."

"I'll knock you out," I reply with the cock of my brow.

He waves a hand. "Just kidding—but not about the apples."

Mom steps out onto the porch and tosses a bucket of water into the driveway. She straightens up and wipes her brow. "Hello!" she chirps.

Vincent nearly trips over himself standing up.

"Hi, Mrs. East. Do you need help with anything?"

"Oh, love. It's just Rosetta."

Vincent looks down at me with a Cheshire grin, distorting his features. I mouth a resounding *no*.

"Maybe when we get to know each other better, Mrs. East."

I hate him.

Evie steps forward. "Rosetta—can East come with us to pick some apples? I promise he'll bring some home to you."

She gives me a look and winks. "Absolutely—I'm tired of him sulking around this house."

"Mom," I whine.

"Just kidding but it'll do you good to get out and have some fun with your friends."

Evie laughs. "I plan on putting him to work."

"I'd love to make a dutch apple pie. It's one of East's favorites, with a dollop of cream, of course."

She offers a smile and disappears back inside the house. Vincent spends more time than he should staring at the door.

"Seriously?" I exclaim while smacking the side of his arm. He laughs through it.

"Every apple I pick will be for her." He extends his hand like he's reciting Shakespeare.

"I'm done with you." I walk toward the gate,

grabbing the latch and opening it up. It fights against me, but I muscle it to the side. You'd think colder weather would shrink the metal, but it doesn't seem to help this old iron one bit.

Evie walks past me with a grin while Vincent approaches. I pull the gate toward me and he grabs the bars while sticking his face through two of them, "If you want me to stay here and help your mom, I will."

I jerk on the gate and he groans while pulling his head out.

"So, what's up with this farm?" I ask as we all walk down the sidewalk in a straight line.

"Um—it's The Farm."

"Oh, sorry." Rolling my eyes.

"Seriously, they have the best apples this time of the year, then we move into pumpkin season!" Vincent skips a step and reaches toward the sky.

I control my laughter as Evie leans in closer to me. "Vincent is obsessed with pumpkins—carving them. He thinks he's Michelangelo."

"Hey, I'm not that good yet, but someday I will be." His pace decelerates. He locks in step with me again.

"I think jack-o'-lanterns are cool. I enjoy carving them, but I'm not that great at it. All I get is triangle eyes and a crooked mouth."

"Same here, so don't beat yourself up over it."

97

"There's a contest every year and I'm gonna win it this time." Vincent proclaims a premature victory, but he's welcome to be confident. I've never seen his carving skills in a pumpkin, so I can't say one way or another if he'll win or not.

"The grand prize is one hundred dollars."

"Whoa," I mutter, suddenly interested.

"Yeah, it's a donation from, well... It's a donation."

I narrow my eyes. "From who?"

Vincent blows out his cheeks and shoves his hands in his jean pockets. He's wearing some acid-washed jeans and high-top Nikes with a green swoosh and black laces. They've seen some miles, but nothing feels better than a broken pair of tennis shoes. I glance at Evie. He couldn't be more different than she was if he tried. The only thing that makes them believable is his obsession with horror movies and her need to hunt down anything supernatural.

"Westson Construction," Evie offers.

"Oh." I look down at the sidewalk as we continue to get further away from my house.

"But anyway, I'm going to win it this year."

I nod. "I hope you do."

I'm not sure why knowing it's Keller's dad who donates the prize each year is bothering me so much.

No. I do. It's because of Keller West.

The one boy I want and can't have.

CHAPTER
SIXTEEN

KELLER WEST

I roll up to Shy's house and put the car in park. I can't believe it's mine. After everything that's happened, it almost makes things better.

Almost.

Shy exits, wearing a long plaid shirt belted at the waist over a pair of light jeans that cuff at her ankles with elastic. Her black pirate boots glide along until she stops dead—mouth agape while gawking at me in the car.

"What the F'n H is going on?" she exclaims.

I grin. She hates to curse, so this is about as close to it as she'll get.

I step out and lean against the side with a sense of pride. "It's mine."

"No way!" she squeals while rushing toward it. She places her hand against the body and slides it along, eyes wide with wonder.

"Yes way," I clarify.

"How? What did you do, Keller? Did you steal this car?" She places a hand on her hip.

"Shy, I'd never do that without you."

She leans in. "Better not! But seriously, where did you get this car? Did you rent it?"

"No, my dad gave it to me."

She stops dead. "He did not give you this car— your dream car? The car you've wanted since you were, like, old enough to know what a car was?"

"Yep—same one. It's mine."

She approaches me with a strange look on her face. "Did he—I mean—" she pauses. I know she doesn't want to upset me.

"No, he didn't cheat on Mom. If he had, I'd beat his ass. I hate cheaters."

Her expression changes while she's biting her lip.

"Unless you know something, Shy. Do you?"

She shakes her head. "No—I haven't heard anything."

"Okay good. I'd like to think this is a good thing."

She grabs the door handle, and I rush in to do it for her. We stand closer than we probably should until I open the door and let her climb in. I rush around and get in on the other side just as she's popping the glove box open and looking inside.

"I haven't had time to put anything in there yet."

"There's a receipt."

I face forward and turn the key in the ignition. The engine hums. I can feel the vibration through the wheel.

"I don't want to know how much it was."

She stares at the paper in her hand and then shoves it back in the glove box. "Good, because it's probably hush money."

I turn to face her. "Hush money?"

She stares out her window. "Yeah—you know. A bribe."

"Shy."

"What?" She turns to face me. "He hurt you."

"I know, but he's trying." I'm surprised to be defending him, but I promised I'd try.

"I'm not okay with anyone who does that to you."

"I appreciate that. I do, but I want my mom to be happy, Shy, and if having Dad home does that, then I'll have to go along with it."

"Okay fine. I get it." She surrenders, not wanting to.

"Let's go get those apples, okay?" I pivot or she'll dwell on it.

Her eyes brighten. "Cool."

"Cool."

We pull up to The Farm and I can smell the apples through my open window. My stomach growls. I'm happy to have a little of my appetite coming back. I need to bulk up a bit more before our next game.

I put the car in park and ask the obvious question before we exit the car.

"Shy, what's going on between you and Brian?"

She refuses to look at me, but she's fidgeting with her hands. It's a nervous habit she's always had when she doesn't want to talk about something.

"I don't love him, Keller."

"Shy—I thought—well, I don't know what I thought."

"It's just," she glances at me, "it got weird when you were in the hospital. He got clingy."

I shake my head. "That's something Ty says."

She sighs. "I know, but it's true. He wanted to talk about the future and I just—I couldn't."

I run my fingers through my hair. "Why?"

She locks eyes with me. "Because I don't see him when I think about the future."

I know this is my opportunity to fix things between us, it's the doorway I've been waiting for, but I hesitate—I'm not taking it. Not yet.

"The future is a scary thought."

"Yeah—I guess." She's disappointed. I can tell.

I open my door and so does she, refusing to let me help her this time.

She walks around to the front of the car and

reaches in, taking my hand. I don't fight it, but it still doesn't feel right.

I don't know if it ever will.

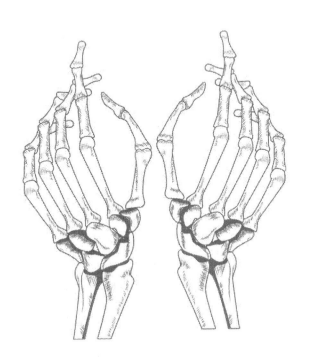

CHAPTER SEVENTEEN

AUGUST EAST

The three of us stand shoulder to shoulder under a wooden archway that has a sign nailed to it that simply says *The Farm*. I guess both Evie and Vincent were not being coy when they told where we were going. I guess if I had a farm, I may consider calling it something this simple, too. I mean, it's easiest.

I can smell the apples in the air. I've never experienced that before. I never visited an apple orchard back east. I could've, but a place like this seems like something a baker might like more than me. I suck at cooking. I won't lie. I can burn water in a pot.

I feel Evie thread her arm into mine and we move forward like the cast of *The Wizard of Oz*. There's no yellow brick road, but there is a gravel road leading down a long lane of maple trees. The leaves are turning colors. Splashes of yellow and red stand out against the blue sky. I can see gray clouds off in the distance and it smells like rain. Another storm is coming.

"Hey, East!" a girl calls out to me with a wave and then another girl does the same. I offer a wave and nod, but I don't know them.

Evie leans in closer to my ear. "I told you kids were happy to get out early that day."

"I guess so." A few more smiles and waves greet us as we make our way down the road. I can see a large white barn with ivy clinging to the sides. It's beginning to creep its way across the front. But the doors sit wide open. I can't see inside the barn from here, but it reminds me of a painting you'd see in some gallery celebrating America. The barn isn't the only building. To the right, I can see a house with a nice big wrap-around porch and a swing. And there's a smaller building with a sign on it. It has wagons gathered in front of it, filled with wooden baskets.

"Vincent, grab a wagon, please," Evie begs.

Vincent doesn't hesitate to leave us standing there while he collects a wagon, and tosses an extra basket on the bed. He drags it back over to us.

"Better?" Evie asks.

I look at the ground, "Yeah."

"Good—I'm glad. It's weird seeing you so sad."

My gaze lifts, "I'm not."

She tilts her head.

I sigh. "Okay, maybe a little."

"Anyway, isn't this place awesome? They sell apples this time of the year and then pumpkins," she counts on her fingers, "then trees. They take your live tree back and replant it—isn't that cool?"

She nudges her chin. "They're over there."

I look to the left and can see a small forest of different sized pine trees. I love the idea and hope we come and get one for the house.

I pause, biting my lip.

If we're still here in December.

"I have to tell you something."

Evie's brows nearly meet with worry.

"Dad says we might move to Arizona."

"What?" her voice carries on the wind and I swear everyone stops talking.

I lean in. "Might—I don't know for sure."

"That's some bullshit," Vincent whines while glaring at me.

"I'm not happy about it."

"Why?" Evie asks with a huff.

I adjust my weight from one foot to the other. "Because the plant won't be opening back up after, you know, but anyway, he's been offered a job there."

"Your mom has a job," Vincent interjects.

"She does, but—not too morbid, but no one's dying around here."

106

Evie laughs. "I guess that makes for some unpleasant business."

I rub the side of my arm. "Unfortunately."

"But the house is yours, right?" Evie asks.

I dismiss it with a wave, "Yeah, it is, but we still have to eat."

"Charles Porter was rich," Vincent shares, "or so I've heard."

"Well, he didn't leave it to us."

"Or maybe you just haven't found it," Vincent whispers.

Evie rolls her eyes. "I will not listen to that crazy nonsense again, Vincent."

"What crazy nonsense?" I want an answer.

Vincent exchanges a strange look with her, so she tells me, "Some people think he hid it in the house—"

"Hid what?" I'm perplexed.

"His money—jewels, gold," Vincent croons.

I roll my eyes. "This isn't pirate treasure in The Goonies."

Vincent rubs his chin. "Man, that's a good movie, but not so scary."

I massage my palm, "It's great, but there's no treasure in the house."

Vincent shows some pride. "I know—for a fact — that he didn't have a bank account."

My brows meet. "That's weird."

"Right?" he baits me some more.

Evie grabs the handle of the wagon and gives a tug. Vincent allows her to strip him of his duties. "I'm not doing this—I want some apples."

I blink through Vincent's claims. If—and that's a big **if**—there is any treasure in that house, then my parents should know. Maybe that would stop them from wanting to move? We could stay here—make this a home, be happy. My mind sparks with a glimmer of hope. I don't want to move to Arizona, not because I hate the state—but because I actually like it here. I like my new friends, and there's Keller, who, even though I know I can't have him, I still don't want to be away from where he lives. I know it sounds sad, but it's true.

"Boys," Evie says.

"Fine." Vincent huffs while taking over once again. He pulls the wagon beside us as we make our way toward the rows of apple trees. The smell is getting stronger and my mouth waters. I can't help it. They smell sweeter than any I've ever had before. I'll definitely give some to mom. She'll make some apple crisp and serve it with ice cream. My hand slides across my stomach as it grumbles.

People seem to gather. I can understand why. We reach the first tree and Vincent snatches an apple from a branch and sniffs it first, closing his eyes.

"I can taste the pie already," he mutters.

I look up at the tree and follow his lead, grabbing one apple, then two.

"We're only allowed three baskets full. It's one basket per person," Evie clarifies.

I can understand, looking down the rows and seeing most of the town has migrated here. My eyes wander over the crowd. I look for him when I know I shouldn't, but I don't expect to see him here. I go back to hand picking the apples I want. Knowing I only get one basket makes me more conscious of what I'm doing.

"We should look at more trees than one," Vincent demands before he leaves us. He rushes across the row. The apples don't look any different to me, but maybe he knows something I don't.

"He's right, some apples are sweeter, and some are more tart. Here," she lifts two apples, "smell one, then the other."

I take both. I place one apple close to my nose and smell the sweet aroma that seems to define this place. Then I sniff the other and it smells different.

"But they both came from the same tree," I state.

Evie grins. "It's like siblings. We're not the same, are we?" She eyes Vincent, who's hopping up and down desperate to reach an apple that's a bit too high on the branch. I watch a girl offer him a small wooden step stool and he takes it.

"I get that."

We go back to picking apples and I glance behind me and the blood rushes from my face.

I see him—actually, I see them—holding hands, walking this way. They haven't seen me yet, but it'll happen and I don't know what to do.

I turn to Evie in a panic. "Um, where's the restroom?"

She nudges her chin toward the small building that sits behind the army of wagons and baskets.

"I'll be back."

"Like Arnold Schwarzenegger?" She laughs through her joke.

"Yas." I attempt a poor impression of his accent.

She giggles, but I have to go right now, before Keller and Shy see me. Luckily, there are enough people here now that I can weave in and out of the small crowd. I reach the small building and have to turn to the side as a girl comes running out, laughing. Her friend is close behind. They momentarily gawk at me. I know I'm probably at the heart of some pretty juicy rumors by now, but I don't even care. My thoughts are consumed with one person, and he's currently out there, right now—holding Shylo Martin's hand.

CHAPTER
EIGHTEEN

KELLER WEST

Shy is leisurely leading me toward the large white barn covered in ivy. We parked outside the gate. The owners of The Farm insist on it. They don't have vehicles on their property. They bike everywhere and sled in the winter with the help of their horses.

From here, we have to walk on foot, but there's something peaceful about going down this gravel road lined with trees. I forgot how much I loved coming here.

It feels like a memory more than from my childhood. It's deeper, but I didn't dream about this place when I was in the hospital, so it confuses me why I feel such a connection with her. I glance at the gate. The sign says 1885. I knew it was old, but something about that settles in me like an old friend. I shake it off. I'm wondering if I should talk to Delilah about everything. I know she'd keep it between us, but I don't want to sound like I'm crazy.

Shy squeezes my hand, so I bring my attention back to her.

"Where are you?" she asks.

"I—I'm right here, Shy."

"No, you weren't."

I part my lips. It's stupid of me to think I can lie to her. She's always been great at reading me.

"I missed this place." I look up ahead and see a few groups of people heading toward the big white barn.

"Me, too! But I also missed you," she admits.

I bite the edge of my lip, then release it. "Same," is all I offer. My response feels empty. My gut churns with guilt.

She tugs on my hand and stops me from walking. A couple passes us by, probably in their twenties. They have their arms wrapped around each other. They're happy—in love. Something I wish I could do with her. I know she wants that from me.

"I need to talk to you about something."

My muscles tense up. That's never a good sign. But Shy is one of those girls who's always been honest with me, no matter what.

"It was you."

I swallow hard.

"What do you—"

Shy interrupts me with the shake of my hand, "Don't be dumb, Keller. I mean, it's you I see when I think about the future."

My heart nearly stops in my chest. This is the moment, isn't it? She's offering me the out I've needed all along. All I have to do is tell her I love her—which I do, and all of my problems will be over.

So why am I hesitating? His eyes—mouth—face, float through my mind's eye. His smile consumes me. I can hear his laughter echoing in the wind. August East haunts me like a ghost.

"Keller."

I snap out of it, embarrassed that I let my mind wander. "I'm here."

She sighs. "Listen, I know."

I glance around us, fearful that someone will listen in.

She steps closer to me and places a hand on my cheek. Her touch is soothing. I've never denied it.

Her bright eyes search mine. "And I don't care."

I feel awful. I know she's willing to compromise, but am I ready to let her do that for me?

"I love you, Keller. I always have and I always will, and I know we could be happy together, if you'd just let it happen," she begs.

I close my eyes. I feel her soft lips brush against

mine. It's not passionate. It's like a warm blanket on a winter's day. That's why Shy is for me. She's safe and predictable. I know what I get with her. It'll always be the same. Today—tomorrow—in the future she so badly wants to give me.

I shake my head, gritting my teeth as her forehead rests against mine. My hands slip behind her back, cradling her against me. It feels normal, right, and yet it isn't. This isn't me. It'll never be me, but I can't have everything, can I?

"I love you, too," I whisper, wanting her to know.

"Good." She tears up, and I let it settle in between us. Brian will be upset, but manageable. Everyone else will be happy, but that's expected.

But East.

I take a short breath. He doesn't even want to be with me anymore, so why do I care what he'll think?

For a few seconds, I wonder if this is what would make him want me again, and it makes me feel even worse. I open my eyes and stare at Shy, who is now happier than I've seen her in a while. I draw her in close, pushing August East out of my mind, and kiss her. It's hard at first, but I ease into it knowing that it's what she wants.

I pull back and she's grinning. Her eyes search mine. I've given her the one thing she always wanted, but she'll never have all of me. Not when I know he's there.

She backs away, taking my hand with her, and we walk down the gravel lane again. She laughs twice, shaking her head, then biting her full lip. She's so pretty and smart. Shylo Martin could have anyone in the world, and yet she keeps coming back to me. I know it should be a sign, but I'm torn. I love her—but will it ever be enough?

"My mom is going to flip."

"Mine, too," I admit, because she knows me better than most. I think back to her showing that old photo album in the garage and telling me about Henrietta. My heart sinks like the Titanic that killed her.

I think about how happy she looked sitting next to her sister and knowing she was born a boy, just like me.

But my dad would kill me if he knew I liked boys, too. And he'd probably lock me away if he found out about the nail polish and lipstick. My expression darkens.

"Hey."

I escape my thoughts when Shy moves in front of me, walking backward but holding onto my waist.

"Yeah?" I speak through a grin.

"You make me so happy." A huge smile curves her lips. It is nice to see her this way. I guess I should be grateful that I can make her feel this way. But my thoughts are like a slingshot. I keep bouncing around and it's unsettling.

115

"I promised my mom that I'd get her the sweetest apples this year, so I'm gonna need help."

My eyes spark, "I'll do my best."

"You better!" she exclaims.

"Plus—you'll get to enjoy her apple cobbler."

"Unfair."

She twists away from me while grabbing my hand. I don't know if she'll ever let it go again.

"I never said I wouldn't use bribery, Keller Kennedy West."

"I respond well to it," I admit.

She giggles next to me as I try my best to accept this as who I am. It can be.

I just have to make it happen.

We reach the end of the tree-line and I scan the crowd. Many people have shown up to get their apples. I keep looking when I shouldn't, knowing what I'm searching for. Finally, I see some familiar faces I want to see. Evie is reaching above her head and Vincent has jogged up to her with some apples cradled in the bottom of his shirt.

But my heart is a little heavy when I realize they're alone. East isn't here—but shouldn't I be relieved?

Shy lifts her hand and calls out, "Hey! Evie—Vincent!"

And just like that, we're headed their way as a couple again.

Keller and Shy.
Normal.
Expected.
I only hope it's real.

CHAPTER NINETEEN

AUGUST EAST

Ipush past a group of girls as they check out a table of Fall decorations. I can smell cinnamon and nutmeg in the air. The shop is small, but filled to the brim with door wreaths, wooden dolls, pot-pourri, candles rolled in flowers and more. Everywhere I look, there's something new. But I'm not here to shop. I came to hide.

I pinch the bridge of my nose.

"Hello."

I open my eyes to a young girl, maybe all of thirteen, wearing an apron that just says **The Farm** in black ink set against white fabric. She has doe-like eyes and porcelain skin. If she didn't blink, I'd think she was a life-size doll.

"Can I help you?" she asks.

I scan the room. "Could I use your bathroom?"

"Sure, it's that way." She points toward the back of the shop, so I leave her with a smile and nod, acknowledging her help, but I don't have time to talk. I step into a narrow hallway and see a line. I don't really have to use the bathroom. I just want to splash some cold water on my face.

I hear the silver bell ring that sits above the shop's door, and my heart skips a beat. But it's just a few more girls chatting away arm in arm. I should run, but I can't. Running now would be ridiculous. I have to face him, eventually—especially if I'm going back to school.

I wonder if that's even a good idea, but again, I don't want to become a hermit like Charles Porter. I miss being around other kids and feeling normal. I want normal. I long for it. I want a schedule and things to distract me. I need homework and conversations. I want a life.

The line moves and I take one step. Just one. I sort of hate these moments. I spend too much time thinking about everything. About Keller and Shy. About the possibility of moving. About how bad I feel.

I feel a nudge from behind and think nothing of it, but it happens again. I glance behind me and my blood runs cold. It's Shy. I wish I could think fast enough to eliminate the awkward energy.

"Of course, there's a line," she grumbles, looking

at her multi-colored nails. She's painted each one a different color. Blue, green, yellow and orange. It's fun. Like her, but I shouldn't be focusing on it.

"It's not too bad." But it feels strange to admit it.

We all take a step forward and now I'm one person away from the door. I can hang on for a few more minutes. I'm sure of it. All I have to do is hold it together until I can get in the room and drown myself in the sink. Maybe they'll be a window I can crawl out of, but what would it matter now? She's right behind me.

The girl exits the bathroom and I slip inside, happy to get away from people. I feel a bump from behind and I'm pushed forward. Shy slams the door behind her and now I'm stuck in this tiny space with her.

What the actual hell?

"Shy!" I exclaim.

She pushes off the door and steps up to me. For one second, I think she's going to kiss me, but she doesn't.

"East—we need to talk."

My nerves kick in. "I'd rather not." I take one step back.

"Do you not think this is weird for me, too?" she asks.

"I really don't know what you're thinking, Shy." I wish I could dissolve into nothing.

"We can't pretend like nothing happened."

I laugh, I probably shouldn't, but is she serious. "Um, how?"

She adjusts her stance. "We have to."

I narrow my eyes. "I'm so glad you have this all figured out."

"You don't have to be sarcastic, August East."

I fold my arms over my chest, "How are you so, I don't know, calm?"

"I have to be."

"Why? Because of who you are?"

She shakes her head. "Keller is here, and he's with me."

"And? I'm with Evie and Vincent."

She narrows her eyes. "No—he's *with* me."

It takes a few seconds, but when the truth hits me, it's like a lightning strike. "Oh, shit," I mumble.

I turn and see myself in the mirror above the sink. Her reflection is behind me. I want to scream. How could he be with her? How could she not tell him what happened between us? How?

But I know why.

Shylo Martin is a lot like me in so many ways. Maybe that's why he likes her. Maybe it's why he liked me? I can't be sure.

I don't know why I'm ever worrying about this shit. Honestly. I can't be with him. I know I can't, and yet this is killing me. It's like poison in my veins.

I splash cold water on my face, leaving my hands in place, but I finally let go. Like everything else, I have to. I have to stop fooling myself.

"East." Her voice is soft—consoling.

I turn to face her. "What?" I lean against the sink, white-knuckling the edge.

A knock comes at the door. My eyes lock onto the handle.

I need to push past her and run. Yes. Run. Run fast and far.

"We need to come to an understanding." She sounds so sure of herself.

I laugh—can't help it. She doesn't seem happy with my reaction. "About what?" I ask.

"That night," she whispers, glancing behind her like anyone could hear.

Another knock on the door makes me flinch. I could scream. She's done this on purpose to pressurize me.

"It doesn't look so great that you came in here with me."

"East—stop it."

I bite my lip. There is a small window. I wonder if I can get through it. I probably can't without her help.

"I don't know what you want, Shy."

"I want to act like it never happened."

Her words could kill me if I let them. But I

understand. It was a mistake. She was as desperate as I was to hang onto Keller, and we didn't know that he was going to come back to us. But he did and now we have this mess.

My mess.

Our mess.

I feel so much guilt I can't stand it.

"You didn't tell him, did you?"

She swallows hard. "East—promise me now that we're going to forget all about it."

"Evie and Vincent know."

"I lied."

I grip the sides of the bathroom sink.

"But you—"

"I lied!" she nearly screams at me.

Her demands trigger something deep inside. I push past her and rush out of the bathroom. I can hear her calling out to me as I hit the door running and I see him—standing with Evie and Vincent, like a brilliant star in the distant sky.

I end up standing right in front of him, fighting to catch my breath and he's staring at me like he wants to talk, but he's lost for words.

But I'm not.

"I slept with Shy."

I wait. There's nothing. Vincent and Evie are stunned into silence. I don't blame them. And his

123

eyes—Keller's eyes, they're dull. I stole his shine. That flickering light that makes him who he is. I'm shocked it isn't pulsating in my hand.

Holy shit. I'm the villain in this story. Keller will always be the hero. Always.

Keller parts his lips as Shy rushes up behind me, but he doesn't pay attention to her. He focuses on me.

"What?" his voice cracks. It breaks my heart.

"Yes, we slept together while you were in the hospital. I'm a terrible person."

He shakes his head. There are people close enough to hear us. I could've done this in private, but my emotions got the better of me.

His gaze settles on Shy, who's fidgeting with her hands. "Keller," She mutters, moving in closer.

"I never want to see you again." His expression changes as he looks at me. "Including you, August East."

And that's that. He turned and walked away, leaving us standing there among the apple trees.

CHAPTER TWENTY

KELLER WEST

Walking back to my car was the most painful thing I'd ever done in my life. Each step felt like glass slicing through my heels, but it was really just the pain of knowing that he—that she, that they.

Shit.

I'm a fool.

"Keller! Wait—please."

I turn to see Shy rushing toward me, out of breath.

I stab a rigid finger in her direction. "Don't, Shy."

"Keller, let me explain, please."

I laugh.

"Keller," she states like she's in control, but she's not.

I raise a hand, signifying for her to stop. "Shy, I love you. You know that. I've loved you as far back as I can remember. You've always been in my life. I've always given you the benefit of the doubt—when you dated Ty Miller," I grimace, "and Brian, who isn't your type at all—but this shit. This takes the whole damn cake. All of it."

She wrings her hands, stepping closer. "I was scared." She speaks through the tears.

"So, it's true?" I ask.

Her eyes are filled with sorrow.

"Man. I must be the stupidest guy in the world."

"Keller."

I look up to see Evie and Vincent have joined us. Great! Then I see him. August East. I jab a finger in his direction.

"Go away."

He stops dead, not knowing what to say, but how could he explain this?

Shy ignores that they've arrived.

"No, you're not. I wanted to tell you, I was going to tell you, and then I didn't because I'm a coward."

I shake my head, folding my arms over my chest. "We've always been honest with each other—always, Shy!"

East tries to intervene. "Keller—wait."

"Seriously, shut up." I spit it out like venom while pointing in his direction.

Vincent raises his hands. "I'm not making excuses for them, but we all thought you died."

I pinch the bridge of my nose. "I was in a coma. I wasn't dead."

He lifts his arms and lets them drop. "There are plenty of people who never wake up from comas."

My eyes turn to thin slits. "Do you think I don't know how you feel about Shy, Vincent? How you probably sit around in your room at night fantasizing about her liking you back when you know it'll never happen?"

His head lowers. I've hurt him when I didn't mean to. All of this anger should be directed at East and Shy.

I lick my lips and stare at East. "Your hair looks like shit," I lie, but it's all I have.

East reaches up to finger at the back of his head. I don't actually hate his hair—it suits him, but I will not admit it.

Evie steps in, completing the circle. "Keller, we know you're hurt, but you don't have to be rude to my brother."

"So says the freak who thinks ghosts are real."

She can't respond to me. I've hurt her. I can see it in her eyes. But my rage won't let me apologize.

"So, do you love him?" I ask, because it's important that I know, but what I really want to ask is if August East *loves her.*

"No—not at all." Shy says without hesitation.

"Then why did you do it—why would you both—I

just don't get it." I stare at the ground. I want to be anywhere but here right now. I hate when my thoughts are jumbled. They did this to me. Both of them.

"I'm so sorry. I never wanted to hurt you, Keller. I would never want that. I just—I went there that night, to his house, and he was alone and upset, and so was I, and then I—I'm the reason it happened. He tried to tell me it was wrong and we shouldn't, but I pushed him and honestly, it meant nothing. I didn't feel anything and I don't think he did either."

August steps closer, "That's exactly what happened, but I'm to blame, too, Keller. I let it happen when I shouldn't have. I have no excuse, I really don't, and I know you'll probably spend the rest of your life hating me and it's fair."

I hiss, "But still—it happened."

Shy's brow wrinkles as she begins to explain, "It did and I don't know what else to say to you except that it was a huge mistake and I feel awful!" She looks around the circle, that's now become a place to speak our truth. Shy balls her fists. "And now he hates me, too, and I've ruined everything."

East sucks in a harsh breath, "I hate you? Why?"

"Because I know you blame me for it happening and you're right—I did this. It's my fault. I'm jealous and scared—and too many other things to mention because I know you love him."

East doesn't correct her. In fact, he says nothing—nothing at all. His silence speaks volumes.

I gasp, he loves me.

Loves me?

Like loves me now—not past tense?

I try to control my emotions.

I snicker, "Right." I can't show how I feel.

She rolls her eyes. "I love you, but you're so dumb sometimes."

"Trust me, I know." I give her a once-over, and she takes another small step, closing the gap between us.

"Keller, if I could change things, take it all back, I would. I'd go see Maggie and have her do some witchy spell and change everything for us. I'd erase dating Ty Miller and Brian James—and going to The Mill House that day. I would've stayed in cheerleading and never left you. But I can't and that isn't real life. All of those things happened, and I don't know what else to say. I wish I could make it better, but I can't. I just make everything worse—but he doesn't deserve for you to hate him. Hate me." She pauses while everyone remains silent. "And I just wanted to protect you."

"Shy," I tilt my head, "you can't spend your whole life trying to protect me from the world."

She laughs through the tears. "Says the boy who always has to be the hero."

I can barely breathe. Evie takes her hand, and she

129

nods at me. They walk away. I lift my hand and Vincent steps out of the circle. "I'm sorry." I offer. He acknowledges my apology, "It's cool, man."

I know I was cruel.

"But it isn't." I grab his arm, and we look at each other for a moment. I want him to see my face. To know that I regret what I said. It was wrong.

"I'll survive—I always do. I have a helmet and a mouth guard."

"Lunch tomorrow?" I ask.

He's reluctant to agree, but does. It'll take time for my words to dissolve. I know that, but I'll try to fix this. I know I can.

He steps away and leaves me alone with East.

What now?

CHAPTER TWENTY-ONE

AUGUST EAST

The rain lightly taps against his windshield as we sit in silence. Blue skies can sure turn gray pretty fast. I stare out the passenger window. I agreed to get in the car with Keller, but I don't know what to say now. I don't know if I ever will.

"How could you do that to me?" he asks.

His question feels like a knife.

"I don't think you want an explanation," I admit.

He grips the wheel. I can see his muscles flex, "I wouldn't ask if I didn't want you to explain it to me—I want to know what happened. Every detail."

"Keller," I half-whisper.

"I want to know!" he nearly shouts.

I blink through it. I understand his pain.

"I was scared. I thought you would never wake up again. And Shy, well, she's the closest person to you and I think I just wanted to feel something—anything."

"That's a piss-poor excuse, East."

I sigh, cupping my chin and resting my elbow on the window ledge. "I realize that now, but it's all I got."

"You didn't ask her to come over?" he asks.

I shake my head, looking in his direction, "No— she showed up at my house and then, well, things happened."

"Tell me," he insists.

My brow furrows. "Keller."

He looks at me, eyes glossed with tears. "Tell me."

I part my lips. "She—we were in the kitchen and she got closer to me and to be honest I couldn't hear most of what she said, which wasn't much, but she climbed onto my lap and then—"

He reaches over and takes my hand. I feel him squeeze it, so I stop talking. The rain is coming down harder now.

"Come here," he tempts me.

I narrow my eyes, but he moves his seat back, to make room for me on his lap.

"Keller."

"Please," he begs, so I comply, giving him what he wants.

I climb onto his lap, straddling his waist. He reaches up and cups my face. "I don't hate your hair."
132

I sniffle. "I do."

"Don't—it looks amazing."

"I thought I lost you." I bite my lip while his thumb moves across my cheek, gathering a tear.

"I know but I'm here now. I'll always be here, East. I can't help it."

His admission soothes me.

"You should hate me."

He smirks. "I know you keep trying, but I don't."

"I don't deserve you."

He sighs, tilting his head. "I wish you could see what I see. You're so beautiful."

I close my eyes, reaching up and covering his hands with mine. "You should leave me behind—live your life, be happy."

He leans in. I can feel his breath against my cheek. "You make me happy," he whispers.

I gasp as his lips crash against mine. He's gentle at first, but his need for me intensifies as the seconds tick by. His tongue slips past my lips, toying with me. I moan, he tenses. My knees press against his thighs. I can feel him against me. Exciting—wanting more, but we can't do anything here. The rain isn't enough to protect him from being seen with me.

I force him to stop. "Wait—wait." I can barely catch my breath. He's wrecked me, like he always does.

"I want you," he admits. Keller's chest rises and falls as if he ran a marathon.

My fingers twist through his curls on the back of his head. "I want you, too, but someone could see us."

"And?"

I narrow my eyes. "It could ruin you."

He grins. "You've ruined me already."

I shake my head, climbing off of him and slipping back into the passenger seat.

"I—East, you know I was kidding."

I stare out the window, then back at him.

"But it's true—whether you know it or not."

He turns in his seat and grabs my hand, pulling it against his chest. "I don't believe that."

"Keller—you're a star here—your whole life is set; all you have to do is take it."

He holds onto my hand. I can feel his heartbeat racing. "I need a promise from you."

I bite my lip.

"I'm serious," he adds.

"I'm listening."

"Never leave me again."

I can't believe he's asking me this.

He grips my hand. "East—promise me. Never leave me again—if this doesn't work out, then let it be me—let it be my fault. Give me the choice."

134

I know he deserves this from me, it's the only gift I can give him. "Okay, I promise."

He lifts my hand and presses his lips against my palm. It sends a wave of pleasure through me. I'd love to climb back onto his lap and show him how much I love him, but I can't. Again, I'm reminded that we're boys. It pains me, but I promised him I'd give him the choice, and even though my insecurity tells me he'll eventually leave,I'm going to treasure every moment I have with him now.

Arizona seeps in. I need to tell him, but I just want him to be happy—for as long as possible.

CHAPTER TWENTY-TWO

KELLER WEST

We sit in front of his house. I want to rush inside and hide away in his room. Thought, like memories, floats across my mind of a different time and place. I remember having water tossed in my face and how I stayed in this home for days with him. I almost feel homesick for something I know wasn't true—or was it?

Maggie spoke to me in my dreams, but does it mean that any of it actually happened?

He grabs the door handle and I speak up, "I have tickets to the Horror Movie Festival at the theater I work at during the summer break."

He grins. "I love horror movies."

My head inclines, eyes locked on his, "Come with me, it's next weekend, on Saturday. There are three movies—Fright Night, Teen Wolf and Nightmare on Elm Street. I know you've probably seen all—"

He chimes in, "You had me at *I have tickets.*"

I draw my bottom lip inside my mouth, then scrape my teeth against it with a little pressure. I'd love to kiss him right now—even walk him to the front door, but I know I can't. I hate it.

"Good—great!" I can't hide how happy I am.

"Vincent loves horror movies," East adds.

I tap the wheel. "Yeah—I should ask him to come, too, along with Evie. In fact, I will—or you can, either way, it's cool."

"I think that would be nice," he agrees, but he looks like something's on his mind.

"What's wrong?"

East adjusts on the seat and looks me dead in the eye, "I have to tell you something."

"What now?" I ask with a nervous chuckle.

He shakes his head, staring at his lap. "Oh God, no—" he glances up at the house, "my dad wants us to move to Arizona, I mean, they're talking about it."

My stomach churns. "What? When?" I try to calm down, but it's hard. I feel like we just got a second chance.

"I'm not sure, but I know we'll be here through Halloween because my mom wants to have a party."

"Wow."

"Yeah, I know."

"I mean—is it set in stone?" I ask.

"No—no plans yet, but he got offered a job and the nuclear plant closed down here."

I wring the wheel, feeling the pressure against my palms. "Your mom has a job."

He taps the door handle. "I know, but few people die around here."

I laugh, so does he. It's morbid, but he's right.

"I think we should spend as much time together as we can, then."

He tries to smile, but I can see the sadness in his eyes.

"Plus, you promised you'd never leave."

"I did." He wipes his eyes.

"Hey—it'll be okay. I know it." I lie, but I have no choice.

He looks to the house and back to me. "Do you want to come in?"

My breath hitches, "Yeah."

"Come on. I'll give you a tour of the house. You've never really had one. I'll show you everything."

My eyes spark with mischief, "Everything, huh?"

He smiles, "Well, what I can."

"Bummer." I jest.

He opens the car door and bolts toward the gate. The rain is still coming down. I park the car and follow him. We laugh as he struggles to open the gate and we have to push on it together. He slams it shut and
138

we rush up the steps and under the protection of the porch awning. I shake my head and the water sprays. He brushes his fingers through his hair and does the same. Water streaks his face and I want to kiss him so badly it makes my bones ache. I control myself as he opens the front door and I step inside.

The heat hits my face first. My eyes follow the sound of crackling wood in the fireplace to the right. The smell fills my nostrils and makes them flare. Most homes in Whynot have a fireplace, but the ones in this house are large and hold much more wood.

East approaches a metal box and opens it, retrieving a piece of wood. He tosses it on the fire and uses the poker to adjust it on top of a smoldering pile. The sparks fly, my gaze follows.

"Dance with me."

I hear a voice on the wind, turning to see East dressed as he was in my dreams. His white shirt is stiff and resting high against his neck, but his sleeves are rolled up, exposing his arms. I reach in, letting my fingers run along his skin, gripping him tight as he laughs and draws me against his chest. He spins me in the center of the room. The clock chimes above our heads. It's midnight.

"Keller?"

I blink out of it and look to East, who's rejoined me. The vision is gone. Something about it soothes me and breaks my heart at the same time.

139

I know I'm demanding honesty from him and I feel like he deserves the same from me, but what would I say? Should I tell him about the life we probably never lived? The fantasy I created as I rested in that bed at the hospital? It sounds crazy, but is it? Could it be another life that we lived together? Maybe it would explain why I feel so strongly about East. How I immediately loved him—everything about him. Maybe it would explain why I've always been drawn to this house. Even before he came here.

"Are you okay?" he asks.

"Yeah, I just get lightheaded from time to time since—" I pause.

His expression saddens.

"Don't," I whisper to him before a voice interrupts us.

"Hello!"

We turn to see East's dad covered in smudges of dirt and what appear to be red stains all over his shirt.

"Hi," I say. East sticks by me. He reaches in and takes my hand. His dad smiles. I feel at ease. I guess this is the only place in this town where we're completely safe to show how we feel.

"You didn't tell us we'd be having someone else for dinner."

I raise my free hand. "Oh, no. I'm good, but thank you."

140

"What do you have all over your shirt?" East asks.

He looks down and grins. "Ah! Well, your mom wanted some maple syrup, and I milked the tree."

"In the garden?" East's voice shakes.

"Do we have another tree?"

I smirk, East doesn't.

I clear my throat.

"That tree is dead, Dad," he states.

"Clearly not!" he shakes his shirt.

"It looks dead." East looks to me. I don't know why he hates the tree so much, but he must have his reasons.

"I promise you, it tastes delicious."

"Paul would agree with you, Dad."

His dad's expression changes, like he's been insulted. East promptly follows up his statement, "He tasted it the first day we were here."

"Mmm, then perhaps he'd like a jar so we can avoid him licking the tree."

I cover my mouth with the side of my hand, but my eyes are smiling. Clearly, East's dad doesn't like Mr. Rider so much and, honestly, I can't blame him. I don't like it that East was in the car with him and how much he's been in this house, but it doesn't matter now. I'm here, and I plan to be here as much as I can.

"So, East tells me you're thinking about moving to Arizona."

There's a weird silence that settles in the room, but his dad finally relaxes and looks to East. "It isn't set in stone, but we're discussing it."

"I've been to Arizona, it's hot."

"So I've heard." His dad adds a playful wink.

I wish I could say more, but we visited Arizona once when I was little. We have a cousin there. It's not an awful state—not even a terrible place to live, but I'd never admit it. Not now.

He pivots. "Did East tell you about the party?"

I glance over at East, then back to his dad "I think a Halloween party will be amazing here." My eyes lift as I look up the sprawling staircase.

"I agree and, of course, you're the first guest invited."

"Thanks."

East squeezes my hand.

"Well, East is going to give me a tour of the house. I've never seen all of it, Mr. East."

"You can call me Steven."

I swallow through the informality. "Okay."

"Come on—I'll give you the tour the best I can," East says, before pulling me along with him. We pass by his dad and he stares at me. I catch myself staring at his shirt. He looks like he murdered someone.

We move down the hallway and I glance over at the kitchen. My jaw clenches. I don't know if I'll ever be able to go into the room again. East notices and quickens his pace. We end up in the garden. He closes the door behind us and I step in and take a deep breath. The vegetation smells good, but there's also this underlying scent—sickly sweet.

I peer up at the glass ceiling. "This is amazing." My eyes follow the long crack in the glass, running the length of it.

"I don't really like it in here."

"Really?" I walk over to stare at a collection of flowers. I reach in and his hand grabs mine, stopping me.

"That's poisonous—all of it is, except for the roses and that damn tree."

"Poisonous?"

East pulls me back so we're standing side by side. He points. "That's hemlock, and that stuff there is oleander, and along there—that's nightshade. We also have venus flytraps—I mean, I love that movie trailer for *Little Shop of Horrors*, but I don't like having meat eating plants in the house."

"I like it too; it looks like it's going to be great."

He nods while staring at the garden. His mood has changed. I can tell he doesn't like this place at all.

"Why not just dig them all up and plant new stuff?" I ask.

He shakes his head. "Mom loves it—Dad, too, I

143

guess. They don't want to change anything in here and the roses are all wound up in everything."

I offer my advice. "Maybe you could just accept them as they are."

He sighs. "No—you're right, and you'd think I'd know that."

We stand in silence for a moment longer.

He laughs. "I saw an eyeball in the roses."

"What?"

His head bobs, "Well, it was Owen—Maggie's cat, but for a moment, I thought the roses were staring at me. But Evie picked him up and took him back to her. I forgot to ask how she was doing today, but, it's been a little crazy."

"Yeah," I admit, not wanting to really talk about Maggie, but knowing I should if we're going to be honest with each other.

"I want to talk about—" we both speak at the same time, laughter follows.

"Okay—you first," I demand.

He shakes his head while teasing me. "No, tell me."

I eye the tree and see the benches. "Can we sit down?"

He hisses, but agrees, "I will, but only for you. I really don't like that tree."

"I noticed."

144

We sit down under the tree, and I feel a chill roll through me. There must be a draft in here. Not surprising, since it's an atrium.

"Tell me why you hate this garden, East."

He looks down at his feet. "I thought we decided you were going to talk first?"

I lean in. "Please?"

He grins, leaning back on the bench and staring at the door across the room that lads back inside.

"I think you could get me to do anything."

I bump against his shoulder while leaning back against the bench next to him. "I'll cash in on that."

"I'm counting on it."

I feel flush. "So, what happened?"

He rubs his palms against the tops of his thighs. "I had a dream—a nightmare, whatever you want to call it. I'm sure it was brought on by my seizures, but it seemed so real and ever since it happened, I really don't feel that comfortable in the house—except in my room and the library upstairs."

"What did you see?"

He looks at me like I'm the first person who will totally believe him.

"I told Delilah about it at school and she asked me if I wanted to be hypnotized."

"Hypnotizing someone is used to remember something that really happened, East—not a dream."

145

He leans forward. "I don't know if it was a dream."

"Okay—what happened?"

He turns to face me, so I adjust to mimic him. He takes a breath, glancing over at the tree sitting right behind our heads. "Please tell me."

His eyes widen, "I heard my name, so I left my room and followed it to this room," he looks around, "and I could smell it, feel it; it seemed so real and then I watched a child—the same one from the painting upstairs across from my room, run past me and climb up onto this bench."

I swallow hard, but I have to know what's upsetting him.

"Anyway, the kid had something in their hand and then they—well, the child ate it and fell asleep, but it wasn't sleeping—the child died because it ate something poisonous from the garden."

"East." I lean in a little closer. I place my hand on his and run my thumb across his soft skin.

"And then a woman came rushing in, dressed like she was from another time, and screamed when she saw the child on the bench. She scooped the baby up in her arms and sobbed, then she took what was left and ate it, falling asleep, too."

"Holy shit."

East swallows his nervous tension, "I know, but then Charles Porter came into the garden and he saw
146

both of them and wailed like someone was stabbing him—his grief stopped me from breathing. My chest hurt; my legs felt weak. I dropped to my knees as he scribbled symbols on the cobblestone and then the tree caught fire and flames rose and cracked the glass ceiling. But then something happened."

"What?"

"The child woke up."

"Woke up?"

"Came back to life."

We both yelp when a bird hits the glass ceiling and twitches before coming to a stop. I grimace.

"I hate this garden."

"I can see why, but East, do you think any of it was real, like it could've been something that happened in this house?"

He smirks. "Like a vision?"

I don't match his humor, so the smirk fades.

"I'm serious."

"Keller—do you believe in that sort of stuff?"

I knead my shoulder, "I never did before, but now, I don't know. I saw things when I was asleep. Things that seemed real. I could feel it, taste it—smell it."

"Maggie is someone who makes a living doing what she does, Keller."

"But it doesn't explain how I knew to go there when I woke up, or what about the card in my pocket?"

"She could've come to the hospital and talked to you while you were sleeping and placed that card there."

I relax on the bench. "I don't think she'd do that, would she?"

East seems determined to discredit her. "I'm sure it's tough to be a psychic in a smaller town. Pretty much everyone has probably talked to her, that wanted to anyway. I mean, this was an opportunity to bring in some business."

The muscles clench in my jaw. "I understand what you're saying, but I saw things—felt things—and she told me she was there to help me come back."

"Again, she could've told you that while you were in the hospital, right?"

"I just—"

"I just don't want her to take advantage of you," he adds.

"I get that, but I was here—with you."

"What?" His eyebrow arches.

"Yes, in this house. This is where we met, when the town was still new and a train ran through it. I wanted to buy this house, so I met with a man here, inside the gate, and you came out and tossed a bucket of cold water in my face before apologizing."

Confusion distorts his expression, so I go on.

"And you offered to dry me off, give me some new

148

clothes, and I ended up staying here with you. I remember it like it was yesterday, East."

He's studying my mouth, then eyes.

"I know I sound crazy, but—"

"I don't think you're crazy at all."

"So, you believe me?"

"I want to believe and there's—there's more to this house. I've seen more than just Charles and his wife and child."

"I'm listening."

He grabs my hand and pulls me up onto my feet. He walks to the side door and opens it, allowing me to step out first. I can see a path leading behind the atrium.

CHAPTER TWENTY-THREE

AUGUST EAST

I stare into his eyes and listen. Something deep inside me is telling me to believe him. I feel it. It's hard to explain. It's almost like an echo, a ripple through time. I take a scant breath, grabbing his hand.

I lead him to the side door and usher him out before me. I stare at the path leading to the cemetery behind the house.

"I've been here before," he whispers.

"Did you come here before we owned the house?"

"No," he says, leaving it at that. But he walks the path and I follow. He seems to know where he's going. I would ask him, but again, it feels right, like I should allow this to happen.

He stops in front of a large stone. The words are faded, what little we can see of them. There are thorny vines and bright red roses wrapping it.

He reaches in and grabs a vine, careful to avoid the sharp thorns, and drags them away to expose the gravestone.

"Porter," he whispers.

I stare at the lettering and run my fingers over the name. I grit my teeth as a flash of memory reveals sobbing and rain. I can see black umbrellas and sad expressions. But everyone is dressed like they're from the Victorian era. Then I see the back of a man's head. He's wearing a top hat. He's holding a cane. His dark, loosely curled hair is sticking out from under the hat. He won't move aside so I can see the wordage on the stone. He reaches in and places his black gloved hand against it. His tears fall. I catch a glimpse of his mouth. I know those lips.

"East."

I blink out of it.

"Are you okay?"

"Yeah—I just, I don't know. It felt like a—"

He finishes my sentence for me, "Memory."

I nod. "Yes."

"Same. This is what I mean."

He turns to face me. "Every time I'm with you, it feels right—but it's not the first time. I don't mean now—in this time, either."

"You think we've been here before?" I ask.

"Yes. I know it. I can feel it."

"I have to show you something else."

He follows me as I lead him to the mausoleum. We stand there in silence as his brow furrows.

"What is this?" he asks.

"Come, look." I step up and push on the door. It opens for me. A sweet smell rushes out and my nostrils flare. It's a fresh scent of roses.

I step inside and Keller follows me. I approach the empty coffin sitting in the middle of the small space and look inside. Fresh roses have been placed in the box. I gasp.

"What?" Keller rushes up but sees nothing but the roses. He reaches in and picks one up and the petals fall off of it. They're not new. But who placed them here?

"This is creepy."

"There's more." I walk to the door and nearly close it so he can see the pentagram with roses drawn on the wall and over the door.

"What the hell is this?" he asks.

"I think it's meant to keep something out of here."

Keller steps up and touches the dried paint. "Or something in."

My blood runs cold. He may be right, but what would be placed in here—or who?

"I never thought about that."

He turns to face me. "I think we need to talk to Maggie."

"Keller."

"I'm serious. She needs to know what you've seen, too, and about this place. Maybe she'll know what this symbol means and why there's an empty coffin."

"I mean, there may be a vampire."

"Mmm, are you a vampire?" he asks.

I swallow hard. "Are you?"

He grins while leaning in closer to me. "Would that benefit me?"

"Yes—one hundred percent."

He laughs. "But seriously—this place gives me the creeps."

"I don't know—it isn't so bad," I admit.

"East—it's where they bury people."

I massage my neck, "I don't get freaked out about that kind of stuff."

"Oh, right. I guess it wouldn't be strange for you." He narrows his eyes while approaching the door. He reaches up and grabs the lock. "Is this what I think it is?"

"Yeah—it's a lock." I confirm.

His eyebrow cocks. "On the inside of the door?"

"I'll admit that's weird."

He steps back, studying the pentagram. "Just a little."

"Okay."

He looks at me. "Okay, what?"

153

"Okay, I'll talk to Maggie about this stuff."

"Really?"

"For you." I admit.

He steps closer to me, taking my hand. His eyes lower. He's thinking again and I hate it. I'd love to read his mind. I know that would ruin any surprises, but I want to know everything about him.

"I—East, I don't know what's going to happen."

I take a short breath, "I know."

"I don't expect you to be okay with it, either. But I promise I'll try."

I step in closer to him, making him look at me, "There is no pressure at all. None—even though kidnapping you has crossed my mind."

He snorts, but even that's cute about him. "Why am I not surprised?"

I lick my bottom lip, drawing it inside. He makes me crazy. One moment I'm depressed, the next I'm higher than I've ever been. If this is really love, then I don't think I'll ever get used to it, and that's okay.

"All I want is as many moments as I can have with you," I admit, because it's true.

I shift my weight from one foot to the other. It's easy to forget where I am when I'm with him. It's dangerous and exciting. I have to watch what I do in public. I know Keller promised he'll try, but I don't want him to ruin his life in this town. I know who he is. I
154

know what people expect of him. I won't be the reason he can't be happy.

He sighs. "I want every moment with you."

He leans in and our foreheads rest against each other. He lets out another sigh. He sounds desperate. Frustrated. I can relate. He reaches up and cups my face. I close my eyes. I could get lost in him forever. I want that more than anything, but right now, this has to be enough.

"I never want to lose this—lose you." He breathes through the words. I can feel his energy shifting.

We are alone. The door is closed. My mind is racing. I want to show him more—I want to let him in.

"You can't move to Arizona." He pulls me closer.

"I don't want to go."

"I won't let you." He laughs through it, but I know he's upset. "I mean, how is that going to work? We'd be on the phone every minute of the day."

I want to laugh, but I can't. The idea of leaving this place upsets me the more I think about it.

He sniffs, so do I. I know he wants to cry and I wouldn't blame him.

"Listen," I place my hand behind his head and let it slide down the back of his neck, holding his forehead against mine, "I'll do everything I can to stay."

His eyes search mine for confirmation, "You swear?"

"Of course." I lean in and brush my lips against

his. He winces like it hurts. But I understand, it hurts more than anything else now. Knowing this could end and I wouldn't have him is killing me. I didn't want to admit it to myself, but it's the truth. I love Keller West more than anyone else in the world.

"I love you," I whisper.

He nods, "I love you, too, August Elliot East."

"Are we using middle names now?"

"I think so." He wipes the edge of his eye.

"And yours is..." I wait.

"Kennedy. My mom loved JFK. Thought he was the shit, actually. It made my dad mad, but I thought it was funny. I think he wanted to name me, but mom insisted."

"I love it," I say.

His lip curls. "Oh, yeah?"

"Yeah," I declare.

He rocks us back and forth while holding onto my waist. Keller glances around the room. "You know, we're like alone." He's hinting at more.

"I noticed."

He walks me back against the wall, reaches in and grabs my wrist, and lifts one of my arms above my head.

"What are you doing?" I whisper.

His eyes burn with desire, locked on my mouth.

He leans into my ear. "Seeing how far you'll let me go."

156

I tremble.

"Keller, we're in a mausoleum."

"Mmm hmm," he growls.

His lips move against the side of my neck, and then I feel his teeth graze my skin. I moan.

"Oh—so that's it." He toys with me.

"What?" I lift my shoulder. He places his hand at the base of my shirt and works his fingers underneath, brushing my skin.

"This—" Keller is determined to wreck me.

"So, you think I want to have some boy attack me with a coffin in the room?"

He watches my lips move. "I know that's what you want."

"How do you—" An uncontrollable groan cuts off my words when his hand grazes the front of my jeans.

"Shit." I breathe out.

CHAPTER TWENTY-FOUR

KELLER WEST

We sit on the floor of the mausoleum shoulder to shoulder against the door.

East places his face in his hands and moans.

I lean forward with a smirk on my face. "What?"

He leans his head back and stares up at the ceiling, then over at me, but his chin is still elevated and I'd love to kiss his neck again.

"I can't believe we did that here."

I take a long breath and release it. "I don't think it's so bad."

East bumps against my shoulder. "And that thing you did with your tongue? Evil. All of it."

"Oh, yeah?" I raise a brow.

"Um, yes."

"Oh, shit." I groan, staring at his neck.

"What? Do I have a spider on me? If I do, don't kill it. We'll just—"

I cut him off. "No—I gave you a hickey."

East's eyes widen. "No way!"

"Yes way—it's right there." I poke at the small red splotch.

"Well, I'm sure you have one lower," he claims.

I laugh. He's probably right. I lift my shirt while standing up and he hisses.

"Oh, yeah—actually two." He holds up his fingers in a sloppy peace sign.

"I guess I owe you one more, then."

I rush in and we wrestle. But it finally eases, as I end up half on top of him, staring down at his pretty face.

"I wish we could stay here forever." His eyes fill with worry and sadness.

"Hey, we promised we wouldn't do this, right?" I urge him to stop.

He fights back the tears.

"And we're going to make sure you don't move to Arizona, right?" I add.

"Yes," he agrees, but it may be a lie.

I know East isn't in control of what his parents decide to do. I've lived with that my whole life with my dad, but for now, I'd like to pretend that we're okay. That this is day one of forever with him.

"We should probably get out of here." He suddenly becomes the logical one.

I hate that he's right.

I get up, pulling him with me.

"Have dinner with us tonight."

I hesitate, not because I don't want to.

"Or—not," he huffs, "if you have plans."

"No—it's just, I—I want for this to be out in the open, I do, but—"

His chest rises and falls, "Listen, we don't have to tell anybody, I mean, our friends know—Shy, Evie and Vincent."

"They all do?"

He grins. "Well, yeah."

"Okay—that's a good thing, right?" Hoping he agrees, but trying to control my nerves.

He faces me, crossing his legs. "And Delilah—and her wife, oh, and my mom and dad."

"Jesus, East."

"Keller—it's fine. Not a single one of those people would tell anyone in this town."

I let out a defeated sigh.

"What?" he asks.

"I feel like a jerk for caring if they do." I admit.

He reaches in and takes my hand. Our fingers intertwine, "Don't. I get it. I never had to come out to anyone, really. I've been like this since I was little and my parents never yelled at me or told me to stop doing anything. They supported me all the way. I guess

I'm lucky. A lot of kids get kicked out, and end up homeless."

I swallow hard. "My dad—well, you saw him. He's all *men do this and women do that*. He believes that."

"I know, I'm sorry you've had to hide how you feel." He pauses. "Does your mom know?"

I look down in my lap. "Yeah—I think so. We had a weird talk in the garage. She wanted to show me old pictures of my uncle, but he—he dressed like a girl."

I let that sit between us, but East isn't bothered by it. It just adds to his charm.

He grins. "I wore my mom's heels when I was little, and her pearls. I even got into her make up and made a hell of a mess. I had it all over my face."

"You did?" I ask.

"Yeah—it was fun."

I pause, carefully choosing my words. "How—I mean, did it make you feel any different at all?"

"It made me happy. I don't say *this is a boy, and this is a girl* with anything. That's not how I see the world, Keller. I like you this way, or with lipstick and nail polish. I'd like you in heels—or no shoes at all. It doesn't matter to me. What matters is what you want—what makes you happy."

I squeeze his hand. "I do like nail polish and lipstick." I hold my breath. I've never admitted it to anyone before.

161

"I think that's cool." He moves in closer to me. I can feel his knee against my thigh.

"You don't think I'm a freak?"

He laughs, but it stops. He leans in and touches my chin, lifting it so I have to look him in the eye. "I think you are perfect in every way."

I snicker.

"I'm serious, there's absolutely nothing wrong with you, Keller West. There never was, and never will be."

I feel a tear roll down my cheek. It's such a re-lief to hear it from someone, anyone. I've carried this with me for so long that it felt like an anchor dragging along the bottom of the ocean. I knew it would even-tually drown me, but now—well, I have hope, and it's all because of East.

I sniffle. "I just—it's hard to admit that I feel like this, and for the longest time I hated myself for it. I always thought something had to be wrong with me."

He wraps his arm around my shoulder. "The only thing wrong is that there are people in this world who hate boys like us for just being who we are. For existing."

I shake off the emotions before they get the better of me.

"You know what? I am hungry. I'd like to take you up on dinner. I just need to use your phone and call my mom, so she knows."

"Deal." He leans in and kisses my cheek, then my lips. He lingers. I'd love to stay in this place with him forever, but I know I can't.

"I love you," I whisper.

"I love you, too," he whispers back.

He stands, pulling me up with him.

We look at the empty coffin.

"I can't believe we did that in here." I laugh.

East snickers. "It's my favorite place now."

I grin. "Mine, too."

CHAPTER TWENTY-FIVE

AUGUST EAST

We enter the side door to the garden and stop dead when I see movement. I don't want to give anyone outside of the ones who know the wrong impression. I shake loose from Keller's hand. He grimaces, but then realizes why.

"Hello?" Keller asks.

Paul pops out from behind the tree.

"Oh, hello there!" He wipes his forehead with a handkerchief and tucks it away in his back pocket.

"What are you doing in here?" I ask, approaching the tree.

He steps down and looks up at it. "Your parents asked if I could take it down, but I'm having issues."

I narrow my eyes. "What type of issues?"

"It's an old tree and the roots go deep, so tearing it out will not be possible. But I could chop it down to a tree stump and then drill holes into it and fill them with salt."

"That seems cruel," Keller exclaims.

I roll my eyes. "Have you seen this thing? It looks like it's bleeding."

"I know, but being ugly shouldn't be a reason to kill something."

"Why are you trying to make me feel guilty?" I ask.

Keller scratches his head, "It's still producing maple, East. It's not dead." He thoughtfully defends it.

"Wow, well," I turn to Paul, "I guess we shouldn't *murder* it."

Keller laughs. "You can do whatever you want, I just think it's part of the house now."

I hate that what he's claiming is true. I'm only freaked out by this tree because of that dream I had. I don't know for sure there was anything to it. All I know is my blood seems to run a little colder when I'm in the garden and I blame this creepy looking tree. Besides, Keller has strange stories of his own. He seems to go back and forth as much as I do with whether he believes any of it.

But I understand denial.

He bumps me from the side. "Plus, it'll be cool for the Halloween party."

"Halloween party?" Paul asks. I forgot he was still

165

in the room with us. I guess I should be more careful. I don't want to out Keller to anyone. He should tell people—or not tell people—when he decides. That isn't up to anyone else. Even me.

"Yeah, my mom is inviting the whole town—I'm sure."

"I think that's wonderful. Charles always refused to do anything for Halloween. He was a real party pooper about it."

Keller gives me an odd look. He doesn't know about Paul and Charles, but I'll fill him in later.

"Was he religious?" Keller asks.

Paul laughs. It echoes in space.

"Charles? Oh no. Not at all. He was obsessed with angels and demons, but he never stepped foot in a church." He pauses with a mischievous twinkle in his eyes. "He claimed it burned his skin."

"Creepy," I mutter.

Keller guides the conversation elsewhere.

"Mmm, I think this place is going to look badass for Halloween," Keller eyes Mr. Rider, "I mean *awesome*."

Paul waves a hand. "I don't care if you curse outside of class."

Keller relaxes a little more.

Paul looks at the tree, "I have to break it to your parents about this tree. Your mom will be happy,
166

though. She didn't seem too keen on me taking it out of here."

"Really? I thought she hated it?" I ask.

"No—she sort of sounded like you, Keller. Talking about it still producing maple and not being dead."

"See?" Keller whispers while bumping me from the side. I feel his fingers brush against mine and it sends an electric pulse up my spine. I know Keller is trying his best to make sure that I know how he feels about us, even when it could expose his true nature.

"I'll see you tomorrow at school." He directs his goodbye to Keller.

I chime in, "I'll be there too."

Paul smiles. "That's good to hear." He jogs toward the door.

I turn to face Keller.

He suddenly kisses me, and I stop him with a gasp. I glance behind us, but Paul is gone.

"He could've seen us."

"But he didn't."

"You're dangerous."

He grabs at my side, making me laugh more as we enter the house. I hear multiple voices and head toward the living room. I look behind me and Keller is staring into the kitchen. It knots my stomach.

"Sure!" he says, while stepping in. He emerges with a tray of snacks. My mom is notorious for offering them when we have guests. He passes me by with a cheerful grin. It's good to see him happy. I spot the hickey on the side of his neck and flip his collar up, trying to hide it away. But I don't know if he really cares while he's here in my house. It makes me happy to know he feels safest here.

My mom wraps my waist and rocks me back and forth while laying her chin on my shoulder from behind. "I like him," she whispers.

"I do, too."

She lets me go and takes my hand, leading me into the living room where I see Megan and Delilah sitting on one couch. My dad has a drink, probably scotch, in his hand and is waving around an unlit cigar. Mom doesn't like for him to smoke, so he quit after the fire back east. But he still likes to hold one when he sips on his drink. He even places it in his mouth and takes a puff. Habit, I guess.

"So, you've lived here your whole life?" Dad asks.

"Yep, born and bred." Megan confirms.

Delilah leans into her side. They're holding hands. "I'm only here because of her."

Megan smiles. Delilah kisses her cheek. It's sweet to watch them together. I'd love to sit down and do that with Keller and know none of them would care one bit, but he's not ready for that yet. I hope someday he will be, but that'll be up to him and no one else.

Keller sets the tray down on the coffee table between the couches. Dad reaches down and takes a stack of meat, cracker and cheese. He nibbles on it before taking another sip of his drink.

"It's nice to see you up and around, Keller," Megan says.

Keller stands tall. "I'm feeling fantastic." He glances at me and I look down, rubbing my neck. I don't know if he's trying to say it's because of me, but I hope it is.

"And I hear someone is returning to school." Delilah beams.

Our eyes meet. "It's that or become a hermit."

Delilah grins. I'm happy to see she will not be awkward with me after the whole fire thing. I have to believe it *was* a faulty wire and nothing more. I probably smelled the smoke while I was hypnotized, and it made things worse. Just like how dreams can be influenced if you have the TV on.

Megan acknowledges Keller, "Thank you for whatever you said or did."

I feel flush. Keller looks at me and back at Megan. "I just told him to stop being stupid."

The room erupts with laughter. It's a lie, but effective.

"So, how long have you two been together?"

I almost choke on air, but my dad is asking Megan and Delilah.

Delilah looks at Megan, "We've been together for fifteen years, married five. It took a decade to convince her I was serious."

Megan chuckles. "Delilah dated a lot more than I did. It took time for me to feel comfortable coming out to people."

"I get that," Keller agrees.

I'm shocked he's taken part in the conversation.

"It's a personal decision. Be ready and comfortable knowing that people may not react the way you want them to."

Keller sits down on the chair. "Did you have people react badly?"

Delilah tucks a strand chuck of hair behind her ear, "My parents disowned me—said I was evil and going to Hell."

Megan rubs the top of her hand. "And my parents said they knew, and it would not change a thing."

"And with East—well, his dad and I knew from the time he was little and it changed absolutely nothing," Mom adds.

Keller is listening to everyone, taking it all in.

"I—." He looks at me. My heart flutters. He continues, "I don't know who I am yet."

Delilah nods. "And that's totally fine. You're young. You have so much ahead of you. I want you to know my door is always open if you ever want to talk to me about anything—anything at all."

"I appreciate that." He grins. "Sometimes I wonder if I'll end up in a seminary."

"A priest?" I exclaim.

"I've considered it before—when I was sick of playing football. I knew my dad would never yell at me if I did that—and I felt guilty."

I sit down on the chair adjacent to his. "You have nothing to feel guilty about."

"That's not what they told us in church."

I lift my hand and let it fall. "And this is why we don't go to church."

"Not all churches are biased. Delilah and I go to a church that accepts everyone as it should be."

"Really?" Keller asks.

"Yes, because God never damned homosexuality, he was talking about men laying with boys. It was about pedophilia, but try telling that to some of them."

Mom chimes in, "This is why we've avoided the whole mess. East can choose on his own. If he ever joins a church, then it'll be up to him. Not us. We don't need a book to understand right from wrong."

"I can respect that." Megan says.

A knock comes to the door, so I decide to answer it. I approach as a second knock comes, then a third. I open it to see that it's Maggie. Her hair is wet from the rain. She appears to be upset.

"Maggie?"

"East—I hate to bother you, but have you seen Owen? Evie returned him to me earlier and said she found him in your rose garden."

I shake my head. "No—I was just out there and I didn't see him."

"Oh, dear. This isn't like him to be so skittish. Maybe he's mad at me." She rubs her arms and I can see her teeth are chattering.

"Do you want to come inside and get warm? I can help you look for him after dinner if you want."

She hesitates, looking inside the house behind me, "I won't lie, this house has always sent a chill up my spine."

"It *was* a funeral home."

"True," she leans in, "the dead are so chatty. It's hard to sleep."

"Come on inside. You look cold."

"I'm sure he'll come home on his own." She seems nervous.

"Come in," I insist.

Laughter erupts inside the house. Maggie looks past me. "I don't want to intrude."

"I promise it's fine. My mom loves to feed people. It's her thing. Maybe it's because she spent so much time with dead people. She loves conversation."

Maggie laughs, then takes me up on the offer and steps inside the house. She's immediately drawn to the
172

same spot on the floor where the pentagram used to be etched into the wood. She clears her throat.

"Do you have something I could drink?"

"We have water, wine—my dad's scotch."

"Wine would be lovely."

I turn and see a shadow in the hallway, then it steps forward. My mom's face comes into view.

"East—introduce me to your friend."

"This is Maggie, Mom."

"Oh! The one who rose from the grave?"

Maggie steps in closer, the firelight illuminates her face. "I apologize for not giving you some business."

Mom chirps with laughter. "That type of humor deserves a drink. I'll grab the bottle."

Mom spins on her heel and she's off to the kitchen, leaving Maggie and me in the foyer.

Her gaze lingers on the stairs, like she's staring at someone. My eyes follow, but I don't see anything.

"You can come into the living room if you like. Everyone else is in there."

Maggie blinks out of her stupor, "Lead the way."

CHAPTER TWENTY-SIX

KELLER WEST

"I just don't know." I rub the side of my neck.

Maggie takes another drink of her wine. "I'll be honest. I came to see you in the hospital, but just the one time. The rest—well, I had to meditate to reach you. Your mom asked me to come see you. She loves you so much, but didn't want your father to know."

Delilah is riveted by the conversation. I know she hypnotized East, so this is something she must believe in. I'm still on the fence. A lot of stuff can be suggested to people when they're sleeping. I don't know why being in a coma would be any different.

"Dad doesn't believe in anything he can't see or touch. I'm shocked he went to church, but I think he fears God and that's about it. Maybe that's why I really considered being a priest."

Maggie tilts her head. "That doesn't surprise me. You have an aura about you. You believe in more."

"I don't know what I believe." I admit.

"So, what happened?" Delilah asks.

Maggie looks at me. I'm terrified she got me to tell her everything that I saw while I was laying in that hospital bed.

"This won't be in any book—but I entered his world—that world in between ours and the dead, and I showed him how to come back."

Her explanation isn't complete. I still remember the days I spent in this house lying in bed with East. I can still smell my grandma's cooking, and then there's the warning. The darkness that scared me awake. I don't remember exactly what it was, but I know I never want to encounter it again.

"I placed a card in his pocket and told him to come see me and that's exactly what he did."

I shake my head. "You could've placed that card in my pocket at the hospital."

She adjusts on the couch to stare me dead in the eye, "That's true, but there are two things you need to know about me—one," she gulps down her wine, "I can handle my drinks, and two," she places the wine-glass on the table and places her hand on her heart, "I never lie."

Silence settles in the room.

"So, you want me to believe that you met me in this *in between place* and guided me back home?"

"I don't want you to do anything, but you know the truth. I know you can feel it." She states.

"Can you show me?" Delilah asks.

"I can—I can show you all." She looks at her bag. It's large. I wonder what's in it. She reaches down and produces a board. It's made of wood—brown with black lettering. She places it on the coffee table and the lights flicker in the room, but it's storming.

We all lean in to look at it.

"Is that a Ouija board?" Delilah asks.

Maggie lays a teardrop shaped piece on the board with an eye painted in the center.

"Yes, it is."

"I don't like this," Megan grumbles.

Delilah looks to comfort her. "Honey, it's just a game board."

"Oh, it's no game," Maggie insists.

Delilah tilts her head. "So, you think this thing can talk to the dead?"

"Oh, it does more than that. It talks to the dead and other things."

"What sort of things?" East asks.

"Dark things."

My blood runs cold. I'm taken back to that moment when the darkness snaked around me and Maggie sent her warning. But again—how true can it be? If something like that was lurking around Whynot, then I'd think we'd know.

"I'm game," Delilah insists.

Both East's parents have been quiet. Finally, his dad leans forward. "So am I." He toasts, then downs the rest of his drink.

"We need more than two people." Maggie kneels down by the coffee table and eyes me. I take a breath, then lower to my knees next to her. She places her fingers on the teardrop piece with the eye. I look to East, who joins me.

"Mom?" East asks.

She shakes her head. "I'll watch."

East stares at me. "It'll be fine," I urge, trying to calm his nerves.

His dad joins in, placing his fingers on the piece. There's no more room.

"What do we do now?" I half-whisper, like it's listening.

"Now we ask our questions."

I have a question.

Evie steps into the room with a book in her hand. It's the leather journal from the library. She opens the book and fingers through the pages, her eyes widen. "Ask Charles why he tried to open a doorway to hell."

I remove my hand, as does everyone else. I stand and East mimics me.

East is stunned. "I'm sorry, what?"

Evie hands him the book. "Look at the page. Right there, it's an incantation. I deciphered it the best I could, but it seems like he was trying to open a gate."

East's mom laughs. It's low at first, but then it boils over. She waves her hand, drink sloshing against the side of the glass.

"What's so funny?" his dad asks.

She steps closer to the board. "I've spent my life with the dead and I can tell you there's nothing magical about it at all. There's no discussion—no confusion, no shadows and specters, because death has an air of finality like no other. It settles into your bones like an old friend and robs us of our last breath. It comes for us all."

My blood nearly runs cold. She seems to be speaking with no emotion at all, but then she blinks before taking another sip of her wine. I study her eyes. They appear dilated. I don't want to say anything to East, but I wonder if she's taken something. I assume if she was struggling, then he'd confide in me, but maybe not.

"Or perhaps we're haunted." She rolls her hand and some laughter from the rest of the room follows.

Stephen rises and East follows. Maggie is left alone with her fingers on the teardrop-shaped piece. She lifts her hands and rises to her feet.

"Perhaps we can do this another time."

"Perhaps," Rosetta parrots her sentiment.

We all flinch when a loud buzzer rings throughout the house.

"Ah, the roast is done." Rosetta sets her glass down and exits the room.

Delilah and Megan look at each other.

"I'll be going—I have a cat to find."

"Again?" Evie asks.

Vincent steps in. "I'll help."

"Thank you." Maggie touches his arm. He grins. Maybe his obsession with older women has shifted away from East's mom.

Evie looks to East and hands him the book. "I swear I'm right," she whispers, leaving it in his hands.

He doesn't respond, but tucks the book away in his arms. Finally, he speaks. "Charles was obsessed with angels and demons—Paul told me."

"Trust me, I know. That journal is full of them"

"Everyone has a hobby."

We all turn because Megan has spoken up, "Like Delilah, she loves to shove ships in a bottle."

"I do, but it's a little different." Delilah says.

Megan shakes her head. "I just don't think it's fair to talk about someone who's passed away and can't defend himself."

My muscles relax. She's right. We shouldn't be taking his things and reading into them.

179

"I mean—maybe he wanted to write a book, and this was his research?"

"You write, don't you Evie?" I ask, knowing the answer.

Evie sighs. "I do—but," she looks to Maggie, then back to me, "I don't know, maybe I'm looking for something that isn't there."

"It's a common thing," Megan adds, gripping Delilah's arm for support.

Delilah clears her throat, "This is true. It's called inference. It's when you put together clues that prove what you think is right. Sometimes we can be so desperate to explain something that we only see what we want to see."

Delilah's gaze settles on me. I sigh. It reminds me of how I dream of being with East, and here, in this house, it's easy for me to think that we'll get to be together.

"I think I'm going to go home." I force a grin, but it's painful.

I head for the door and East follows me. I feel his hand slip into mine and it forces me to stop. I face him and he lets go. I wish he hadn't.

"I thought you wanted to stay for dinner?" he asks.

"I have an early practice tomorrow."

"What time?"

"Earlier than you get up."

He bites his lip. "What time?" he whispers.

"Six."

"In the morning?" he chirps.

"I told you it was early."

"Mmm. I might be there."

I lean in. "I doubt it, but thank you."

"For you, I would do anything," he murmurs close to my ear.

I want so desperately to kiss him. To touch his face, look into his eyes—but again, I let the moment come and go.

I open one of the two doors and look back only for a moment. A sadness seeps in as I rush down the steps. The further I get away from him, the lonelier I am. I look back and he's waiting for me.

But will it always be this way?

CHAPTER
TWENTY-SEVEN

AUGUST EAST

I wake up with a groan and rush to get dressed as speedily as I can. I skip down the stairs and head for the front door.

"East."

I nearly stumble when I hear my mom's voice. I turn and she's standing in her robe with a drink in her hand. I narrow my eyes but soon realize that it's orange juice. I can smell it from across the room. I won't lie and say that I don't suspect it's spiked.

"Why are you up so early?" she asks.

I clear my throat and thumb behind me. "Keller is practicing and asked if I wanted to watch."

"That's so sweet of him, but love, be careful."

I narrow my eyes; she's never warned me before.

"I'm pretty sure people know about—"

"Not you—for him. For Keller."

I close my eyes. I let it pass because I know she only wants to protect us.

"I'm not going to run out onto the field and kiss him, Mom."

"I know, but—" She pauses.

I step closer to her out of curiosity. Her skin looks paler and eyes are sunken.

"What?"

"I spent some time speaking with Maggie last night and she told me some things about him."

"What things?"

"Honey," she approaches me, "Keller is a sweet boy, but he isn't like you."

I nod. "Yes, that's why I like him. I don't want to be with someone just like me."

She tilts her head, cradling the glass against her chest and rolling it back and forth ever so slightly. I become transfixed on it until she speaks up again.

"Keller will finish high school and get a scholarship to play football."

I narrow my eyes. "I know he plays football."

"But what you don't seem to realize is his path is set, my love. He has a future."

I shake my head. "Why are you doing this now?"

She steps back and takes a sip of her drink. I glare at it, then snatch it from her hand. She flinches. I place it to my nose and smell it. It has a powerful scent. It's more than just orange juice. She grabs it from my hand and scratches my skin. I hiss, drawing my hand in to look at it. I see a small trickle of blood.

"Oh—East—let me see."

I tuck it away. "Is this about Arizona?"

She bites the corner of her bottom lip. She takes a quick breath and reaches out, but I won't let her touch me.

"East, I only want you to be happy."

"I am happy, Mom, but you wouldn't know because you're constantly—" I stop short of calling her an addict.

She stares at her glass and tosses it to the floor. It shatters. "Is that what you wanted?" she shouts.

I back away, running to the door and leaving it open behind me as I rush down the steps and toward the gate.

"East—I'm sorry!" she yells.

But I'm not listening. I climb up the gate and jump down on the other side, not bothering to open it.

My pace slacks off when I'm halfway down the street. I wipe a tear away with the jacket sleeve.

I hate seeing her like this. She's never been this way. Maybe it's this town. Maybe it's the house. Maybe I should stop being so damn selfish and let them take us away to Arizona, where we could start again.
184

But I don't want that. I want to be as close to Keller as I can, for as long as I can, which, if my mom's right, could only be a couple more years.

But I'd take it with gratitude if it means I get more moments with him.

I round the corner and run straight into something hard. I stumble, then feel a hand on my elbow. I look up to see Paul. His hair's a mess. He has dirt on his shirt. I notice a scratch on his arm, so he pulls his sleeve down to conceal it. I don't know why.

"East—I'm so sorry. Are you okay?"

I sniffle. I wasn't done crying yet. But I'm not crying out of sadness. I'm angry. I hate feeling this way. I take a short breath.

"I'm good." It's a lie, but I don't think I should confide in Mr. Rider. We've had a couple of awkward moments and I blame myself for it happening at all. It just seems that he shows up when I'm at my lowest point and I feel weak.

He leans in closer. "Your eyes are red."

"Allergies."

He straightens, realizing I will not tell him.

I give him a once over. "What are you doing out this early and why are you all dirty?"

"I—" He looks down at himself. "Oh, I guess I am a mess."

"Yes—and you're bleeding." I point to his arm. "I
185

saw the scratch on your arm." I feel like I'm accusing him of something, but it's easier than dealing with my anger about what my mom just said to me.

"I was helping Maggie find her cat."

"Owen."

He grins. "Yes, Owen."

"Did you?"

"Did I what?"

"Find him?"

Paul hesitates. "No, but I had a good fight with a stray."

I look around. "Funny, I've never noticed stray cats in town."

"It would be easier if you were outside more."

I laugh. "Sure, I—I have to go."

"Where?"

I grin while passing him by. "I've joined the football team."

"What?"

I walk backward, teasing him. "I mean, look at me."

"They'll crush you."

I wave a hand. "Don't underestimate me."

"I never do," he shouts as I leave him behind and head toward the school.

CHAPTER TWENTY-EIGHT

KELLER WEST

I stare at the gate, but only see a few girls have gathered to watch us practice. The cheerleaders have shown up, though. Shy is among them, wearing her uniform with a pair of leggings underneath the short skirt. It's chilly this morning but I appreciate the cold when we practice. It's easy to feel like your body's on fire.

"Go, Wolves!" Shy shouts with a raised fist.

I grin. She was always the most enthusiastic cheerleader on the field. Sometimes I wondered if she was trying to prove something. Who knows? Some people are desperate to impress others. I've never been like that, but to be fair, nothing's been that hard for me here. My dad played football. He was a star quarterback. My mom cheered. I come from royalty as far as people from this town are concerned. It's unfortunate, but true. Sometimes I wonder why I'm so ungrateful for that when I see kids like Evie and Vincent struggling to fit in. I've never felt that way in school. People move out of my way. They wish they could be and yet I don't care.

I'd honestly give it all up if I could be with August East. But I'm a coward. I can't seem to convince myself that it's what I truly want.

Maybe I want it all.

I feel a bump from behind and turn to see Brian standing on the field with his helmet in hand. Things have been strange between us. I hate it, but there isn't much I can do to make it better. I love Shylo Martin, and in some ways, I think Brian loves her too, but it's probably for different reasons. Brian is the kind of guy who's a collector. He wants the awards—the trophies.

But we haven't talked since I woke up. He hasn't called once. I don't even know if he came to the hospital. It makes me feel like a fool for ever liking him to begin with. In many ways, Brian was a placeholder for a life I wished I could have. But I never fantasized about spending my life with him. Not once.

He didn't show any interest in Shy until we were no longer dating. It's like he couldn't help himself. But Shy—well, she's good at getting her way. Some people call it manipulation, but I know she loves me. In a lot of ways, Shy is like Brian. They both want me to pay attention to them. It doesn't matter how I feel about anything.

"So, are you with her now?" he asks.

I swallow hard. I knew it was coming, but he's chosen a strange place to ask me.

"No—we're not dating."

"But people saw you two together at The Farm."

"We did go, and we broke up there."

"So, you were dating her, then?" he states.

"I don't count it."

"You're something else," he grumbles while tapping his helmet against his leg.

"Did you even come to see me in the hospital?"

His head tilts, but he doesn't say anything.

"Nice." I huff.

"You knew how I felt about her, Keller."

I smirk. "So, you didn't come to see me."

He steps closer. "This isn't about you."

"Why didn't you come?" I yell at him.

"Because I didn't want to!" he shouts.

I blink through his cruelty, but think back to those moments we had together. Maybe this isn't about Shy at all. Maybe it's about us. I try to appeal to him.

"Brian—"

"No, man. You could have anyone, but you just can't help but grab those same old scraps."

189

I narrow my eyes. "Scraps?"

He snickers, glancing over at Shy.

"Not cool, Brian."

"What? Didn't you hear? She pity fucked that faggot."

Every muscle in my body tenses up. That disgusting word should never be used to describe anyone in this world—most of all August East, whom I love. And who the hell is Brian James to be calling him that when he begged me to kiss him?

My anger rises to an uncontrollable pitch.

I lunge at him, crying out like a wounded animal while knocking him to the ground. Our helmets go flying across the field. Our teammates form a circle around us as we roll around. He gets in a couple good hits on my side, and I moan, but finally I catch his lip and bust it wide open. It immediately starts bleeding, but he smiles, blood staining his teeth and shakes his head at me. "I know why you like him," he hisses in my ear.

I could die. I want to push him into the dirt and bury him deep. I could. I hate him for doing this to me. He knows what it would do. It would ruin me—ruin my family. It could cost me everything.

"Shut up," I hiss back. I feel a hard tug from behind and the assistant coach has me on my feet. The team scatters as our head coach approaches us like a

190

galloping horse. He's a big man, intimidating to some. He doesn't bother me because I've dealt with my dad. But everyone else has their heads lowered and helmets in hand.

"What the hell is going on?" his voice booms.

Brian stumbles to his feet, spitting blood on the ground. I hold my breath, waiting for him to make his accusations known, but he doesn't. Maybe he thinks I'll tell everyone about the way he used to beg me to kiss him on the field. Maybe he knows I won't go down without taking him with me. I don't know if I could do that to him, but if that's what it takes for him to keep his mouth shut, then so be it. I can play the villain.

"Bench, now!" he barks at Brian, who backs away, pointing a finger at me.

I hate him. He isn't who I thought he was, or maybe he's always been this way? Maybe it's me who's changing?

Coach gets in my face. "What are you doing?" His face contorts with irritation.

"He was being rude about a girl," I admit.

Coach barks at the team with the twirl of his finger above his head. "Give me five laps!"

They all groan, giving me the stink eye. I don't blame them. They did nothing wrong. Coach focuses on me. I glance at the sideline and see Shy standing

191

there with her arms tucked away. I'm sure she knows what happened between me and Brian. She isn't stupid.

"Son, you have a bright future. I'd hate to see you throw it all away for a little tail."

I swallow the bile. Shy isn't *tail* or any other derogatory term.

"I'm not dating anyone."

"Not what I hear." he glances over at Shy. "That girl is trouble, West. She's got you all messed up in the head." His rigid finger taps against my temple.

I look away and see East moving along the fence. Coach is right. I am a mess, but it isn't because of Shylo Martin. His eyes follow my gaze and he leans in my ear, "Or new *friends*." He emphasizes the word and my jaw tenses. Does he know? Maybe he was suspicious? Maybe people are gossiping? I don't know, but I hate that he's mentioned East at all. But I see Evie and Vincent walking up behind him. Maybe he means all of them? It doesn't make it any better. It's a classist thing to say. It doesn't matter what other people think about them. Evie and Vincent are my friends, and I have no intention of dropping them because of popularity.

My eyes lock on his. "I'm going to win this next game and the one after that—and the one after that." I speak as if I'm trying to convince myself, even though I know I can. I just have to focus.

He grabs my helmet off the ground and shoves it into my chest. "Then do it, Keller. Show me, and the world, what a badass you are."

I grit my teeth and forcefully shove my helmet on. The howl starts low and then rises to a fevered pitch as he backs away from me. The rest of my team howls along with me. If they run laps, then I run laps.

That's what a leader does.

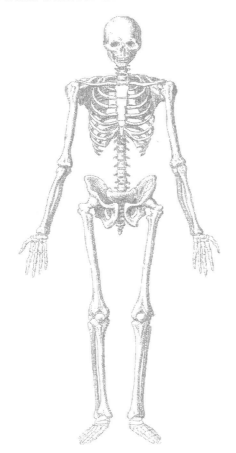

CHAPTER TWENTY-NINE

AUGUST EAST

I watch him run around the edge of the field. He's glanced at me a couple of times, but he won't linger. I wish he would stop and talk to me. I feel a bump from behind and turn to see Evie has joined me. Vincent is still yawning while rubbing the side of his head.

"What are you guys doing here?"

Evie grins while unscrewing the cap on a thermos bottle. "I'm here with hot chocolate."

"Oh—wow, thank you."

"I bet it was about Shy," a girl states to her friend. They're standing next to us, pressed against the fence.

"Of course, it was, I mean, Brian was dating her and then she got with Keller."

I try to ignore it, but I'm curious.

"What did we miss?" Vincent asks.

One girl eyes him and then gives up the information because she clearly loves to gossip.

"Keller attacked Brian on the field."

"Oh!" The girl's friend rolls her eyes. "Brian was talking to him before they ended up on the ground and pummeling each other like cave dwellers."

"The ground?" I ask.

"Yes, they were rolling around hitting each other and I know it was because of her." The girl stares at me like she's waiting for a reaction. I won't give her one. I know her type. She must live to talk shit about people.

I look over at Shy, who's doing a high kick. She catches me staring.

"Probably." I want to end the conversation with them before they trick Vincent into admitting things. It would be easy enough. He's so honest about everything. I respect him for it, but it doesn't do me any good when I'm fearful of the rumors.

For him—not for me.

I feel a cup slip into my hand and the sweet scent of chocolate fills my nostrils. My stomach growls. It's the distraction that I need.

The girls get bored with me and walk away arm in arm.

"I hope they end up wrinkled like prunes," Vincent grumbles. He was listening in, but must be too tired to take part.

I chuckle. They probably will be. They're both nearly orange from frequent trips to tanning beds.

"Drink—everything gets better with hot chocolate," Evie claims.

"It's true," Vincent agrees.

I take a sip and hiss through the heat, but it's good. Fall is here. The leaves are changing and the temperature has dropped. What was once rain will soon make way for snow now that we're moving through October. My stomach tightens. Will we be here after Halloween? I wish I knew.

I look back to Shy, who's trying her best to ignore me and then I see Keller stop on the field, looking in my direction. I stare into the cup and see the reflection of the sun rising, skimming across the surface.

I hate to think that my mom was right. I'm having a hard time believing in her ability to give me advice right now while she's under the influence of anything. I want her to be well. I want everything to be as normal for us as it can be, but I think I'm fooling myself. There probably is no happy ending for me. Not here, not with Keller West, so I seem to be delaying the inevitable.

I look at Keller, but he's stopped to talk to Shy. She touches the side of his arm and I feel a little jealousy lapping at the corners of my mind.

I shouldn't be, right? He wouldn't do something with her to get back at me, would he?

I have to stop letting my thoughts get away from me.

"So, when am I getting an invitation?" Vincent asks.

"To what?"

He takes a sip of hot chocolate and grimaces from the heat. "Um, the Halloween party?"

"Oh, I would think soon. Mom was making the invitations."

"I'm going to be a vampire." Vincent's chin bobs like he's announced something important.

I grin. "But which one?"

"Duh, Dracula—Bela Lugosi. That's the only one."

Evie snickers. "You think girls will want you to bite them."

"They will, trust me. Girls love a sexy vampire."

"No girl wants that."

Vincent rolls his eyes, but then stares longingly at Shy. "You're wrong." He scoffs.

I shove my hair back, "Maybe someday—if a director does it right for teenagers."

Evie cocks her brow. "What's the right way?" she asks.

I lean against the fence and take another drink. "I don't know, maybe a vampire should be like us."

She lowers her cup. "Like in high school?"

"Yeah, a vampire that goes to school and does normal teenage crap."

"That's actually pretty cool." Vincent says.

"But how would this teenage vampire walk around in the sunlight?" Evie tosses the question at us like she's about to claim a checkmate.

I snap my fingers. "Rain!"

"Rain?" she asks.

"Yeah—clouds. No sunlight."

"Mmm, well, let me know if you know some boy like that."

I look back at the field and see everyone packing up. Practice is over. I swallow hard. Should I stay and try to talk to him or leave?

"Hey, are you going to the Horror Festival?" Vincent asks, drawing me out of my thoughts.

"Are you serious?"

Vincent extends his hand to Evie, wanting more hot chocolate, she fills his cup. "I guess that's a yes."

I brighten. "I actually have access to free tickets."

"Really?" he asks.

I let him suffer for a few seconds. "Want to come with me? Both of you." I invite Evie, too.

"I'd love that!" he nearly yells it back at me.

Evie shoves a finger in her ear and wiggles it. "Inside voice, Vincent."

He rolls his eyes. "Those tickets ain't cheap!"

He's right. They are expensive.

Vincent speaks with his hands and the hot

chocolate spills over the side of his cup, he switches hands and shakes off the hot liquid, but doesn't miss a beat. "It's an all-day horror extravaganza with three movies—*Fright Night, Nightmare on Elm Street* and, what seems to be a palate cleanser, *Teen Wolf.*"

"Awe, I love Michael J. Fox." Evie swoons.

"Yeah, they also have actors dressed up in the audience and plenty of snacks—all you can eat. People participate while the movie is going on."

"Like *Rocky Horror Picture Show*," I reply.

"Which is also amazing, by the way." He says.

"We've never had it here—not yet, anyway. Some people in town think it's too g—" He stops before finishing the word, but I know what he means. There have been people protesting that movie since it came out ten years ago.

"Well, they're dumb. Eventually *Rocky Horror* will be everywhere. They don't seem to realize that telling everyone they can't have something makes everyone want it more." Evie glances at me. "It's reverse psychology."

"True, and it's awesome. I saw it once back east with friends." I admit.

"Do you—I mean," Vincent pauses, looking to Evie for support.

Evie takes over for him. "Do you have any friends back there?" she asks.

I take a sip, "No, they all died in the fire, and the couple who survived didn't want to talk to me again."

"God, I'm so sorry." She touches my arm.

Vincent leans in. "It's not your fault. I mean, yeah, the fire started in your house, but from what Evie tells me, there was a storm and the wind made it spread."

I clear my throat, trying to push what memories I have left from that night out of my mind's eye. "It was. It was a terrible storm, but I—well, Keller invited me and he wanted to invite both of you, too." I want to steer us away from the fire. It's in my past. I need to let it go.

"Yeah?" Vincent looks to the field.

"Yeah, he told me I could ask, so if you want to come, we can all meet up at the theater on Saturday."

"It's a date!" Vincent yells again.

Evie pinches the bridge of her nose but doesn't chastise him this time.

"Thank you," she says.

Vincent does a little dance to celebrate.

"I wouldn't want to go without you guys."

Her head cocks. "Yeah?"

"Yeah, I mean we're friends, right?"

She fights her enthusiasm. "Yeah—sure."

I turn to look at the field and see that the last of the football players are leaving. I'd love to run out there and find him—talk to him—hold his hand.

But I can't and I think I need to face that truth.

200

CHAPTER
THIRTY

KELLER WEST

I've spent the last two days avoiding East at school. We've passed each other with looks that tell me he wants more, and I get it. I want more, too. But that fight with Brian is festering inside of me. His ugly words—his accusations. All of it.

Brian didn't come back after the fight. I assume his mom freaked out and took him to the emergency room. Each time Brian gets a cut, scratch or bruise, she flips out. I get it, I guess, but it drives him insane. I know at least that much.

I look up when an assembly is requested in the gym over the loudspeaker. I don't know why. It's Thursday. Most of the assemblies happen on Fridays for games. Books snap shut as kids head for the door. They waste no time getting out of studying. I stand up, grabbing my books, and head for the door as I look back and stare at Brian's empty seat. Something about it bothers me.

I enter the gym and scan the bleachers. Shy offers a wave. I follow her invitation. Once seated, I look down the line, but I know who I'm looking for—August East.

The side door opens and our principal comes walking through, his dress shoes clicking against the waxed floor. He pauses in front of the small podium and adjusts the extended mic. Some feedback rings out, and I wrinkle my nose.

He taps the mic twice and then clears his throat. "I called all of you here because we need to discuss a situation."

I notice Delilah is standing to the right of him, along with Megan and Mr. Rider. I have no idea what's going on.

"Oftentimes, being a teenager can be stressful. For some, this stress will cause them to do things they normally wouldn't do."

I stiffen up. I'm not sure why. It's not like what happened between me and East would be announced at an assembly, but my paranoia seems to always get the better of me.

Our principal continues, "And one of our own—a student here at Whynot High—has seemed to succumb to these stresses."

What the hell is he talking about?

I look around and every face is as stunned as I feel inside. I wish he'd just say it!

"What?" someone yells out from the crowd of students and a little laughter follows.

Our principal taps the podium, clearly annoyed, but he gets over it and looks to Delilah like she needs to step in. He lifts his hand, and she walks up to him and he relinquishes the mic.

Delilah looks out at as many of us as she can and then licks her lip before speaking. "Brian James is missing."

The words linger in the air, heavy and dark.

Missing? Brian is missing? How? When? Why?

I catch a couple of girls looking at me. I was the last person who got into a fight with him, as far as I know.

Great—wait! They don't think I know something, do they? Holy shit. I'd never do anything to him, or anyone else.

She immediately follows up her statement, "Now, the police are investigating this, but, as far as we can tell so far, it seems he's run away."

I narrow my eyes. "Run away?" I whisper.

Shy hasn't said a word, but she is fidgeting with her hands. I reach down and stop her by placing my hand over hers. She seems grateful, but it changes nothing.

"Now, we would like to speak to a few of you today, with the help of Detective Marshall Brant."

She waves a hand, and a man emerges from the crowd. He's been sitting in the front, on the bleachers, with the rest of us. He turns and offers a nod. He's dressed pretty normal. Jeans, blazer, tennis shoes. I would've never guessed he was a cop.

Shy let out a heavy sigh. I squeeze her hand and she glances over at me, but she's upset. I get it. We've known Brian since we were all little. He's always been here, like the rest of us. I catch Detective Brant looking at me and hold his stare, because I have nothing to hide. He looks down and away, taking a seat.

Delilah looks at all of us.

"There is nothing to worry about. I promise you."

I take another breath. I think I forgot to breathe.

Our principal leans in toward the mic. "Okay, children. You can return to class now."

The chatter is gone. We move in silence toward the door. Brian James is missing. Those words are ringing in my ears. Missing? How? Brian was a lot of things, but I never took him for someone who would run away. But maybe he'd had enough? His mom drives him crazy and we just, well, he hit me. I hit him. He seemed to hate me.

Shit.

This doesn't look good.

CHAPTER THIRTY-ONE

AUGUST EAST

Holy shit," Evie whispers as I sit in silence next to her at the impromptu assembly.

"Missing—is that code for dead?" Vincent asks.

Evie shushes him. "Vincent—don't."

A girl glances behind her and looks at me. I swallow hard. I don't have anything to do with this. Nothing at all but Keller was fighting with him on the football field.

Shit.

I stare at Detective Brant after he stands up. He doesn't look like a detective. I didn't think they wore jeans and blazers with tennis shoes. But who am I to know what they really look like? I never talked to one—just the police.

Oh, shit—shit. Shit!

The fire.

I try to control my breathing. I may hyperventilate if I don't get my emotions in check. All I know is it doesn't look good for me. Brian clearly doesn't like me and I tried to break his face in gym class.

Oh, man. I need to stop freaking out. I didn't do anything. I know I didn't do anything to Brian James. I look down the line and I see Keller sitting next to Shy. His hand is on her lap. Jealousy sours my stomach, but it's the least of my worries right now.

Delilah looks at all of us.

"There is nothing to worry about. I promise you."

Everyone stands, but it's eerily silent, like the air has been sucked out of the room. I nearly stumble, but Vincent helps me stand. We move along, finally breaking free, but not fast enough. I feel a hand on my shoulder and see Delilah. Her expression says more than any words could. I look past her and see the Detective speaking with Megan and the principal.

"Do you have a few minutes?"

I look around. "Sure."

I follow her out the other side of the gym and down the hallway. We end up in the library. I guess it's better than the police station. I take a seat at a long table and Delilah sits down next to me. Detective Brant enters the room. He remains silent. Maybe this is how he gets criminals to crack. It's probably a good plan. It's making me nervous, and I didn't do anything wrong.

206

He takes a seat across from us and grins. I look at Delilah. I've seen enough movies to know I should probably have a parent with me, but I'm afraid to say it for fear of looking guilty when I'm not.

Detective Brant offers a smile. It seems genuine.

"So, August, how do you like Whynot?"

I adjust in the chair. "Good—it's nice."

"Not like the east coast."

I swallow, glancing at Delilah and back to him. "No—the ocean is missing."

He grins, looking down at the table as he intertwines his fingers. I see a wedding ring. At least he's married.

"Yes, it is. Plenty of water there to put out fires, I guess."

I narrow my eyes. "Our house burned down along with the town that we lived in."

"Many people died."

"Most."

"Friends of yours?"

"I lived there my whole life, so yes."

I'm annoyed now. He has no right to ask me any of this. What happened there—it wasn't my fault.

"It was an accident," I state, "a horrible accident."

He lets me sit with what he's said. I feel that he's trying to upset me.

"Tragic loss. I extend my deepest condolences."

I don't respond. I think I hate him, but I guess this is what he does. It's his job.

"So, tell me about what happened in gym class."

I shake my head. "It was dodgeball."

"I know, but Brian got hurt, didn't he?"

I nod. "Yeah—a lot of people get hurt in that game. It's brutal."

"True, I remember," he twists his finger next to his head, "you never get that sound of the ball out of your head, do you?"

"No."

I pick at my nails under the table. Then my knee shakes. I don't like where this is going.

"Did you not like Brian?"

"Did?" I ask. "I think asking *do I like him* would be more appropriate, right?"

"Yes—I apologize. I didn't mean to speak about him like he was no longer with us."

"Is he?" I ask.

Detective Brant leans forward. "Is he what?"

"Still with us?"

He leans back in the chair, forcing it to creak, "I make no assumptions until I know all the facts."

"But he isn't dead, right?" I ask, because I have to know.

"There is no body," the detective clarifies.

The door opens and my mom comes rushing in.

She steps up to me and kneels down, cupping my face. Her eyes are filled with fear. But then she pulls me up with her and wraps her arm around my shoulder, glaring at the Detective. "How dare you interrogate a child!"

Detective Brant stands, rubbing the side of his neck. "Mrs. East, it was just a few questions. We're talking to everyone."

She shakes her head. "This is illegal and if you ever bother my son again, I will sue you into the ground."

She pulls me along with her, as the Detective calls out behind him, "It's nice to see you, Rosetta."

I narrow my eyes as we step into the hallway.

How does he know her name?

"Mom?" I ask as we sit in the car. She has yet to drive away, but she's gripping the steering wheel.

"Yes, love."

"Who was he—I mean, he knows your name?"

She sighs, then releases the wheel.

"That's Detective Marshall Brant. He investigated the fire back east."

I shake my head, glancing out the window. It's frosting over from the heat inside the car.

"I don't remember him."

"He talked to me and your father after we claimed the insurance for the house."

"Oh."

She looks at me, reaching up and cupping my cheek. "There was no reason for him to talk to you then or now."

"I would have if he wanted."

She tilts her head. "My sweetness. You are perfect."

Her words don't sit well with me. I'm perfect? What does she mean?

"Mom, I don't remember much of anything from that night."

"And that's a good thing."

I adjust on the seat, looking down into my lap. "I don't know if it is."

She reaches in and takes my hand. I look at her as she kisses the top of it and holds it against her chest.

"This boy—Brian James. Did you not like him?"

I bite my lip, I feel like she's wanting me to admit something to her. "I don't think about him—I never did."

"But you hit him with the ball in gym class?"

"I did, but he was slaughtering the team. I just did what I had to do to save us."

"A hero," she whispers.

I don't feel like one. I've never thought of myself that way. But I guess I've always been willing to place myself in the way of danger to protect the people I love. I felt that way in the tunnel, but Keller took it from me and the door ended up hitting him instead of me.

"I'm no hero, Mom."

She removes her hand and starts the engine.

"Should I go home?" I ask.

"Yes, today you should and besides, you can help me with the invitations."

"The party?"

"Yes, I think it's exactly what we all need," she states.

Maybe she's right.

I feel myself sink into the seat as she takes off with a heavy foot. Dad hates her driving. It makes him nauseous, or so he claims. Honestly, I think he just assumes she'll wreck the car with us in it.

We move down the street and I see Mr. Rider standing on the sidewalk. He watches us pass by, but his eyes look hollow. Something about it is unsettling, and then I think about the dirt on his clothing and the scratch on his arm.

But I've seen too many movies and my imagination is getting away from me.

CHAPTER THIRTY-TWO

KELLER WEST

S ince you were kids, huh?" Detective Brant asks me.
I keep my eyes on him, there's no way I'm going to
give him the impression I'd ever do anything to Brian.

"Yes." My chin rises. I have nothing to hide.

"But you didn't always get along," he adds, drumming his fingers on the tabletop. I wish he'd stop. It's annoying the hell out of me, but maybe that's the point.

"No, because best friends don't. Not real ones anyway."

He looks to Delilah and back to me. "So, the last time you saw him was when you were beating him on the football field?"

I chuckle, but it fades. "Yes, I saw him at practice and then he wasn't in school. I assumed his mom freaked out when she saw his lip because I busted it."

"Why would that upset her so much?"

I lean forward. "Because she's terrified she'll lose him."

"I guess sometimes being paranoid has its reasons."

"Listen, do you know anything about what happened to my friend or not?" I'm losing patience with him.

"I know he went to football practice and got into a pretty good fight with his best friend and then he left the field and that's it."

My brows meet. "Wait—he never went home?"

The detective shakes his head, pulling out a cigarette, but he doesn't light it. He just holds it between his fingers. I don't smell smoke on him, so I assume he's trying to quit.

"No—he got his ass handed to him by you and then poof," he spreads his fingers, "he disappeared like magic."

"Well…" I run my hand across the top of the table.

The detective leans forward. "Yes?"

My gaze lifts to meet his blue-gray eyes, "Brian was sick of his mom. She hovers. But I never thought he'd actually leave."

"Did he ever mention leaving to you before?"

I sigh. "Yeah—a few times, but like I said, I never thought he'd do it."

"This changes things a little bit."

I lean back and glance over at Delilah. She's been a quiet observer this entire time. I guess it's good to have someone with us. I'd hate for him to say I said something I didn't, just so he could solve a case.

"I just—I don't know. He was pretty upset."

"About the girl—" the detective looks at his notes, "Shylo Martin, correct?"

I swallow hard. "I mean, yeah, I guess. They broke up."

"Then she started dating you."

I adjust in the chair, it creaks against the wood floor, "No—we're not. She's my best friend, like Brian is."

"*Was*—since he doesn't seem to be here."

"I will not talk about him in past tense," I protest.

The detective stands up. He's got about four inches on me and his shoulders are broad. It wouldn't surprise me if he played football when he was in school. Probably a defensive linebacker, like Ty Miller. They're built about the same.

I wonder why someone built like him is doing this. Maybe I don't want to know.

"Fair enough." He walks to the window and stares out across the town. He wags a finger. "That East boy lives in that big house on the hilltop, right?"

I'm visibly confused. "The Mill House? Yeah. His family lives there."

214

He turns, taking a seat on the window ledge. "What do you know about him?"

I lean in, placing my arms on the tabletop, "He loves horror movies, and he's funny—got a good sense of humor."

The detective folds his arms over his chest. "That's all well and good, but I mean about his past."

"I know he lived back east, in Maine, and their house burned down."

"Did he talk to you about what happened?"

I shake my head. "He doesn't like to talk about it and I honestly don't blame him."

The detective rises, walking toward me like he's about to tell a story, "Rosetta East and her husband Steven were in some debt."

I look at Delilah. She remains silent, but nudges her chin in the detective's direction like she wants me to listen to what he has to say.

"A lot of people have bills."

"Yes—this was a considerable amount of money. Thousands of dollars."

I feel uncomfortable for the first time since I've been talking to him, so I fold my arms over my chest. Subconsciously closing myself off to him.

"I don't know anything about that," I admit.

"Their house burned down, and they collected some insurance."

215

He lets that settle between us. I don't like what he's implying.

"They lost everything. The house, their belongings and people died."

"That's right, people died. In fact, all of their friends. Every single one of them." He states with aggression.

I push my chair back and place my hands on the table. My chin lifts and I lock eyes with him. "That was an accident. They would never do something like that on purpose, especially East."

The detective takes a seat, allowing me to be taller than he is. His expression changes in a matter of seconds. "Of course not. I mean, that would be horrendous." He tosses me a newspaper that's back dated. The fire is front page news. I see their names in bold black type. I push it back to him.

"What East says happened is what happened."

"But he doesn't talk much about it, does he?"

I shake my head and look at Delilah. "I should probably tell my mom and dad that I'm here."

The detective straightens in the chair, he waves a hand, "No one is holding you here against your will, Keller. You can go if you want."

I head for the door but he calls out behind me, "I just thought you'd be interested to know about your boyfriend, is all."

I cringe, balling my fist at my side. He has no right to threaten me so I keep going, exiting the room and pressing my shoulders against the outside wall. I close my eyes, taking a few deep breaths. I barely breathed while he steered that conversation in a direction I didn't want to go.

He can go to Hell.

CHAPTER THIRTY-THREE

AUGUST EAST

I sit in my room staring out at the school and then at Keller's house. I hear a light knock on my door.

"What, Mom?"

"I'm not old enough to be your mom, East."

I turn to see Shy has come to see me. I stand up, grabbing a few pieces of my clothing and tossing them aside like it's going to make any difference.

"What are you doing here?" I ask.

She takes a small tour, walking along the wall and staring at my posters. I've managed to get a few up, but nothing like I had when I lived in Maine. She pauses in front of *Nightmare on Elm Street* and tilts her head. "It sort of feels like a nightmare, doesn't it?" She turns to face me and her eyes are swollen. She's been crying. Something in me shifts. I know Shy has her ways of manipulating situations to suit her, but I know she'd never wish that Brian was gone. She isn't like that at all. Her wicked nature begins and ends with wanting to be loved. I see that now.

"I think he ran away from home." I don't know if I'm trying to convince her or myself.

"You think so?" She wipes her eyes with the edge of her sleeve.

I take a step closer to her, but I need to keep my distance. I've been here before with Shylo Martin when she's upset. We won't be repeating any past mistakes. "I know he was upset about you and Keller, and his mom seem to be a little overbearing."

She snorts. "A little? Try maximum overdrive."

"Maybe he had enough. Sometimes people make decisions in the heat of the moment and do stupid shit." I stop, because I could also be talking about us.

Shylo nods. "No—you're right."

I take a seat by my window and she joins me. I study her profile. She really is one of the most beautiful girls I've ever seen in my life. Anyone would be lucky to have her. I'm just not that person for her. Even if Keller and I never spoke again, I know I couldn't be with her when I know she's always wanted to be with him. I don't think that'll ever change. I get it. He has this way of trapping you and never letting go. It's infuriating.

"I never did anything with him." Shy admits.

"Who?" I ask, before realizing I should've just let her speak and stayed quiet.

Shylo sighs, fidgeting with her hands. I reach in and stop her from digging at her fingernails. I've been there. They'll start bleeding. She looks at me, her eyes solemn. She has no intention of trying to do anything physical with me this time. That time has come and passed for us. I'm relieved. I don't need to worry about it anymore.

"Brian."

"Oh."

She rolls her eyes. "Not that he didn't want to, but I—I just didn't want to, ya know?"

"I get it. I've felt that way." I support her the best I can.

Her lip curls, "Probably with me, huh?"

I remain tight-lipped. I don't want to offend her, but I had no intention of sleeping with her.

"Man, I'm the worst, right?" she asks.

I shake my head, removing my hand from hers. I didn't realize I was still holding onto her.

"No, we—listen. We made a mistake, is all. We were both upset and then things happened and I don't regret it."

"No?"

"Of course not, Shy. I care about you, I just don't—I mean, we're not—" It isn't coming out right.

220

She steps in to help me. "I understand, it's the same for me, don't get me wrong, you're cute—like so cute and funny, but it's I never imagined my life with anyone but Keller because it's all I've ever known."

I take a short breath. I hope she isn't here to tell me she wants to fight for him because I don't know what I'll do. I may give in and let her have him if she pushes me, because I don't even know if we'll still be here after Halloween.

"But," she adds, "just because you've only had vanilla ice cream doesn't mean rocky road wouldn't be nice, right?"

I chuckle. "Rocky Road might be a great way to describe me."

She reaches out and touches my arm. "No!" she laughs through it, "I didn't mean you, it could be strawberry sherbet, or chocolate chip. What I mean is," she huffs, "I think I only want Keller because I'm still here, in Whynot. But if I go to school, out of state and meet new people—I don't know. There're more flavors of ice cream out there."

I look down at my hands. "I hope I'm not the reason you feel like this."

"Oh my God, no—no, East."

I feel flush. I must've sucked that night.

"And it was amazing," she adds.

I perk up, even though I shouldn't. But nobody
221

wants to think that someone hated being with you. I want what happened to be part of our past, and not shape the future in any way.

"I thought it was great, too, but I never want it to happen again."

She extends her hand so I can shake it. "Deal."

"Deal."

We sit there for a moment in a peaceful silence. I'm so glad to finally have this behind us. I didn't want to lose Shylo Martin as a friend. I really care about her.

"So, do you really think he ran away?"

"I mean, yeah, but he'll probably come back soon and apologize to his mom and everyone will think he's a badass for leaving."

Shy tries to smile. I lean in to make her look at me. "I'm serious."

My face is a little too close to hers, but nothing's going to happen. I know we've reached an agreement that will stand firm between us.

"East?"

I stiffen up when I see Keller standing in my doorway. I stumble to my feet, but he walks out of sight. I roll my eyes and look at Shy.

"Let me go after him," she offers.

"Are you sure I shouldn't?"

"No—we need to talk this out once and for all.

And I want him to know that absolutely nothing was going on between us right now."

I want to run out of the room and find him, but I think she's right. Shy should talk to him first and have her moment with him, too. Then maybe—just maybe—we can finally move forward.

CHAPTER THIRTY-FOUR

KELLER WEST

"Damn it!" I pace in front of his house, wondering what I should do when Shy steps out and looks at me with such compassion.

"What the hell, Shy?" I exclaim with one hand raised toward his window.

She approaches me without saying a word, but once she gets to me, she wraps her arms around my neck and forces me to hug her. I'm confused and angry, and completely at a loss for words. She backs away and looks me over.

"We need to talk."

"You think? I mean, what was going on?"

"Nothing and everything." She effectively confuses me even more.

"I mean—do you—does he—are you—?" I try to ask, but it comes out like I've forgotten how to communicate with anyone.

"I don't, he doesn't, and no," she clarifies.

I narrow my eyes, "So, what was going on then?"

She looks back at the house, "I came here because I felt awful about Brian—and East, and you."

"Shy, Brian only likes you because of me."

She sighs. "I know, and I only liked East because of you."

I let out a sigh and place a hand on my hip.

"This is a freakin' mess."

She sniffles through the laughter. "No—it is, but not anymore."

"What do you mean?"

"I just made a deal with East that we're friends and nothing more and never will be anything more than that."

"Oh." I'm stunned.

"And I know it looked like something was going to happen, but it wasn't. I wasn't going to kiss him and he wasn't going to kiss me."

"No?" I ask.

She shakes her head. "No, and as far as we go, you're off the hook, Keller. For good. I'll never show up at your house crying, or trying to get you to kiss me, or grab my boobs again."

I nearly blush. "Well, you do have nice—"

She tilts her head and I raise my hands. "Kidding—sort of."

"I appreciate the compliment, but what happened is in the past, and I have to start thinking about the future and honestly, I don't know if that's in Whynot, Ohio," she admits.

I understand how she feels. I was just thinking the same thing, but I can't tell her that for fear of it getting back to East.

"I get that, Shy, and listen, I'm sorry."

I eye the house, and she shakes her head. "Don't be. I deserved that. What I did was wrong. And we're sorry, Keller. He's sorry." She approaches me and places a hand on my arm. "He is, and you should go talk to him now. He's sort of freaking out thinking you thought we were about to do something dumb again."

"I guess I should."

She walks toward the gate and I call out to her, "Shy?"

"Yeah?"

"Do you think Brian ran away?"

She sighs. "I mean, have you met his mom?"

I let out a bit of laughter. It feels good.

I turn back toward the house and stare at the door. I decide to run up the steps, but before I can knock on the door; it opens. East is standing there looking at me with his curly blonde hair and two different colored eyes. I'd love to kiss him right now and apologize for

226

being such an idiot, but I can't. It's an awful reminder of our reality.

"Hey," he says.

"Hey."

"So," he looks past me and Shy offers a wave before walking down the sidewalk, "I take it she told you?"

"Yes, and I'm—"

East reaches out, grabs my hand and jerks me inside the house, he slams the door shut and pushes me up against the door. His lips crash into mine, but I can't fight him. I don't want to fight it ever again.

He pulls away, but his mouth lingers close to mine. My chest continues to rise and fall. He's the only person in the world who's ever made me feel this way. I get this electric current running through my body each time he touches me. It grows stronger and stronger, telling me one thing.

I'm screwed.

"What?" East asks with a smirk, tugging at the edge of his full lip.

"Did I say that out loud?" I ask.

"It sounded like—I want to be screwed."

I laugh, pushing him away from me in jest. "No—I said, *I'm screwed.*"

The mischievous glint in his eyes makes him even prettier in the soft light of the room.

"So—do you think he ran away?" I ask, straightening my shirt.

"Brian? I think so, I mean, Shy said his mom is crazy protective of him."

"Yeah—no, she is, but it's, I don't know. It just seems weird." I rub the side of my neck.

"Did that detective talk to you?" he asks.

I tilt my head. "You, too?"

"Yeah, he was fun," East grumbles. I can tell Detective Brant upset him, but to be fair, he upset me, too.

"I think he dislikes me," East admits.

"You? No, he really dislikes me. He reminded me of my dad, all big and burly."

"Big isn't always bad."

I blush. "Anyway," I clear my throat, "I bet Brian will come back in a week or two. He might've gone to hang out with his cousin. She lives in Illinois."

"Then why isn't the detective there?"

My shoulders sag, "I guess he has to check everything out. I mean, it is his job."

East leans against the staircase. I love the way the light plays off of his skin. He's beautiful. The most beautiful boy I've ever seen.

I look behind him. "Where are your parents?"

"Grocery shopping for candy. My mom is still insisting we have this Halloween party at the house."

"That's right—I mean, Halloween is in like two weeks."

"Don't remind me," he grumbles while sitting down on the bottom step. I join him, bumping into his side. He finally smiles.

"I'll be coming to this party, so I guess it won't be all bad."

"Mmm, guess not." He toys with me.

I bump into him even harder and finally he falls off the step, dragging me down with him. We roll a couple of times and I end up staring down at him.

I say nothing. I can't. All I can do is appreciate this moment, what few we have together.

"What?" he asks. His brow furrows with worry.

"I never want this to end."

He reaches up and gently glides his thumb over my bottom lip. "It won't."

It may be a lie, but I don't care.

He reaches between us, and my mouth sits agape. I can barely breathe as his hand moves languidly at first and then it accelerates, tightening—forcing me tense up.

"What if your parents come home?"

"What if?"

He tightens his grips. I moan.

"Please—" I gasp.

"Please what?" he asks.

My eyes gloss over. "Please don't stop."

His grip tightens at my side. I reach down and find him waiting for me.

He shakes his head no. "Don't."

"But I—" I can barely focus.

"Let me do this for you," he whispers in my ear.

I look at the fireplace and the room tilts. Sparks of light consume me before I fall against him.

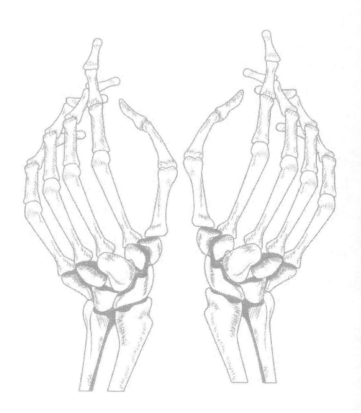

CHAPTER
THIRTY-FIVE

AUGUST EAST

I toss a grape at him, and he laughs, grabbing it and
throwing it back. I lean over and he misses. I shove
one in my mouth and chew, trying to avoid grinning,
but it's hard. Keller West makes me so happy I can
barely stand it.

I perk up when I hear the front door. Keller stiff-
ens. I wish he wouldn't. My parents won't mind that
he's here, even though mom's opinion has shifted.

I get it, but I don't want to.

I step around Keller, grabbing at his side. He
moans. I know he's ticklish now. I plan to take advantage of it.

I enter the hallway. Keller lingers in the kitchen. I
wish he would come with me.

Dad is juggling five bags, and mom has four. I rush
to help, taking two from her. Dad refuses, stumbling

toward the kitchen. He pauses in the doorway, offering a grin aimed at me.

"Keller! Could I get some help?"

Mom and I exchange a look, but she says nothing. I let her go first and follow her into the kitchen. She places the bags on the table. Dad chose the counter. There's plenty of space in here for everyone, and anything she wants to buy.

I rifle through the bag.

"Your mother bought the entire candy aisle."

"Half," she chirps.

"All." Dad cocks his brow.

"I expect everyone to be here for the Halloween party, plus we'll have trick or treaters."

Keller gives her a strange look.

"What?" she asks.

He raises a hand. "Kids don't come here for candy."

She stares at the bags stuffed to the brim with all sorts of sweet treats, "I'll have to do some sort of positive marketing campaign."

She turns and places a hand on her hip, pointed at me and then to Keller. "Which should start at the school."

I narrow my eyes. "Mom—seriously?"

"Yes, seriously, East! I know Keller is very popular there, he could—I don't know, convince them they should come."

232

I part my lips, ready to defend him when he steps in, "I'd love to help."

She touches the side of his arm. I look at Dad, but he won't talk. Mom has always steamrolled us for her creative ideas, and she's a master at making us feel guilty if we fight it.

"Wonderful!" She claps her hands together.

"So, what can I do to help now?" he asks while surveying the bags.

"Oh, we'll handle the candy—I know how boys can be," she pauses, glancing over at me, "with candy."

"Mom," I whine.

"Here." She walks over to a drawer and produces a stack of cards. She holds them out to Keller, and he takes them.

"I have a job for you."

He turns them in his hand. "These are cool. Look." He holds one up to me. The card is coffin-shaped with a skull at the top, and has a place for the date, time, place, details and RSVP. There are quite a few, with matching red envelopes.

"You boys can fill them out for me and then get everyone to come to the party."

He nods. "I'd be happy to help."

She looks at me and I smirk. "Cool."

She hands me two black pens.

I wag them in my hand. "Come on, we can do them in the living room."

I lower to my knees next to the coffee table and Keller mirrors me on the opposite side. I wish he'd sit next to me, but I get it. He may be comfortable here, but he's not ready to show any affection toward me. Hopefully, that changes. But it'll be up to him. I won't pressure him. That would be wrong.

We both look up when mom steps into the doorway. "For the detail line I'd like for you to put *'Bring your soul.'*"

"Mom."

"East," she places a hand on her hip, "it's Halloween."

I bite my lip and look at Keller.

He perks up. "I think it's cool, Mrs. East."

I narrow my eyes but she's beaming. "Thank you, Keller."

She exits with a skip, I sigh. "Don't encourage her creepiness."

He adjusts his weight from one foot to the other, "She's just having fun."

I purse my lips. "I guess."

"I mean, this is the first party at The Mill House, so it might take some convincing."

"No, they'll come out of morbid curiosity and then ask me to show them where the bodies are stored."

He snickers, placing the pen on the first card. He fills them out and I tilt my head, placing my chin in the palm of my hand. He catches me staring at him.

234

"What?"

"Nothing—just you."

"Me, huh?" He's visibly embarrassed, but I love it. I want him to know how much I care for him.

I eye his wrist. He's never stopped wearing the black rubber bracelet I gave to him. He notices and lifts his hand.

"I never take it off."

"Me either." I lift mine and he grins.

I pick up the pen and begin filling out the card. I lift one and eye it from the side. "This is actually pretty cool, but don't tell her I said that."

"I'd never share your secrets."

I swallow hard. I know he wouldn't. I can trust Keller more than he could trust me. I don't think I'll ever forgive myself for what I did with Shy, but he's forgiven me, and that has to mean something.

I study his profile. He's as beautiful as Shylo Martin is—probably more, at least to me. I can't believe he's with me. I've never thought of myself as cute, just interesting. My quirks seem to appeal to some, but it only matters if I appeal to him.

"So, you said you were here, in this house, with me, in your dreams."

He stops writing and wiggles the pen back and forth in his fingers. He finally looks up at me.

"Yeah," he admits.

"Could you tell me about it?"

He adjusts like he's somewhat uncomfortable.

"Or not." I look back at the card I'm working on.

"It was in the 1800s. I could tell because of the way we were dressed. I came to this house with every intention of buying it. I met a man here, in a top hat. He was going to give me a tour of the house. But I already knew that I wanted it because my dad had me convinced that I needed a place like this for status to get a wife."

I cover my mouth, muffling a laugh. Keller tilts his head. "Do you want to know?"

I lower my hand. "I'm sorry—I am! Go on. I promise I won't laugh again."

He scowls at me. "Anyway, my family owned the train that came through town. I could hear the whistle blowing when I was standing at the black gate." He pauses, like he's recalling a real memory, "Anyway, I was standing at the base of the steps and you rushed out and tossed a cold bucket of water in my face."

I shake my head, fighting back laughter.

His eyebrow cocks.

"It was funny, Keller."

"So, you freaked out, of course, and then offered me a towel and some dry clothes. I came inside the house." He stops like the stories over.

"Is that it?"

He writes on the card. His cheeks are getting red. I lean in. "Keller—what happened next?"

He takes a measured breath and glances at the doorway.

"They can't hear us—this house has walls that are three feet thick."

He relaxes. "You had a fire going. The house was really warm. The man who was going to give me a tour was irritated, but stayed in the foyer. He sat down in the chair next to the fire. But you told me to come upstairs."

My eyes spark, "Did I?"

"Yeah—and I—I followed you to your room. It was the same one you have now and the same bed. You offered me a towel. I dried off and changed my clothes. The end."

I let my hand fall on the table. "Bullshit."

"East." He sighs through some laughter.

"I had you," I wave my hand at him, "in my room and that's all that happened?"

He rubs the side of his neck, "You unbuttoned my shirt and then showed me something—a tattoo on your skin—"

"What was it?"

"The pentagram with roses."

I straighten up. "The symbol in the mausoleum?"

"Same one."

"Well, that's weird."

"Sort of, but I already knew about the one in your living room, so I probably just had it stored away in my memory."

"Mmm, I guess, but what happened next?"

He leans in closer to me, so I push forward. There are only a few inches between us now.

"I stayed in your bed for days."

"Oh, really?"

He licks his bottom lip. The moisture remains. I'm so tempted to taste him again. He drives me insane.

"Yes, I did, but eventually I had to leave, knowing I couldn't stay here with you."

I sit back. It's not the ending I wanted, but the one that makes the most sense.

"That sucks," I admit, staring at the stack of invitations.

"It was a dream," he clarifies, "that's it."

I feel his hand on top of mine.

"Yeah," I whisper.

CHAPTER
THIRTY-SIX

KELLER WEST

I pull into our driveway and see Brian's mom stand-ing on our porch with my mom. I get out as they both stare at me. Seeing her makes me uncomfortable, but I really don't know anything about Brian.

I pause as his mom rushes in and gives me an un-expected hug. She's never been this affectionate. Ever. But I guess things have changed now.

She steps back as my mom gives me a strange look.

"Would you mind speaking with Mrs. James?" she asks.

If it was anyone else but my mom, I'd probably say *no* and run, but I can't. They've ambushed me.

Mom opens the door, and the light pours out. It's nearly twilight, my favorite time of the day.

I step in and the smell of roast and potatoes hits me. My stomach growls. I forget to eat when I'm with

East. My appetite is completely suppressed. I've read about it and it seems like loving someone can do that. It makes me grin thinking about it, but I have to hide it as Mrs. East takes a seat on our brown couch. Mom sits next to her, so I sit down in the chair. I look down and see one of my game cartridges in the shag carpet, so I pick it and keep it in my hand. At least it'll give me something to fidget with as we talk.

"So, I know that you and Brian had a fight at school."

"It was on the football field. He was upset about—," I look at my mom, "him and Shy broke up."

"I know, and I'm glad; that girl is nothing but trouble." Mrs. James makes her opinion known.

My jaw tenses, I hate how judgmental she is about Shy. It makes me wonder if she doesn't like the color of her skin, but I won't throw that in her face right now—not with Brian missing.

"He was just upset about it," I add.

"Because she started dating you," she adds.

I clear my throat. "Not really, I mean, we talked about it, but we're not. She's my best friend."

Her brow cocks. "I thought Brian was your best friend."

"Sure, yeah. We just don't talk as much as we used to, and Shy—we still talk."

"And the strange boy on the hill—along with those weird children, Evie and Vincent Rice."

I narrow my eyes, swift to defend them. "East is cool and so are they."

She clears her throat, clasping her hands on her lap. I stare at her neatly pressed pink dress suit and pearls. Her shirt is buttoned high, with frills cupping her chin. She's wrapped herself in fabric like an old piece of hard candy at Christmas time. The ones you avoid in your grandparents' crystal bowl.

"You must know something," she insists.

I shake my head. "The last time Brian and I talked, he was busy insulting my friends."

"You have a bright future, Keller," she looks at my mom, who is also irritated, but trying to remain calm, "perhaps he was only trying to protect your reputation."

The muscles in my jaw tighten. I'd love to tell her what a piss-poor job she's done raising Brian. How he snuck around wanting to make out with me and only dated Shy for status. Not to mention the way he spat out that disgusting slur against East on the football field. All of that is a reflection of her.

But I remain silent. I don't want her to go to Detective Brant and tell him she thinks I did something when I didn't.

"Listen, I'm sorry Brian left, but I know he loves you and he'll be back. He just got upset, is all."

She adjusts on the edge of the couch, tucking her low beige heel behind her ankle. It's been a long time since I've seen her. All I know is what Brian tells me and the fact that she leads a women's church group.

I'm sure she thinks I'm the devil.

She pulls out a tissue and dabs the corner of her tearless eye. She isn't even crying. It makes me wonder if she really cares about Brian, or just misses controlling everything he does in this life. "I'm sure you're right. But he's been led astray. He isn't a bad boy. He's kind and giving. Pure."

I have to hold back the laughter as I think about him grabbing my hand and trying to shove it down the front of his pants.

I hold my breath.

She stands up and I do the same. Mom joins us, cupping her elbow. She straightens her shoulders.

"I know you'll tell me if he calls."

"Of course." I say.

"And I'll help distribute the flyers you brought." Mom adds.

I notice a stack of black and white flyers on the coffee table with his face on them, along with his information. I placed my half of the invitations for the Halloween party right next to them without noticing.

She eyes the coffin-shaped invitation and snatches one up before I can stop her.

"Bring your soul?" she asks, like we've insulted her senses.

I grin, rubbing the side of my neck. "It's a joke. That's an invitation to a Halloween party."

"A party?"

I pause, shoving my hands in my pockets. "Yeah, at The Mill House."

"So, I guess they think this is appropriate while my boy is missing?"

I clear my throat to the side of my hand. "Mrs. James. Brian is okay. I know he is. He probably went to see Lucy in Illinois."

She yelps with laughter. "Lucy! She's a terrible girl."

I fold my arms over my chest. "I mean, it's the closest family he has—so I'm assuming he went to see her. She has her own place in Chicago."

"My Brian doesn't need to be wandering around some evil city."

"I don't know if he did, but I'd call her and ask. She may tell you if he reached out to her."

"Mmm." She side-eyes me while heading toward the front door. Mom shakes her head at me. I have an apologetic look on my face.

I hear the door open and close and mom returns, placing her hand on her hip.

"Keller Kennedy West."

"What?"

"You know what."

I reach in and grab a flyer, looking at Brian's face. It's not even a current photo. He still has braces. I flip it in my hand. "This is an old photo. I don't even think she wants to find him. She just wants the pity."

Mom's shocked, but trying not to laugh.

"She's a mother."

My brow cocks. "I know, but look." I shake the flyer and she takes it from me. She tilts her head and lowers it to her side.

"She's just upset."

I slump down in the chair. "She's awful. She drives him nuts. I know because he told me."

Her eyes spark with irritation, "Maybe that detective should talk to her more and not harass children."

I lean forward. "So, you know he talked to me?"

She nods. "He came here and talked to me, too."

Confusion spreads across my face. "About what?"

She takes a seat on the couch, placing the flyer back on the stack. "He asked about how long you've been friends and then mentioned the fight you had with him."

"Oh, that."

"Yes, that—want to tell me what happened?"

I hesitate. "He's mad about Shy."

"But he never cared before," she says.

I lift a hand. "Exactly!"

"What was said?"

I bite my lip then release it. "I think he only wanted to date her because I did."

"Mmm, did he tell you anything else?"

I pinch the bridge of my nose. "Nah—I mean, he was just rambling because he was mad."

She lets that sit between us. I should tell her what he called East, but I know it'll only open the door to more conversations about my twin aunts. I don't want to go there with her. I felt awkward when we talked in the garage and even worse now that Dad's home.

"So, how's it going with Dad?" I ask, wanting to change the conversation.

She straightens, placing her hands on her lap. It's an unnatural look for her. "Good."

"Good, huh?"

"Yes."

I want to tell her I think letting him back into our lives is a big mistake, but it isn't my place. I need to keep focused on getting done with school and then I can leave and it'll no longer be my problem.

Not that I don't care about my mom, but she's an adult, and it isn't up to me what she does or doesn't do with her life.

CHAPTER THIRTY-SEVEN

AUGUST EAST

I pass by a telephone pole with a flyer stapled to it with Brain's face on it. I step up and then I notice a second flyer with a picture of a black cat. It's Owen.

I narrow my eyes, reaching in to adjust the paper, ready to read it when a car pulls up close to the curb.

It's Keller.

I grin, rushing to lean in on the passenger's side. Keller is wearing his football jersey and a pair of jeans.

"Is it school pride day?" I ask.

He laughs. "We have a game tonight, but I know you don't like sports."

"I'll be there."

"Yeah?"

I grin. "For you."

His eyes shift to the telephone pole. I tap my hand. "Did you see Owen is missing again?"

He nods. "Yeah—I saw it when I was hanging up the flyers for Brian with my mom."

"You hung them up?"

He taps the steering wheel, then grips it tight. I watch his knuckles turn white. "His mom stopped by the house last night and told me I should."

"She didn't ask you?"

He snorts, rubbing his chin. "Mrs. James doesn't ask anyone to do anything. She just tells you, then walks out like she's the Queen of Whynot."

"Well, that was nice of you," I admit, even though I'd rather that he steer clear of anything to do with Brian James. It isn't his fault or problem.

"So, get in. I'll give you a ride to school."

"Are you sure?" I half-whisper.

He leans over and opens the door, forcing me to back up. "Get in the car, East."

"I guess you think you can just tell me what to do."

He runs his thumb across his bottom lip.

"Yep—okay. I'm getting in the car." God, he drives me insane.

He grins as his foot hits the gas. I sink into the cushioned seat, reaching up to hold on to the side strap.

We park and he slips the gear shift into park. He removes the keys and we sit in silence.

"So, I guess I should..." I thumb behind me.

He stares out the window then turns to face me, "What if I told everyone about how I feel about you?"

My heart flutters. "Keller." I scan the parking lot, making sure no one can hear us. It's not like I wish we could, but I also know what people would do. It wouldn't be kind.

"I mean it." He reaches in and tries to take my hand, but I won't let him. He's visibly confused, but it gradually makes way for sadness. He slumps against the seat and fingers at the base of the steering wheel.

"Hey, I wish we could. I do, but I know who you are here in this school, and I also know that your ticket out of here is a football scholarship and you'll get that, but not if—"

"Not if they know about us," he grumbles.

I lean forward. I wish he'd look at me, but he won't. I don't blame him.

"No one wants to tell the world about us more than I do, but I also know how screwed up people are and we are in a smaller town in the Midwest."

He lets that sink in. All of it. He wipes away an angry tear.

"I just—" I reach out, but he adjusts on the seat so I can't touch him. I feel like I messed up, but I'm only trying to protect him.

"I do love you," I whisper.

248

"I love you, too. I just don't know what's going to happen." He looks to me for comfort.

I wish I had the answers, but I don't.

"Listen, I think," I grab his hand and hold it, "we should enjoy the time we have. Every single moment, every day we get to see each other like this. And we have time—it's not like you're graduating this year."

"We have two years."

"Two years is more than some people have."

"That's if you don't move." He groans.

"I plan on protesting with a sign in front of my house until my parents get sick of it and decide to stay."

He laughs. I'm happy to see I could make him feel better.

His eyes lock onto mine. "I want to kiss you so bad right now."

"Same," I admit.

"More than that."

I nod. "Always—yes."

He takes a deep breath and releases it.

"I guess we should go inside but I have my part of the invitations with me."

I hand him the rest, except for two, which I plan on giving to Evie and Vincent myself.

"Why?"

I lean in and wink at him. "Because no one can tell you no."

He shakes his head as I slip out of the car and walk backward, biting my lip. He watches me go and I linger on him as long as I can. I finally turn on my heel and my eyes become glossed over. I felt like bawling my eyes out in the car, but I held it in because I can't promise him I'll still be here after Halloween, and it's killing me.

I splash cold water on my face and hear the door open up behind me. I don't look and then notice the shoes on the floor next to me. I look in the mirror and see Paul washing his hands.

"Are you okay?" he asks.

I wipe my hands on the front of my jeans.

"We do have paper towels."

"Oh, yeah," I say.

I don't know why I feel so awkward around him now, but I do. Everything has changed and I don't like it at all.

"Did you see the flyers for Brian?" I ask, like no one has noticed in town. They're on every telephone pole.

"I did, and I also saw one for Owen—Maggie's cat. That's a shame. She loves him a lot."

His comment about Owen seems strange when he's a cat and Brian is a student. One of his students.

"Did that detective talk to you?"

He shuts the water off and shakes his hands off over the sink, then ignores the paper towels. I feel like I've caught him off guard.

"Detective Brant? Yes, he talked to all the teachers."

"I don't know if he believes Brian ran away." I turn and lean on the sink, wanting to see his expression, but it doesn't change.

"It isn't his job to take anyone at their word."

I fold my arms over my chest. "Yeah, that's true, but what do you think happened?"

He grins, finally grabbing a paper towel, wiping his hands. "I think he ran away from his overbearing mother."

I take a short breath. "That's what Keller thinks."

He turns to face me. "How is Keller?"

I stand up, not expecting him to ask me.

"Good, I guess."

"I saw he drove you to school this morning."

I narrow my eyes, "Yeah, I was looking at a flyer for Brian and he stopped and asked if I wanted a ride."

"Hitchhiking is a dangerous thing."

He winks at me and then tosses the paper towel in the trash can. I watch him leave and turn back to stare at my reflection in the mirror.

Something about Mr. Rider bothers me now. The way he was always at my house, hovering, to how he conveniently showed up when the nuclear alarms went off, and running into him covered in dirt with that scratch on his arm.

It makes me wonder if I should've told the detective when he was pressuring me? But how would it look now?

I've read too many books.

CHAPTER THIRTY-EIGHT

KELLER WEST

I see Detective Brant speaking with our principal in the hallway as I'm headed to lunch. I look up and see my face on a banner strung above the lockers. I'm in my football uniform, standing next to Brian and the rest of the team. We have a game tonight and he won't be here for it. I flinch when two girls brush past me, giggling.

"Hi, Keller," they speak in unison.

I half-grin. The girls always get like this on game day. I think it's the football jersey.

I step into the cafeteria and grab a tray. I get some food without thinking about it, but the flat square pizza smells good. They also tossed a brownie on my tray, and corn.

I'm not sure why we get corn with pizza, but whatever. I'll eat it. I'm starving.

I see Ty and a few other guys from the team sitting together at one table. He spots me and waves me over. I catch Evie looking at me from across the room as I decide to keep it civil and take a seat across from Ty Miller. I'm not happy about it, but I also don't want him to target Evie or Vincent.

I see Vincent looking at me, too, but he looks away like he's disappointed. I don't blame him. I'd rather be sitting with them. East walks past us and Ty cups his hand and mumbles the word *gay*. The table erupts with laughter and high fives. I don't take part. It makes my stomach churn.

"Dude, we gonna slam tonight or what?" Ty barks at me.

I reluctantly agree, "Totally."

"That's my man!" he adds in a wolf howl toward the ceiling. The other guys join in. I take a bite of piz-za and skip out on the testosterone-fueled display. I don't need to.

I'm shocked. I used to sit here every day with these guys and ignore how stupid and obnoxious they are. They always show off and make fun of other people.

"So, did you kill Brian or what?" he asks before rolling his slice of pizza and taking a huge bite off the end.

I choke, but wash it away with a drink of my choc-olate milk.

"Dude," I hiss.

He leans in and slaps the side of my arm. "I'm just joking! We all know his head's all screwed up over some tail."

I grit my teeth. I want to grab Ty and drag him across the table, knocking him to the ground and slamming my forehead into his nose until it's bent in two. The fantasy makes my heart skip a beat, but then I blink out of it.

The worst thing about this is what Brian started on the football field about East, and I need to change that somehow.

Not for me, for him.

"East likes girls. He was with Shy and that's what Brian was mad about."

Ty looks awestruck. "What?"

"Yeah," I say.

"Dude!" He places his side fist to his lips and lets out a hearty laugh. It isn't until then that I notice Shy is standing next to the table with her tray in hand. She looks like I've stabbed her through the heart with the sharpest knife, and she's right. I just sacrificed her for East.

I reach out and she walks away. "Shy."

Ty shakes his head, "Man, she is a beast."

I take a deep breath and suddenly my appetite is totally gone.

I look up, and Shy has taken refuge at the table with Evie, Vincent, and East.

I'm an asshole.

Evie is glaring at me as Shy speaks to her. I'm sure she told her what I said. Vincent glances up at me and then tosses his slice of pizza on the tray and walks away.

I'm left stuck here with Ty Miller making more jokes about other people in school and wishing I could sink into the earth as far as I could go.

I spot Shy in the library, looking through a book and jotting something down. I think about turning around and running, but I know I can't. She deserves better than that.

I approach her table, clearing my throat.

She eyes me, but refuses to speak.

I sit down, then pull my chair forward and it produces a noise like fingernails on a chalkboard.

"Shh!" the librarian calls out from behind her desk.

I lift my hand, acknowledging her.

"Hey," I whisper.

Shy purses her lips and continues to write in her open notebook.

"What are you reading?"

She leans in. "How to murder someone and get away with it."

256

"Don't tell that detective."

Her expression changes. "What do you want?" she whispers.

"I wanted to tell you I'm sorry."

She toys with a lock of hair, "No need."

"No, I need to apologize. What I did was wrong."

"I don't need apologies from people who are not my friends."

"Shy." I tilt my head and try to take her hand. She jerks it away and slams her notebook closed. She gathers everything up and leaves me sitting there feeling like the biggest jerk in the world.

I rise, and Vincent sits down in front of me. I let out a sigh, "Listen, I know how awful I am."

"I wanted to thank you," he whispers.

I narrow my eyes. "For what?"

"She hates you now."

I shake my head. "I don't know how that's a good thing."

He lifts a hand. "Because there is no way in Hell you'll ever date her again."

I lean forward. "I don't want to date her."

"There's no way now."

I run my fingers through my hair. His eyes follow. "What?"

"You! You're perfect with that hair and face stuff. How the hell is anyone else supposed to date anyone here?"

257

"Face stuff." I snort.

"Shh!" The librarian has had it with me.

Vincent leans in closer and whispers to me. "Girl, in this school, they compare all of us to you."

"They don't."

His brow cocks. "They do, you idiot."

I let out a sigh.

"But I know why you did it."

I let that sit between us, so Vincent continues, "For East."

"I don't know what you mean," I lie.

"Dude—okay, whatever."

We both look up as the librarian looms over us with folded arms. "Out."

"Yep," we both speak in unison.

Vincent places his hand on my shoulder once we've entered the hallway and the door is closed behind us. "I don't care who you like or what you do, I just want you to know that and I mean it, Keller."

I look past him to make sure nobody can hear us.

"I did it for him. Brian called him a—" I can't even say it. "Anyway, they'd make his life a living hell."

Vincent's eyes dilate, "And you saved him from that. I mean, just tell Shy why you did it and she'll understand. She's popular. She'll survive. These idiots will forget all about it by the end of the day and start talking shit about someone else."

I know he's right, but I hate it. This has to do with popularity and nothing more. Kids like me can survive this kind of crap, but other kids, like East, Vincent and Evie, can't. Their lives would be over here at school and I hate that. It shouldn't be like this.

"Okay." I accept his advice.

"Or, I can," he offers.

"Dude, I got it."

"Okay, but if you change your mind," he calls out as I'm walking away from him.

I lift a hand. "I won't."

"Cool, cool." He places a hand on his hip and offers an awkward wave goodbye.

I step out into the busy hallway and place my fingers to my lips, producing a loud whistling sound. Everyone stops what they're doing and looks at me.

I reach into my bag and pull out the invitations.

"Halloween party!" I yell, and everyone rushes me, taking them as fast as I can hand them out. I have one left, and Shy steps up and takes it from my hand.

I sigh. "Shy."

"Shut up, I get it. Give me the rest of the day to stop wanting to punch you in the dick."

I take one step back. "Sounds good."

She walks away and I relax.

CHAPTER
THIRTY-NINE

AUGUST EAST

I hand Vincent an invitation and he grins, tapping it against his palm.

"Yes!" he exclaims.

I turn to Evie and she eyes the card in my hand.

"Halloween party?"

"Of course."

"I know a lot of people got them today, so I started getting nervous."

I lean against the locker. "I wanted to personally invite both of you."

Vincent sniffs the envelope before tearing into it.

"What are you doing—wait, you know what? I don't want to know."

"So, is this it, then? The big farewell party?" Evie asks.

I swallow hard, looking down at my black industrial boots. "I really have no idea."

"Does he know?" Vincent asks.

"He knows it's a possibility."

Evie opens her locker and tucks her books away. She holds onto the card. I'm glad she wants to come. I want both of them there. I've never even talked to half of these people. I scan the hallway. It's like I'm invisible and that's fine. But, suddenly two girls walk by. "Thanks for the invite, East!" They seem thrilled.

I wave, it's awkward. They giggle and move along. I don't know why I'm so bad in social situations. One on one, or small groups of people? No problem. School full of kids? I'm a mess.

"What time are we meeting for the game tonight?" Evie asks.

My nose wrinkles; I forgot there was one. I guess I shouldn't since every football player is wearing their jersey today, including Keller.

I look up at the banner. I see him standing next to Brian. I wonder when he'll come back to Whynot or if he's decided he never wants to be here again? I guess I don't blame him. His girlfriend broke up with him to be with his best friend. Plus, his mom sounds horrible. I guess I shouldn't judge, but I trust Keller.

"I don't know when it starts."

Vincent laughs. "Man, you really aren't a Midwesterner, are you?"

"No."

Evie steps in. "Everything starts at six, if you want to tailgate. Some people go earlier than that, but I'm fine with six, or even seven."

"I think seven would be fine. I have to tell my mom."

She cocks her head. "You always say that. Do you not talk to your dad?"

I push off the locker and shove my hands in my pockets, "It's just he's usually not home like this so it's a habit. I always ask my mom about everything."

"Are they doing okay?" Vincent asks, but I assume it isn't an innocent inquiry.

Evie scowls at him. "I swear to God, Vincent!"

He threads his fingers through his thick mane of hair, "No—I mean it. I'm over your mom, East. You can tell her that the ship has sailed."

I tap him on the shoulder. "I'll let her down easy."

"I appreciate it." He smirks before shoving a piece of Bubble Yum in his mouth. It smells like cotton candy. I used to live on that stuff before it upset my stomach. I'd accidentally swallow it. But they have every flavor. I was addicted to Bananaberry Split.

"Want some?" he asks.

I shake my head. "No, I eat it."

He grins. "I never tried that."

"Don't." Evie presses.

"I'll be fine, Evie."

"Anyway," she huffs, "do you want us to stop by your house or just meet you there?"

I hesitate, thinking Keller might take me to the game, but then I remember who he is and I immediately get sad.

He can't take me.

"We can walk there together if you want."

She grins. "I'll bring the hot chocolate. We can buy something to eat there. They sell hot dogs, cheeseburgers, nachos and pretzels."

My stomach growls. It all sounds good.

"Should I bring something?"

"Blankets, if you have a couple."

I look down the hallway and see Keller staring at the banner. "I'm sure we have some."

"Sweet, well, I'm going to go help Maggie."

My eyebrow cocks. "With what?"

Evie's expression sours. "She's still looking for Owen and I want to help her."

"Oh, yeah! I saw a flyer."

"Weird how he's missing along with Brian, huh?"

I pinch my bottom lip then turn my hand mid-air, "Everyone thinks Brian ran away to see his cousin."

"In Illinois?" she asks.

"Yeah, I guess. I don't know him well enough to say anything."

She bobs her head, "Mmm, maybe. I mean, it would make sense."

"It does, huh?"

She adjusts her bag on her shoulder. "Yeah, I mean they used to be close when he was little. They lived here, but her mom died and her dad was barely home, so his cousin moved to Illinois with his other aunt. But she was wild and Brian's mom had a lot to do with her leaving town. She called the police on her."

"That really sucks." She studies my expression. "I just know what it's like to have to leave a place you loved."

"I'm really sorry about the fire and losing your friends, East. I don't think I ever told you that, but I am. I should've led with that instead of throwing my magazine in your face or sending you that cryptic note in class."

I lean in. "But I'm really glad you did because we became friends."

"Yeah, we are friends, huh?"

"Absolutely."

"I hope you don't have to move, August East."

I take a short breath. "Same."

"But you know what?" Her eyes brighten. "We have the game tonight and the Horror Festival tomorrow! Then a Halloween party that will be amazing, so we have tons to look forward to."

264

"No, you're right," I agree, "we have tons."

I catch myself looking at Keller again. He seems stuck in thought, but then he glances at me and I think I know what he's doing. He wants to talk. My heart skips a beat.

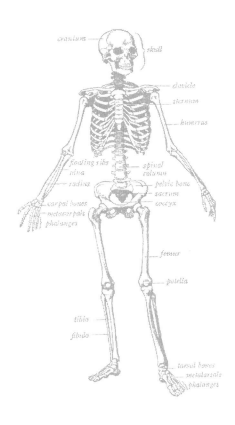

CHAPTER
FORTY

KELLER WEST

I stare at the banner once again. I had looked at it earlier when I passed out the invitations to everyone. But this time I'm hoping he'll see me.

I glance over and East is looking at me. I'd walk over, but he's talking to Evie and it feels like I'd be interrupting their conversation. Finally, she walks away, leaving him alone. I rub the side of my neck. He's coming over. I don't know why I always get nervous around him, but I do. It's like I'm always wanting to impress him, which is weird for me. I don't worry about impressing anyone.

"Hey." He looks up at the banner with the picture of our football team.

"Hey. I handed out all the invitations."

"Thanks, my mom will be happy."

"Are you?" I ask.

He leans in closer to my ear. "Only when I'm with you."

I can smell his clean scent. It's something that lingers with me every time he goes away. I guess it's a good thing. I close my eyes before he moves away. Everything always seems to slow down when he talks to me this way. I wonder if this is how girls felt with me? I guess it doesn't matter.

"Anything new about Brian?" he asks. I get caught up staring at his profile. He's so—beautiful. I don't think he knows it.

I clear my throat. "No, not from what I hear, but a lot of people agree he's probably hiding out with his cousin. She's kinda wild."

"And you know this how?"

My lips part while I think about how she was when she still lived here. "We all hung out together. She's the only one who ever jumped off the covered bridge into the water below. I thought Brian's mom was going to shit a brick."

I snicker. "That would be painful and something to maybe not want to see?"

Keller laughs.

"Yeah—bad visual, especially with Brian's mom."

East turns to face me. I love his haircut. I don't know if a lot of people could pull it off, but it's perfect on him. He has on a Cure t-shirt for The Head Tour, jeans and black industrial boots. I love to go see them in concert, but that takes money and I gave everything I made over the summer to Mom for groceries.

"Do you like them?" he asks while I gawk at his t-shirt.

"Oh, yeah. I do. Not many people listen to them here."

He looks down and tugs on the shirt. "We should go see them if we can."

"I'd love that!" I seem too enthusiastic, so I pull back.

"I'll talk to my mom about it. She knows their road manager; she went to school with him. Funny how she ended up being a mortician, and he ended up traveling around with The Cure."

"They can be a little catatonic sometimes."

He laughs. "Yeah, I guess so—but I will ask."

"That would be cool."

We end up standing there in silence, looking up at the banner again. I feel his fingers brush against mine and I don't flinch. I want to grab his hand and hold it. But I'm stuck like a hamster in a wheel in this town, this school. All of it.

"Do you want a lift home?"

East hesitates. "Actually, I'd love to go to Maggie's."

"Mischief?"

I nod. "Evie went there to help her look for Owen."

"Oh, that's right. Man, that sucks about her cat."

"It does, but if you want to drop me off over her house, that would be cool."

"Yeah, come on. I'll take you there, but then I have to go. Big game tonight."

"I know. I'll be there."

I light up. "You will?"

"Of course—Evie insisted. She's bringing hot chocolate."

"Sometimes I wish I could just sit in the stands." I let that sit for a moment. I'd never admitted it to anyone before.

"They're probably cold and hard—the stands, I mean."

"Yeah."

We head down the hallway—me wishing I could take East out a date tonight, and him probably wishing I could ask him.

We pull up in front of Maggie's house and I lean down to see her lights are all on in the house.

"That's a killer electric bill."

East looks out the window. "Yeah—does she always have them all on like that?"

I tap the wheel. "Maybe it's because she's freaked out about losing Owen."

"Maybe," East adds.

I study his profile once again. "I'd be upset if I lost someone I loved."

East looks to me. His eyes search mine. But they both look green.

"Your eyes changed color."

"Did they?" He turns my rearview mirror and looks for himself. "They do that sometimes. Maybe they changed with the season?"

"Like a tree," I confirm.

"Yeah." He turns the mirror away like I've upset him somehow.

"What's wrong?"

"Other than the tree—I love that house, and this town."

I wait. I'm not sure what's wrong, but I want him to tell me.

"What's going on?" I ask.

He sighs. "I just—I don't want to move!"

We sit there with the truth between us. We both know it's a possibility—probably more than that—but talking about it isn't something I really wanted to do. It makes it all too real.

"East—" I reach across and hold his hand against the seat, nice and low. No one would know. "Whatever happens, we'll face it together."

He looks down at our hands. "But you know if I move then we'll—it'll—everything will change."

270

"Yeah, it would. But we could talk on the phone."

He lets out a defeated sigh. "That's not the same."

"I don't know. I could say some pretty dirty things on the phone if I had to."

He grins, but he isn't happy. Neither am I. I feel like we have this clock ticking over our heads and time is running out.

"East," I whisper.

He wipes a tear. "Yeah?"

"Can we just enjoy what time we do have together?"

He tries to surrender, "I want to."

I lean over. "I love you, but you're doing a terrible job at it."

"Shut up." He laughs through the words.

I shake his hand. "It's not that I don't care—I do. But I don't want to miss out on this," I shake his hand again, "while I'm thinking about you not being here, because you are here now."

He sighs. "No—you're right. I'm ruining this."

I let go of his hand, but he grabs it and places it on his leg, dragging it along—higher and higher. I gasp, so does he.

I hear a car coming and jerk my hand away. It's almost embarrassing how fast I denied him. He grabs the door handle and I speak up, "I'm sorry."

"No—I get it." He exits the car. "I'll still be there

tonight—good luck, break a leg." He rubs the side of his head. "No, don't do that—just win and be careful."

I nod. "Always."

He closes the door and I sit there in silence, watching him climb the steps and then go inside the house. I reach over and turn on the radio and Simple Minds' "Don't You Forget About Me" is playing. I grimace and shut it back off.

"Shit," I whisper.

AUGUST EAST

I watch him drive away, careful to hide that I'm spy-ing on him from behind the curtain. I already feel desperate enough. I keep ruining every moment we have together by bringing up this thing hanging over our heads.

"It's a terrible thing."

I turn to see Maggie standing there with a drink in her hand. It reminds me of my mom.

"What is?" I ask.

"Love."

I swallow the sour taste in my mouth. In some ways, love is a terrible thing. But, in other ways, the best of ways, it isn't.

"Is Evie here?" I ask, wanting to avoid the topic with her altogether.

"Yes, sweet Evie Rice. She's a spunky girl, and yes,

she was here and now she's out there, with her brother, looking for Owen."

She takes a drink and wipes the corner of her eye.

"I'm really sorry about Owen."

She looks me dead in the eye. "I appreciate that, but he isn't dead. I know it."

"How can you be so sure?" I ask before thinking about how it might upset her, but instead of getting emotional, she waves me along, signaling for me to follow her.

I end up in the room where I first saw her body. I thought she was dead. We all did. My eyes wander around. It looks put back together now. The table is covered with a velvet purple cloth and an oversized deck of cards sits on top. The chairs are upright and the fireplace is lit. I notice the pictures on the mantel. They're all of Maggie and Owen in different places. She's holding him, giving him a hug in every photo. It's easy to see how much she loves him.

"He was my husband in human form—in another life, of course."

I turn to look at her. "Owen—your cat?"

"Yes."

I rub the side of my neck. I want to believe her, but it's hard.

"Again, I'm sorry he's gone."

"He isn't gone—come, look."

She sits down at the table and waves her hand toward the empty chair. I reluctantly take it. I wasn't planning on this. I just wanted to help search for the cat.

She waves her open hand over the deck, splits it and then lays down the cards.

I lean in. I don't know what any of it means.

"Look, there's the compass—it means he will be guided home."

"What's that?" I ask, while pointing to the other card. She bites her lip.

"That is The Hermit, it means you pull away from this world for a little while."

She doesn't seem happy to see it.

"I'm sure it doesn't mean anything bad."

Her gaze lifts. "Let me read you—see what the cards say."

I narrow my eyes. "I don't need that."

She tilts her head, picking up the cards and shuffling them. She cuts the deck and places them back together again.

"Are you nervous?"

"I—maybe a little."

"Touch the deck."

I shake my head.

"Touch it!" she shouts, so I do. Maggie seems agitated and I'm regretting coming here to help look for her cat.

She lays down the cards and her expression changes. She looks at them, then up at me.

"What is it?" I whisper.

"You are on a mission—or will be, but you have to understand that with this comes loss."

I lean in. "That sounds ominous."

"Well, this is the present, let's check the future."

She places a card, then a second and a third. I stand up and stare at them with a confused look on my face.

"What does this mean?"

She shakes her head. "I—wait." She lays down another card and another one, and yet another. But they're all the same.

Blank.

"I have to go—" I back away. Maggie keeps drawing cards even though I told her stop.

"Wait, East!" she calls out to me, but I rush out the door and down the steps. All I want to do is forget it ever happened.

I reach my house and push on the gate. The blank tarot cards bothered me, but what bothers me most is I feel like it was a trick she played on me. Maybe that's her game? Maybe she does things like this to get business?

I run in the door and hit the stairs. I still plan on going to the game, but I want to see if Charles Porter has any books on tarot in the library.

276

I approach the ornate doors and step inside. I haven't spent nearly as much time in this room as I planned to.

I walk along the row of books and then find what I'm looking for. I pull it off the shelf and blow on the top. Some dust hits my nose and I cough.

I sit down and open the book, fingering through the pages until I find what I'm looking for.

"A blank tarot card is *The All Believers Card* which essentially means you are not meant to know yet."

I look up. "Well, that's nice," I grumble.

I follow the text and then narrow my eyes. "There's only one blank card in the deck—okay, nice, Maggie."

I close the book feeling like I may be right. Maggie seems nice enough, but I think she may be messing with me.

I don't know why she'd choose—wait, I do know. My mom's a mortician and I live in the spooky house on the hill. Great.

I hear the phone ringing in my room and I drop the book in the chair and run down the hallway, jump across my bed and slide off the side while grabbing the receiver. I have to pull myself up on the side of the bed when I answer, "Hello!" I'm catching my breath.

"East?"

"Hey—Evie."

"I just wanted you to know that I didn't find Owen yet—could you look in your garden?" she asks, wringing her hands.

I grimace. "I—sure." I like Evie enough to do it for her, even though being in the room with that tree makes me uncomfortable.

"Okay." She pauses.

"Now?"

"Yes, now."

"Okay fine. I have to set the phone down, but I'll let you know on the phone downstairs."

"How many phones do you have?"

I count on my hand. "I think it's six."

"Wow—fancy."

I grin. "They came with the house. They seem to be everywhere—actually, there's one more in the basement."

"Can you check? I want to update Maggie before we leave for the game."

I nod, but then remember she can't see me. "Yes—give me a few minutes."

I set the phone down on the side table and run down the stairs. I fly past my dad, having to do a spin to avoid running into him, and then skid across the cobblestone in the garden. A lifted edge on one stone catches my foot and I hit the ground right in front of the Venus Flytrap.

278

I push myself up. "You won't be eating me," I mutter.

I think I see movement and have to step into the poisonous plants, then I see a black tail fly by.

"Owen?"

"Meow!" comes back at me.

I rush to the left—then the right—and finally reach in and almost have him. He jumps out of the roses and heads for the tree. I shake my head, "Owen—I'm not doing this."

He has a flower in his mouth. My heart drops. Everything in here, except for the roses, will kill you and he's carrying it like it's a late lunch.

I lift my hands, cautiously approaching him.

Evie grimaces while cradling Owen and rocking him back and forth. He's purring.

I dab the wet cloth against the scratch on my neck. It's still bleeding. I have a few more on my arms and one on my cheek.

"He tried to kill me."

She kisses Owen's head. "He's a cat—domesticated, not a panther."

"You weren't there."

She grins. "Maggie will be so happy."

I sigh. I want to tell Evie what happened with the tarot cards, but she likes Maggie, and I guess I do, too.

"I'm going to take Owen back to her and then I'll be back so we can go to the game, okay?"

I dab my cuts while hissing. Owen hisses back at me.

"Dude!"

She continues to rock him and then leaves. I shake my head.

"Domesticated." I huff.

CHAPTER FORTY-TWO

KELLER WEST

I stare at myself in the mirror. I'm fully dressed for the game. I can hear other guys entering the locker room, so I shut the metal door and spin the dial.

I perk up when they enter my side of the locker room. I'm faking it, but I know I have to. You can't be melancholic on the football team. They'd eat you alive.

I feel a few slaps to the back and on my shoulders as I move through them, wishing like hell I could be in the bleachers with East, drinking hot chocolate.

I think it's the first time since I started playing football that I've felt like this. It worries me. Not that I'd trade what East and I have for anything, but I can't be like this and win a game.

I slip through a door and into the hallway. I feel the wall against my back and lean forward, placing my hands on my knees.

"Hey you."

I look up to see Shy coming toward me, but she looks different—like I've never seen her before.

She stops in front of me, messing with the bottom of her short white, red, and black cheerleading skirt.

"What—I mean, your hair?" I ask, fumbling over my words.

Shylo has beautiful, dark brown curls with blonde highlights. I love her hair. I always have.

She reaches up and toys with it. It's now stick straight.

"Do you not like it?"

I narrow my eyes. "I—it's just different. I don't get why you'd do that."

She's immediately hurt by what I've said and walks away, so I'm forced to follow her down the hallway. We end up rounding the corner and I grab her arm, forcing her to stop. "Shy—talk to me."

She folds her arms over her chest, tucking her hands into her sides. "What?"

I look at her hair.

"I don't have to ask you for permission to do anything, Keller West."

I shake my head. "Shy—no, you don't! But for as long as I've known you, you've had these awesome curls in your hair—like badass. I love them."

282

She looks down, then back up at me. I can see she's still upset.

"What is it?"

"Keller—you have no idea what it's like."

"What *what* is like!"

"Being the only Black girl in this school!"

I feel like she's slapped me, not because I don't suddenly understand, but because I do.

"Shy—God, I feel like an idiot. I never knew you felt this way."

She sighs. "It's hard not to when no one looks like me."

I grab her hand and slip inside an empty room. I shut the door behind us. She's fidgeting with her hands. I reach in and stop her from picking at her nails.

"You are absolutely perfect, just the way you are."

She sniffles. "I just—I feel like I have to work harder than anyone else to prove I can be like them. That's why I work so hard—I study hard, I cheer hard—I even dated—" she pauses, "and Ty is such an asshole. You know what he asked me? If the carpet matched the drapes."

"Oh, hell no." I try to pull away from her but she stops me, "No—no! Stop, Keller, Just, stop. I knew he was a jerk."

I narrow my eyes. "Shy. Listen. There isn't a girl in this school who wouldn't kill to be you, exactly as you

283

are, and I'm so sorry you feel this way and that I never knew. I feel like a complete asshole because you never said a word to me. And Ty Miller can suck Satan's taint."

"Keller!"

"He can."

She bites her lip. "Listen, my little brother will be okay because I'm going to pave the way for him here. He'll be a star football player and no one will look at him any differently because of the color of his skin."

"Jesus, Shy. Why didn't you ever tell me?"

She picks at her nails, "I don't know."

I back away and rub the side of my neck. "What can I do to make you feel better?"

"It isn't something you can do, it's just my reality. I'm a Black girl in an all-white school, Keller. I deal with it every single day and maybe that's why I'm so sarcastic and act tough, I don't know. Maybe that's why I date football players and put up with shit, but what I know is my little brother and my family are treated better because I work my ass off to be accept-ed—to be popular."

"Shit."

"Yeah."

"Well, if you like straight hair, then do it. I just want you to be happy."

She laughs through the angry tears. "I don't. I hate it."

I laugh too, and step in to hug her. "I love you."

"I love you, too."

"And do me a favor, okay?"

She presses against me.

"Tell me about this shit, okay? I'm here for you, always." I urge her to understand.

"I know." She mutters.

"Do you, Shy?"

She leans back and looks up at me. "Yes. I do."

"Okay—now let's go kick some ass, okay?" I whisper.

"Fine, but I'm not redoing my hair."

"Fine."

CHAPTER FORTY-THREE

AUGUST EAST

I stare at myself in the mirror. I decided to wear a red, black and white shirt to show some school pride, even though I've never been to a football game in my life.

But I'll go for him. A thousand times over again.

I slip on my black hoody with our school mascot and run my fingers through my hair. I look like everyone else. Great, but again—this isn't about me. I want to support Keller. I also want to see him play. I've watched a few minutes of his practices, but this is him doing what he does, and I have to assume he's great.

I turn to see mom standing in the doorway. She's motionless. I step forward and she blinks.

"Honey, you look great."

"Thanks," I look down at myself, "I feel like I've given into peer pressure."

She grins. "That's not always a bad thing."

I tilt my head. She looks like she wants to talk to me. I contain the nerves. "Evie and Vincent are going to be here soon."

"Oh, I was hoping we could talk."

I swallow hard. "About what?" My voice cracks.

I'd rather run past her, but I can't.

"About us."

She takes my hand and leads me over to the window. We take a seat and she doesn't let me go.

"What is it, Mom?"

She sighs. "I—I'm so embarrassed."

"About what?"

"I've been struggling," she admits. "It's the pills to calm my nerves."

"Mom—" I want to console her, but I'm not sure what I should do. I think about Paul and how he offered her the drugs in the shelter. It makes me angry. I know he only meant to help her, but she never stopped.

"It's all done now. I promised your father I'd quit because he's going to take a little break."

"What do you mean by break?"

She taps my hand. "He's going to Arizona on his own for now."

"Wait—by himself? Why?" I'm actually relieved, but terrified at the same time. I don't know what this means.

"Because we need time, and this will be best."

I shake my head, "Are you getting a divorce?"

She pauses, thinking it through. "I won't lie to you, my love, we discussed it, but for now we're going to try this."

I'm stunned. Part of me wants to jump up and down—celebrate. But the rest of me feels devastated. It's always been the three of us. Always. I can't imagine life without my dad. He's always so cheerful, when mom can be serious and I'm, well, I could curl up in a ball and live out my days with a book in my hand.

"So, we're not moving?"

She looks around my room. "The house is ours. Free and clear. Even the taxes are paid for out of Charles' account. We just have to buy groceries and keep the lights on and your dad is going to send money for that."

I stand up and shake my head. I'd cry if I could, but I can't and it makes me feel even worse. I'll miss my dad so much, but I think I'd miss Keller more and I'll never admit it out loud.

"I—I have to meet with Evie and Vincent for the game." I thumb behind me.

"Okay, East. Go have fun and we can talk later. I just wanted you to know. I also want you to understand that Delilah will come here three times a week so I can talk to her. I need her support, and yours."

"Of course, Mom. I'll do whatever I can to help you, but you got this. You're the strongest person I know."

She rises to give me a hug. I hang on for longer than I should.

"Your father is leaving after the Halloween party, but let's try to be a family for a few more days."

The finality of it hits me in the chest. I don't think my dad will be coming back unless some miracle happens, and I'm shocked they could hide this kind of unhappiness from me. But then again, I spend a lot of time on my own. It's how it is for most kids my age. I have a key to the house. I stay gone most days and we end up seeing each other in passing. Even now, with Dad home, I don't see him much more than I did when he was working.

I feel like I should've known.

I knew Mom was struggling, but I also didn't know what to do. I'll never make that mistake again.

I close the front door behind me and stare down the porch. I don't know how I could be so relieved and unhappy at the same time, but here we are.

"Hey!" Evie calls out as Vincent grabs the front gate and shakes it. I walk toward them, pulling my jacket in close as the chill seems to hug everything tighter now. Fall is really settling in.

I pause, looking at her, then to Vincent.

Evie tilts her head. "What's wrong?"

"My mom just told me that Dad is moving without us."

"Oh, man!" Vincent exclaims, but he doesn't jump at the chance to talk about my mom. "Sorry."

Evie wraps her arm in mine as I step up. I feel sort of numb.

"Are they getting a divorce?" Evie asks.

I peer up at the house. "I don't know, all I know is Mom and I are staying here because the house is paid for and Dad will pay for the electric and food."

"A lot of people get divorced now. It's, like, trendy or something."

I lean forward as we walk in step. "That doesn't make me feel any better, Vincent."

"I hate to say this, but you won't be leaving, and I'm happy about that," Evie admits.

I'm glad she said it but I'm not sure how I should react, "I—no, that's true, but I never thought my parents would... I don't know. I'm happy and sad. It sucks. I feel guilty for being happy that I won't have to move, but I know I'll miss my dad."

"It's not like he'll be dead," Vincent blurts it out.

"Vincent!" Evie scolds him.

"No—it's true, he won't be, but I can't believe I didn't know they were unhappy."

"People are great at hiding things." Vincent's gaze wanders in thought.

I know he's right. Look at Keller. The whole town thinks he's someone he isn't. I guess most people are like this unless they allow you into their world. I feel a grin creeping in and try to control it. I can't celebrate.

"Mom's also going to be talking to Delilah."

"Is she a lesbian?"

Evie smacks his arm, and he steps away. "Evie! I'm just asking!"

"No. She's, well... When Dad was trapped in the nuclear plant, she started taking these pills to calm her nerves, and then she started drinking, but she said that's all over with now, and I believe her, but she'll be meeting with Delilah three times a week to talk."

"Where did she get pills?" Evie asks.

I narrow my eyes, thinking about Paul offering her those. It's hard not to blame him, and a small part of me wonders if he did this on purpose.

"She found them in the shelter. Charles had a stockpile of medication."

"I'm sure she's going to be fine," Evie reassures me, tightening her grip on my arm.

"Yeah, I know she will. We all will, it'll just be weird."

"When is he leaving?" Evie asks.

"After Halloween." I clarify.

Her expression softens, "My advice is to spend as

291

much time as you can with him and tell him how you feel before he moves away."

"Yeah, I will."

"Man, it'll be fine. You got us," Vincent reminds me.

I let that sink in.

I do have them. They're my friends and now I have to face a future here in Whynot—and I get to be with Keller.

My heart skips a beat.

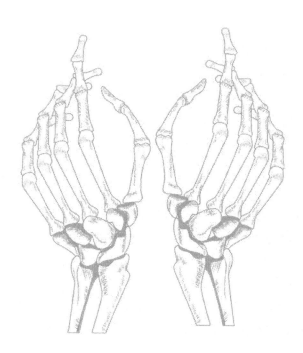

CHAPTER FORTY-FOUR

KELLER WEST

Go—go—go!" I cock my arm back to throw the ball. I see someone wide open and plant my feet. I launch the football with everything I have, straining the muscles in my arm. Time slows down. I can hear helmets slamming together all around me. My team is doing a great job of protecting me. I feel like this may be one of my best games.

Our best games.

It's always a team effort.

My throw goes high. My eyes follow as it spins. Then it lands solidly in my teammates' arms. I draw my fist in, silently celebrating how accurate the throw was. He begins to run. I'm no longer a target, so no one on the opposing team is trying to break through to bury me in the dirt. He keeps running, does a spin to the left—then the right and finally, he crosses the goal line and lifts the ball above his head.

We're officially winning now.

The score changes and the roar of the crowd filters back in. I look to Shy, who's doing a high kick and shaking her pom pom. The band plays and everyone in the stands are on their feet.

I hate to admit I missed this, but I did.

I look through the crowd, searching for his face, but I don't see him. I wonder if East came to see me play. Part of me hopes he did. I'm proud of what I've done tonight. Regardless of how much I hate my dad forcing me to play football, this is where I shine. It's the one thing I do the best—better than anyone else here. I'm in my element. It reminds me that the time will come when I'll have to make a choice. I know I'll be offered scholarships. I'll go away to play at another school and then the thought of asking East to come with me crosses my mind. I place my hand on my hips and look down at the ground. I smile.

Of course, I could ask him.

My team huddles.

I hear a whistle blow from the side and our coach signals that we've reached halftime. It's good. I could use a break. My arm is getting tired and my hand is aching, but the adrenaline is keeping it in check.

We jog off the field and again I look to the bleachers. I finally see his face. He's cheering. I nod, hoping he knows I see him supporting me. If it were up to me, I'd spend half time with him.

The band moves onto the field, and I follow the rest of my teammates into the locker room. I lean against the back wall, catching my breath and taking a few sips of my Gatorade.

I look around the room and still don't see him. Ty Miller hasn't been in the game. I lean in and ask the guy next to me. "Where's Ty?"

He's quick to answer. "Heard he was sick."

"Huh." I mumble.

Ty is one of those guys who will play hard, take his helmet off, throw up on the sideline and then keep going. He's a beast. I guess it must be pretty bad.

"Listen up!" Coach begins his breakdown of the game so far. His words fade as I stretch my shoulder and flex my hand. I look over and see Ty's locker. His name is on the outside, written in black marker on masking tape.

I lift my head. "Hey Coach, where's Ty?" I ask.

He folds his arms. "Good question, West. Let him know that it's his ass when I see him next."

I narrow my eyes. His parents didn't call? Or maybe they did, and it was too late. The game already started.

Coach howls, and the room erupts with a deafening noise. I follow the pack when I feel a hand on my shoulder. I turn to see that Coach wants to talk to me.

"West—keep up that energy!"

"Will do!" I shout.

"Scouts are in the stands tonight," he shares before walking away from me.

I stand still for a moment. The pressure is on. I'm so glad I'm having such a good game. I've heard of guys graduating early and going onto play in college and I wonder if that'll be a possibility for me.

I run back onto the field. We huddle, then break. I dig my heel in the grass. I see a huge guy barreling toward me and I realize Ty Miller could easily take him down.

I end up running down the field. I rarely try to score this way for us, but I have no choice. I hear the crowd cheering as I avoid being taken down. Two more guys fall away and I cross the goal line. My teammates lift me up and I howl at the sky.

I look to the bleachers, but East is no longer there.

I lower my arm, but the guys below me continue to shake me up and down. I know we'll win, but all I can think about is August East.

CHAPTER FORTY-FIVE

AUGUST EAST

I lean in, my jaw tenses. Keller cocks his arm back and then the ball goes flying down the field. I have to stand up with everyone else or I won't be able to see what's going on. The ball hits the target, and the receiver moves down the field, twisting and turning until he scores and I have to cover my ears.

They really love their football here in Whynot.

"Yes!" Vincent is screaming like a crazy man. Evie looks at me and smiles. She lifts her hot chocolate like she's toasting me. I know I should be happy, but that same old paranoia creeps in again. How could I be so lucky to have all of this?

I think about Maine and the fire. I hate that it always lingers in the back of my mind whenever anything good happens.

The crowd cheers again. I look at the field and the

football players are running off. The band takes their place and the cheerleaders begin their routine. I see Shy, but she looks different. Her hair is straight. She's still beautiful, but I love her hair the way it was. No one else looks like her and I think that's amazing. I wonder why she did it, but it isn't for me to judge her. I want people to do whatever makes them happy.

Vincent leans in and yells in my ear, "It's halftime!"

I'm forced to blink from the volume.

"I want a pretzel," Evie admits.

Vincent brightens. "Me too!"

"I can go," I offer.

Evie shakes her head. "No, let me. I want to say hi to Shylo."

I look back at the field and she's getting lifted above a guy's head. The crowd cheers. I can see why people get addicted to this.

I lean into Vincent's ear. "Do they always play this good?" I ask, wondering if what I'm witnessing is normal.

"Dude—yes! Keller is one of the best players I've ever seen."

I bite my lip. He is amazing, but it's more than just football.

He bumps me from the side and points toward the field. "See that guy in the blue and yellow jacket?"

"Yeah!"

"He's a scout."

My nose wrinkles. "For what?"

Vincent laughs. "For football. I bet he's here to watch Keller play."

I clap along with everyone else.

"But he has two more years until he graduates," I shout in Vincent's ear.

"I think they'll take him early."

"Is that a thing?" I ask.

He nods. "Yeah! When you're as good as Keller West."

I let that settle in. Will he leave Whynot early and go play in some college far away? My stomach twists. I want him to be happy—to get everything he wants and deserves—but I also want him to stay here with me until I'm done with high school and I'm a year behind him.

Shit.

The players emerge from the locker room, and I watch Keller return to the field. They huddle and then the game starts again. He gets the ball, steps back— he's looking for someone, but no one is open. So, he decides to run. I hold my breath as he spins out of the way, then again. If he gets hit, I may rush onto the field and that will look bad for him.

Suddenly, he breaks through the last two guys and scores. Everyone on the team lifts him up. He holds the football above his head. He looks so happy. I had no idea football made him feel this way. I naturally assumed he hated it because of his dad, but I don't think that's true. I think he's in his element. He is amazing. Just like Vincent said.

Keller looks up at me. I continue to cheer for him, but who am I but another fan right now?

It makes me feel insignificant in his life because this is so much bigger than me. I can't hold him back from all of this. It would be wrong.

I look down at the scout who's leaning into their coach's ear. They both look down the field. I know they're talking about him.

I just know it.

I should be happy for him, but I'm not.

CHAPTER FORTY-SIX

KELLER WEST

"Hey!" I call out and East stops to look back at me, but he doesn't appear happy. I'm still catching my breath from the game. We won—it wasn't easy, but we did it.

"Hey."

I approach him. Kids are walking by. I hate that I can't grab his waist and pull him against me, kissing him like I always want to do. I don't know if there'll ever be a day I can do that in public or not, but, right now, I want to hold on to the moments we have.

I wave my helmet behind me. "What did ya think?"

"If I understood the game, it might have made a lot more sense to me, but from what I could tell, you kicked their asses." The grin spreads on his face.

"I might've just a little bit." I pinch my fingers together.

"No, you kicked them a lot. You were amazing—really." He offers the compliment, but I can't help but feel like he's not telling me something.

"You okay?" I ask.

He tucks his hands into his pockets and eyes the kids passing us by. I get a couple more pats on the back and I smile. I can't ignore it. People will wonder why the hell I'm not celebrating.

"Oh my God!" Vincent comes running up with his hands in the air. "Man, you are the king!"

Evie stops next to me and bumps me from the side. It's about as affectionate as she gets, but I'll take it. I'm glad they're both talking to me after I skipped sitting with them for lunch. It was a shitty thing to do.

"Thanks." I'm trying to sound humble, because I am.

"The scouts were watching you hard," Vincent adds.

"Yep—I think someone will probably graduate early." Evie shares her opinion so nonchalantly.

East doesn't look happy. He's avoiding the entire conversation, but now I know. Someone told him how I could leave early on a scholarship, but that isn't set in stone and no one has asked me.

"Nah—I'm good graduating here and then I'll go play ball in college."

"Dude, if I had the chance to leave early and get out of Whynot, I would!"

"Then you take it." I look East dead in the eyes. I want him to know that I don't want to leave here any sooner than I have to, and I still plan on asking him if he'll come with me. I just don't know when will be a good time.

"It's a great opportunity," East admits, "I mean, not many kids get to go to college early, and probably even less because they play football."

"I guess, but not me," I state.

"So, are we still on for the Horror Festival tomorrow?" Vincent asks.

"That's a dumb question."

Everyone laughs; Vincent does a little happy dance. "Just making sure! Those tickets are not cheap."

"No, but I'm happy to share them with all of you."

"Is Shy coming?" he asks.

"As far as I know."

Vincent fist pumps the air. I rush my fingers through my hair. It's a mess. It always is after a game.

"Party at my place!" One of my teammates has stepped on top of a car and is belting out some lyrics. He beats his chest and howls at the moon.

"I guess there's a party at his place." I can see East is finally easing up.

Vincent and Evie spin each other around. It seems like everyone is euphoric from the game.

"Wanna go?" I ask East, hoping he will.

303

His eyes narrow. "With you?"

"Yeah, with me. I mean, a ton of people will be there."

"Mmm—a ton of people isn't really my thing."

I lean in. "How about we make an appearance, because I sort of have to, and then we'll sneak out."

His lips tighten. I can see the wheels in his mind turning, "Okay, fine. But just an appearance."

"Like fifteen minutes, tops."

"Deal," he agrees.

I lick my bottom lip, drawing it inside. His eyes lock onto my mouth and he nearly blushes. I know how I make him feel, because he does the same to me.

"I need to change in the locker room. Stay right here, okay?" I yell back as I'm jogging toward the building.

"Maybe."

"You better!" I shout.

We enter the house to a wall of noise. Half of it is music blaring from the living room speakers and the rest is a bunch of my classmates acting a fool. But, I love this. The celebration after a game is the best. It's like a tremendous weight has been lifted.

I've changed into a black shirt and dark jeans with my black boots. I tossed on a peacoat and my hair's still wet from the shower, so it's slicked back—sort of, with a random curl trying to escape.

I'm handed a wine cooler, but I'm not going to drink it. I pass it off to a cheerleader passing me by. She kisses me on the cheek and then we keep going. Finally, I find a quieter place in the house. The library. It smells like mahogany and leather. Maybe even a little cigar smoke. This must be his dad's office. There's an enormous desk sitting in front of the window and a large globe on a stand, and two plants that look like trees. I grab East's hand and jerk him inside the room and shut the door. I press him up against it and kiss him, letting my tongue explore his. He moans, then pushes on me. Forcing me back a couple of steps.

"What are you doing?" he angrily whispers.

"Kissing my boyfriend."

He freezes. "Your what?"

"My boyfriend." I repeat it just so he can't claim he didn't hear me.

"I—wow." He gives the side of his arm a rub.

I lean in, placing my hand against the door near his head. He's pressed against the wood. I could do so many things to him right now, but I won't freak him out. I know having the entire school on the other side of that door makes him nervous.

"Is that okay?" I whisper.

He nods, staring at my lips.

"Good."

"But I—should we talk about this whole early graduation thing?" he asks.

I back away, lifting my hand and letting them drop. "That's not going to happen."

"And you know this how?"

"Because," I grab his hand and spin him into me as he chuckles, "I would have to agree, and I won't."

He pushes off of me and stares me down. "Don't do this because of me, Keller."

"I'm not."

"Are you sure?"

I toy with things on the desk. There are metal balls in strings. I pull one and let it drop. It slaps into the next one and the one on the other end pops up and back. It ticks like a clock.

"Yes, and just so you know, I never wanted to do that even before I met you. I promised my mom I would stay home and graduate here my senior year."

He steps toward me. "But what if—"

I look up. "There isn't a what if."

He lifts a hand. "Just listen, okay? God, you are so stubborn."

"Me?" I snort, giving him a once-over.

"Fine—I can be a little stubborn."

I shake my head and stop the balls from clicking together.

He continues. "What if it's the only way you'll get the scholarship?"

I lift a brow. "Then I won't get that scholarship."

"Really? It's that easy for you?" he asks.

I step around the front of the desk and take his hand, I pull him to me and turn him around so I can wrap my arms around his neck. I lean into his ear.

"Nothing matters to me more than you."

He swallows hard.

East tries to pull away, but I won't let him.

"See? That's what I mean. Please don't make this about me."

I spin him so he has to face me, I lock my legs on the sides of his and he fake struggles.

"It really isn't."

He won't look at me, so I grab his chin and make him. "East—it's not."

I get caught up in his eyes. They're back to normal again. One green, one hazel. It mesmerizes me.

Suddenly the door opens with laughter and I knock East to ground, pushing him away from me. He lands with a surprised look on his face. I did it before thinking. But they would've seen us. I should've locked the door. I'm such an idiot.

"Dude! Are you that drunk?" One cheerleader asks East as he pushes himself back onto his feet.

"Yeah, those wine coolers are tricky."

She toasts him and slides back out, leaving the door ajar.

East wipes off his jeans from the dust on the floor, then looks at me. I could cry, I'm so upset about what I've done.

"East—I'm sorry."

He lifts a hand. "No—I get it. I do." He adds a nod, but he's heading for the door.

"Wait."

He turns back to look at me. It breaks my heart. He's everything I've ever wanted, and I can't seem to have him.

"Stay—have fun. I'll see you tomorrow."

"I'll come pick you up, okay? I'll be there before noon."

"I'll tell Evie and Vincent, so no one sees you picking me up alone."

He steps out and disappears into the crowd. I try to follow him, but he's gone before I can rush out onto the front porch. Someone hands me another wine cooler and this time I decide to drink it because I feel like the biggest asshole on the planet.

CHAPTER FORTY-SEVEN

AUGUST EAST

I hang onto the side of the bridge and stare down at the dark water below. I nearly slip when I hear a voice echo through the wooden tunnel.

"East?"

I step away from the edge and narrow my eyes. A shadow is approaching me, but I don't immediately recognize her, but then, I see that it's Shylo.

I step closer as she makes her way to me.

"What are you doing?"

"I was thinking about jumping."

"That's a little dramatic, don't you think?"

I laugh. "I heard that Brian's cousin did it, so I think it's possible for me to survive it."

"Well, she broke an arm. So, it wasn't all glamorous."

She steps up to the edge and hangs onto the railing.

She takes a seat, so I join her. Our legs dangle over the side.

"I'm going to need you to stop beating yourself up, East."

I narrow my eyes. "What?"

She looks at me with suspicion, "You and I are a lot alike. I think that's maybe why I—well, that thing we did."

"Some people would call that narcissistic."

She cackles, "And?"

I sigh. "I can't argue."

She turns sideways, holding onto the railing above her head. I get caught up looking at her hair. She fidgets with the ends of it.

"I know, my hair is straight. I was having an existential crisis."

I look out across the water and back to her. "Did you see my hair? I cut it myself."

"Yeah—it actually looks good."

I adjust myself on the hard wood beneath me, "Thanks."

"You're welcome."

"And yours looks good, too."

She snorts. "It's shit, I hate it. I only did it because I forgot how badass I am. Keller reminded me."

I look down. I don't want to talk about him, but I know she's going to rope me into it. Shylo Martin is a master of getting what she wants. Maybe I should study her more closely. I might not be so freakin' miserable.

"Did he send you here?"

"What if he did?"

I grin. "I'd think you're both evil."

She leans in and winks at me. "In the best way."

"Maybe."

We sit in silence for a moment and I listen to the water below. It's peaceful and I could be there screaming with a broken arm right now. I should probably thank her.

"East—Keller is a complicated person."

My lip curls, "Oh trust me, I know."

"He's this amazing football star—the best quarterback Whynot has ever had—even beating his dad's record, which was insane, by the way—and then he's also this sensitive person, soft and caring. Loyal to a damn fault."

"That's what I'm afraid of, his loyalty."

Her eyebrow cocks. "He isn't going to stay here forever and you know that. He's too good to stick around this town. He'll leave and go play football and be a big star there, too, and probably go on to play professionally, if he wants. But that's his decision to make. Not ours."

I bite my lip. "I told him that."

"No—what you tell him isn't with words. You are saying stay with me forever, and that's just—it's not his future. And I'm not being mean or saying he should be with me because he shouldn't want to be with me either. I don't want him to be with me. I released Keller once and for all. He needs this. He's earned a ticket out of here after all the bullshit with his dad."

"You did not make me feel good at all, Shy."

We both laugh.

"I'm being truthful. I want you to know that there may come a day where you have to release him too, but for now, could you stop making him insane? Please?"

I push myself forward and she grabs my arms. I look at her. "I'm not going to jump, and I get it. Trust me, I've thought about every day since we met. I know he's better than me—shit, he's probably better than all of us."

"I'm not going to argue with you either."

We sit in silence again.

"But for now, let's have fun. Be happy. Enjoy the time we have, k?"

I nod.

She stands up and offers me her hand. I take it.

"Come to the Horror Festival with us tomorrow. Keller is picking us up before noon at my house."

She places a hand on her hip. "And what if I say no?"

"You won't." I grin as I back away.

CHAPTER FORTY-EIGHT

KELLER WEST

I stare at my class ring in the palm of my hand and shove it into my pocket. I catch my reflection in the mirror. I stayed up too late. I kept thinking about East on the floor in that library. He didn't deserve that. I feel terrible about what happened.

"Hey, son."

I turn to see my dad in the doorway.

"Great game last night! Did you have fun at the party?"

I nod. "Yeah, it was cool."

He steps in and looks around my room. "What are you up to today? I thought maybe we could hang out—toss the ball a few times?"

I swallow hard, hoping he isn't going to ruin my day.

"I can't—the Horror Festival is today, and I

promised some friends I'd be there. I got free tickets for working this summer."

He runs his hand through his thick hair. I see the wedding band on his finger and I'd like to rip it off of him, but I can't.

"Oh, yeah. I forgot. Well, maybe we can do it tomorrow."

I nod. "Yeah—sounds good."

I step past him and he grabs my arm. "I'm proud of you, son."

I accept his compliment, but I don't want to.

"Thanks." My voice cracks. He's too close to me. I can smell his aftershave, and it makes my stomach churn. He lets me go, and I head down the hallway toward the door.

"Honey?"

I turn to see Mom's drinking her *fruity punch*. It makes me wonder if they've been fighting.

"Hey, Mom." I thumb behind me. "I'm heading out to the Horror Festival."

"Oh, that's right! You'd think I'd remember. The video store is closed on this day every year because no one will be there."

"I have to go—I'm gonna be late." I glance at my watch.

She toasts me, "Have fun."

"Yeah, I will."

I grab my keys and hit the door running.

I park in front of The Mill House and stare up at it. I don't know what I'm going to do to make it up to him, but I promise myself I will. It killed me to see him on the floor like that. It reminded me of something my dad would do.

I take a deep breath and grip the wheel.

I flinch when a knock comes to the side window. I look over to see Evie's smiling face. It immediately lightens my mood. I'm sort of glad she found me first. She motions to the lock. I forgot. I lean over and pop it up. She opens the door and stares at me.

"Is he meeting us down here?"

"I guess."

She narrows her eyes. "I'll go get him."

I watch her knock on the front door, then he answers. I take a deep breath and blow it out, tapping the wheel like I'm listening to one of my favorite songs. I jump when Vincent hits my window, and he's wearing a werewolf mask. I nervously laugh at his prank. He lifts the mask and lets it sit atop his head. I get out and lift my seat so he can get in. It's not like Corvettes have a ton of room, but I think we can make it work. Maybe I should've grabbed my dad's truck? But that would've taken more time.

Shy walks up as I'm standing next to the car and she eyes it, then me. "Tight squeeze," she mutters.

315

"Yeah—I didn't think about it."

She waits as Evie and East both join us. We all look at the car.

Evie lifts a hand. "One of us may be walking."

"No—I'll just sit on someone's lap," Shy offers.

Vincent raises a hand, but he's already tucked away in the back. Shy pulls up the seat and Evie crawls in the back with her brother. This leaves East and Shy. East gets in and so do I. Shy climbs on his lap and I hate it, but I will not say a word. I think maybe he's doing it on purpose to mess with me.

I turn the key and we head toward Main Street. It's not like it'll take that long, anyway. Shy giggles as we take a turn. East tightens his grip on the base of her back. The ride can't end soon enough. I know I promised I'd let it go because I've done some stupid shit myself, but it's hard to ignore it when Shy has her arm wrapped around his neck not two feet from me.

I hit the brakes a little too hard when a couple of kids rush across the street, and she nearly slides off his lap. Again, she laughs. I guess it is funny. I just wish I could smile about it.

Finally, I'm able to park. I get out, letting Vincent worm his way out of the backseat. He finally emerges with a grunt. "Man! This car isn't built right."

I smirk. "I still like it."

He adjusts his jacket and pulls down his mask. He

gives me a growl before twisting away. East and Shy are finally out of the car and East is waiting for Evie. He takes her hand and helps her. I guess I could've done the same for Vincent, but I didn't care. I should've, but my mind was elsewhere.

I slam the door and look up at the marquee. The lights are running along the edge, flashing like a beacon. The white board on both sides has one thing listed.

Horror Festival 1985

My heart jumps. I love this time of the year and the Horror Festival Triple Feature is one of my favorite things in the world. I look at East. He's staring up at the marquee, too. He's grinning. I'm so glad he's happy and that I could do this for us. I reach into my pocket and pull out the tickets.

"Let's go." I wag them in the air.

We all happily make our way across the street and into the line that is forming. This is a big deal every year. Not much happens in Whynot, Ohio but this is a constant thing we can rely on.

Evie and Shy are busy chatting away, and Vincent is growling at people and laughing behind his mask. I bump against East's shoulder and he looks at me.

"Are we okay?" I whisper.

"Yeah." He offers a little relief.

I lean closer to his ear. "I'm sorry."

He nods, "I know." He gives me what I need but I haven't done enough.

Evie and Shy reach the ticket booth first and I gently wedge in between them, pulling out five tickets. "This is for all of us." I twist my finger and we move past the booth and into the theater. I hold the door for the girls, Vincent, and then East. He eyes me. I so wish this was a real date, but it'll have to do for now. It's not like I can run around holding his hand and kissing him public. People would die. My dad would flip out and they'd probably run us out of town with lit torches.

I'm not so worried about myself. I worry about East. I at least have my popularity and football, although I'd guess that would diminish. But it would take people longer with me. East would be eaten alive, even with the rumors about him that are circulating now. No one would dare attack him without proof, and I refuse to give them any fuel for the fire.

I step inside, and the fresh popcorn permeates the air. I love the smell of hot butter. There is a hum of excitement. The counter is swarming with kids grabbing popcorn and sodas. They both come free with the tickets. There are already a few plump popcorn pieces on the floor. I hate trying to clean them up. They get ground into the short carpet, but I'm not here to work.

Evie and Shy immediately hit the bathroom. It's a

girl thing, I guess. They all seem to do it. Vincent rushes to the counter. East focuses on me. He seems lost at what to do. I hate it.

"Want some popcorn?" I ask.

"Sounds good. I like extra butter." He admits.

"Same! It's the best, right?"

"I think it's stupid to have popcorn without it. I mean, heart attack or bust." He smirks.

His humor is coming back. Or he may try to appease me, I don't know.

He steps forward, I touch his arm. "I got it."

"Okay—cool."

He lingers behind as I stand in line. Vincent is bouncing on his heels like a little kid on Christmas morning. "Huge bucket and one Coke, please," he says, noticing I'm behind him. "Hey, thanks for this. Really, it's awesomesauce."

I laugh. "Is awesomesauce a superior sauce to the rest?"

"Yeah, I guess. I heard people at school using it, and it stuck."

I look around, "I agree, it is awesomesauce."

Vincent glances over at East, who's standing alone.

"He seems upset—what did you do?"

I immediately feel flush. "Why are you—"

He tilts his head. It's dumb to assume he doesn't know it had to be me.

"I'm an idiot."

He bites his full lip, then releases it, "Sounds about right."

"Hey."

"Well—," he leans in closer to my ear, but the chatter is loud enough that no one would hear us anyway, "I think all guys are idiots."

I follow his gaze and realize he is staring at Shy, who's emerged from the bathroom with Evie. Her lips are shiny with fresh gloss.

"She's a complicated one."

His eyebrow cocks. "I don't know—"

I tilt my head and his mouth snaps shut. I guess we understand each other.

"All you have to do is be yourself. She doesn't like fake people."

His expression hardens, "No way someone as amazing as Shylo Martin would ever go out with me."

I study her. She catches me staring and narrows her eyes. I clear my throat and turn back to the counter. "One large bucket and two sodas, please."

I lean in closer to Vincent as he salts his popcorn. He's grabbed three, being a gentleman. He also has three sodas. "Sit with her."

He eyes me. "Seriously?"

"Yeah—she gets spooked really easily. She'll end up on your lap before the end of the first movie."

He brightens.

"Not like that, man," I add.

"No—I respect her."

I straighten. I didn't realize he was this into her. "Well, just sit with her."

"Thanks," he says as they approach us. He hands Shylo a popcorn and then gives Evie hers. She grins, popping a piece in her mouth and chewing.

"We should find some seats!" he exclaims. His inside voice is non-existent. Shy blinks through his volume. But she laughs while popping another piece into her mouth.

Vincent heads toward theater room one. Evie follows. Shy lingers, but I catch her peering over at East.

"You should sit with him."

"I plan on it." I juggle the popcorn and two drinks.

"I mean alone."

"I have a plan."

"You better."

I tilt my head.

"He talked to me. I mean—Keller."

"I know—shit."

She touches my arm, but then retrieves her soda. "I'm going in, good luck."

"Thanks, I need it."

I look back and East is staring at me. I make my way over to him and try to collect my thoughts before I try to fix everything.

CHAPTER FORTY-NINE

AUGUST EAST

I watch him talk to Shy. They both look at me throughout the brief conversation. I told her what happened. I probably should've kept it to myself, but I was upset and needed to vent.

At least there was no kissing. I think we've moved past that awkwardness. I'm so glad. I like Shy. I want us to always be friends. I don't want a mistake to ruin that.

Besides, she knows Keller better than most people do, and I need her on my side.

He approaches me with a huge bucket of popcorn and two sodas. I reach in and take one before he loses his grip and ends up dropping everything.

I look at the theater room that Vincent, Evie and Shy slipped into.

"I guess we should find some seats, huh?" I ask.

"I have seats for us," he says, nudging his chin to the side.

My eyes narrow, but I follow him past two rooms and then he pauses by a side door.

"Could you?" he asks.

I reach in and it's unlocked. He lets me step inside first and then he follows. I close the door and we seem to be at the base of a set of stairs. I look up, there's a faint light at the top.

"What is this?"

"Come on." He leads the way. My heart skips a beat. I have no idea what we're doing, but I don't hate it. Being alone with him is something I always long for. I hope it doesn't end up like the last time.

I exit the top of the stares and there's a girl manning a film reel. It's larger than I expected. There are elevated seats and glass. A speaker is pumping in the sound. I step up and can see a packed theater below us. I move away, pointing toward it.

She grins, shoving a large metal wheel onto the machine. I can see *Teen Wolf* written on the side of the empty tin. "It's one way glass. No one can see in here."

I swallow hard.

She snaps the reel in place and then extends a hand. I shake it, "Veronica—I'm the manager here."

"East—I got a free ticket."

She grins, focused on Keller. "So, just keep an eye on it, okay?"

He nods, then she leaves the room and rushes down the stairs. I hear the door close behind her.

Suddenly, the commercials kick in and we can hear the roar below us.

"Okay, this is pretty cool," I admit.

Keller smiles, holding out his arm, guiding me toward two of the seats that are elevated so we can see the movie through the glass.

I take a seat and he settles in next to me.

"Oh, wait."

He sets his drink down in the cup holder and hands me the popcorn. Keller finds a switch and the lights go out in the room. All that's left is a small light next to the projector, in case anything goes wrong. I hope it doesn't.

He returns and offers to hold the popcorn.

"I can do it."

He takes a seat and observes the glass. We have a perfect view of the movie screen.

"This is amazing. You did this for me?"

"Of course, I mean, I had it planned out long before this, but I didn't know if you'd come."

"Like how long?" I ask.

"Since the first week we met."

My heart skips a beat. "Oh."

He reaches over and grabs a handful of popcorn. I watch him slip one into his mouth. The butter glistens on his lips. I try to focus on the screen as the last commercial runs. It's a dancing bucket of popcorn and his partner, a full soda.

I feel his hand slip into mine and our fingers become interlaced.

This is what I always hoped for with him. A quiet place where we could be ourselves. The horror movies are an added bonus.

We end up binge-eating the huge bucket of popcorn. I reach in and find nothing but crumbles at the bottom.

"Do you want me to grab us some more?"

"Sure."

He gets up, but I hold on to his hand. His lips appear full and buttery. His beautiful blue eyes pour over me—his skin is illuminated by the small slivers of light bouncing around in the room.

He moves in front of me. My eyes are fixed on him. He tries to step down off the short platform, but I grab his waist. He doesn't fight me.

I grin, fidgeting with the button on his jeans.

He places his hand on top of mine.

"East—you don't have to do anything."

"I know."

I listlessly run my fingers along the top of his jeans.

He flinches at my touch. Soon, I feel him inside my mouth. He reaches down and grabs the back of my head, twisting his fingers in my hair. He moans. I tense up. I hold on to him with such desperation. I know I owe him nothing, but I want this. I want him.

Now and always.

We sit on the floor among a few stray pieces of popcorn. His arm rests around my shoulder and I lean into him.

"That was—" He pauses.

"I agree."

He shakes his head, then digs in his pocket.

I narrow my eyes, but he turns to face me with a balled fist. I look down at it and then into his beautiful blue eyes. His hair's a bit disheveled, but it makes him even cuter. How, I don't know.

"East, I want you to know that I've never felt like this about anyone—ever." He pauses.

"Keller—"

"No, listen, I want you to hear me."

"This isn't because of what just happened, right?"

He sighs. "Okay—that—was amazing, but no. I had this planned before you did that amazing thing with—whatever that was."

I grin.

He takes my hand and presses his against it.

326

"I love you."

"I love you," I repeat his sentiment.

"More—this isn't some puppy love thing. I'm not infatuated with you, although crushing on you seems to be something I excel at."

I grin, he holds our hands together.

"But this is more. It's forever," he admits.

I gasp as he removes his hand, and his class ring is sitting in my palm. I stop breathing. A class ring is like an engagement ring. It's serious business. Guys don't just hand these out to anyone. Most of the girls who get these have string wound up on the bottom of them, so they fit their small fingers. I suspect it will just fit me. Keller and I are pretty evenly matched.

I lift it, and he takes it from me, then slips it on my right hand, ring finger. I investigate with wonder. I'm mesmerized. His last name is etched into the side and it has a big red stone in it. The Whynot Wolf mascot is on one side and a football is on the other.

"Keller—you don't have to do this."

He leans in. "I know—I want to do this, and that makes all the difference."

He takes my hand and places my palm against his lips. I can feel his hot breath against it. He kisses my skin, letting his lips linger. Then he lowers it to his heart.

"I promise you I'll always be here for you. I'll

protect you and stand by you no matter what. I don't care what people think. I know I've been an asshole, but I promise I'll do better. I'll try my best. I just need time to change and I can only hope that you'll wait for me—because nothing matters more to me than you do. Nothing. Not football, not popularity. Not even Shy. Nothing."

I fight back the tears.

"Keller—"

His lips crash against mine and I allow myself to get lost in him, once and for all.

CHAPTER FIFTY

KELLER WEST

I drop Shy off first. She slides off East's lap, but something's changed. Nothing about her sitting on him bothered me at all. I know we've stepped over a threshold now. We've changed. I've committed myself to August East and making this work.

I've never given my ring to anyone. I barely wear it because girls eye class rings in school like chocolate cake. Leaving it off makes it appear as if I'm taken without having to talk about it.

Let them wonder.

I know who has it and he's sitting next to me.

Shy leans back in. "That was a blast!" she chirps.

"Yes, it was!" Vincent yells in my ear because he's moved up behind me. I blink through the volume of his voice, but it's okay. I know he likes her and if I can help him, I will. Vincent's a good guy—I just don't know if he's Shy's sort of guy. He may be too nice. She gravitates toward boys she knows will wreck her.

Like me and Ty Miller.

I pause.

Ty wasn't at the Horror Festival either.

"Does anyone want to come in for some apple cider? My mom made some."

"Yes!" Vincent practically screams. I grin.

"Sure," Evie says.

I step out, Vincent tumbles out of the backseat. I have to grab his arm to stop him from falling.

"Just chill," I whisper.

He straightens his shirt. He won't get Shy falling all over her. I know that for a fact. He has to play it cool. Act like he's not interested.

He steps around the car as Evie exits on East's side. He hasn't said anything. I'm hoping he doesn't want to go in.

We share a fixed moment and then his attention turns back to Shy. "I should probably get home. I promised my parents I wouldn't stay out that late."

"Okay—cool. Have fun." She offers a finger wiggling wave.

I feel flush. She knows, but whatever. Shy would never tell anyone in school. I trust her when it comes to that.

Evie and Vincent offer a wave before following

Shy up the winding sidewalk. Her house is pretty big. Bigger than mine. Her parents have money, but she never talks about it.

My house is pretty modest, but I don't need a ton of space. Although a second bathroom would be nice. Maybe Dad will finally add one on now that he's home.

I climb back in the car and East is already settled in. He pulls out my ring and places it back on his finger. I love seeing it there. Honestly, I don't think any of them would have said a word to us, but Shy would've definitely asked me about it as soon as she got me alone again.

I'll tell her—maybe. I mean, for now, it's nice having something that's just ours.

Me and East.

I pull away from her house and East reaches over and places his hand in the center. I take it, wrapping my fingers in his. We drive down the street as a couple without anyone knowing, and there's something about it that makes me want him more. I don't know if it's because it's dangerous or not. All I know is I've decided that he's who I want in this life—the last one—the next one—all of it.

He makes me happy.

I don't think I've ever felt more at home with someone. I look over and he's staring out the window. The

331

sun is setting. We spent hours together talking about what we like and don't like. We even stopped talking and enjoyed some of the movies after, you know, what happened. But we just held hands after that. We didn't even kiss. It's like we settled into being together. It was heaven.

I pull up to his house and there are a few lights on. I glance up at his window. I sort of wish he'd invite me up. I'd be tempted to stay if his parents would let me, but they know about us, I think, and might be uncomfortable if we slept in the same bed.

But I want that.

I don't even care if nothing happens. I just want to fall asleep with him and wake up to his face in the morning.

I shut off the engine, and he clears his throat.

"So what now?" he asks.

I narrow my eyes. "What do you mean?"

"I have your ring, Keller."

I fidget with my hair. "Yeah—you do."

"Is it really what you wanted?" he asks.

"Yes, one hundred percent—maybe more."

He grins, twisting it on his finger. The light catches the red stone and it reminds me of blood. I was born in January. Sometimes it's the worst month for weather, and sometimes it lets February take the title.

"When's your birthday?" I ask, realizing I never asked him.

"Halloween," he states with little enthusiasm.

"Are you serious?"

He lowers his hand and abandons the nervous fidgeting with my class ring.

"Why didn't you tell me?" I ask.

He bitterly dismisses it, "Halloween isn't the best day to celebrate a birthday. Kids are usually collecting candy, then beaching themselves at home."

"I guess, but I think it's cool."

His brows nearly meet.

"What?"

"My parents are separating," he admits.

My heart drops. "East—why didn't you tell me?"

He eyes the ring. "It was such a good day. I didn't want to ruin it."

"So," I pause, I don't want to sound selfish, but I need to know, "what does that mean?"

He studies the house. "Dad's going to Arizona on his own and me and Mom are staying here."

"Really?" I calm down, and clear my throat to the side of my hand, "Really?" I tone it down, trying to sound sympathetic.

"Yeah, so, I guess I won't be going anywhere anytime soon."

I take his hand again. I'm so happy to know he won't be moving, but I feel awful about his parents.

"But—"

"No, buts," I demand.

He shakes his head. "Listen, I don't want you to pass up any opportunities because of me."

My eyes turn to slits. "What do you mean?"

"Football." He pulls his hand away from me. "East."

He places his elbow on the window's ledge, and stares out the passenger side window. "I know the football scout was at the game."

"I know he was, and?"

His nostrils flare. "I'd never forgive myself if you stayed here because of me."

I grab his hand and make him hold mine, "Everything I said was true, August East."

His head lowers.

"Hey—seriously, look at me, please?" I lift his chin. "I love you more than football."

He shakes his head.

"Please, don't do this," I whisper.

"I feel like I'm ruining your life," he admits.

I lean in closer to him. "You're not—you've made my life better than it's ever been. Ask Shy. I was a miserable old man before you came to town. I went to school, played football, skipped everything and worked at the theater during the Summer. That's it. That's all I did."

"And now?" he asks.

"Now I want to go places—with you. I see a future for us, East. Don't you?"

He doesn't answer, but I know he has to see it.

"Do you want to come inside?" he asks.

I nod before answering. "I really do."

We both laugh.

"Come on." He gets out of the car, waiting until I've reached him on the other side. I'd love to push him up against the car and kiss him right now, but I'm trapped in this town—hiding who I am and how much I love him.

But it won't be like that forever.

CHAPTER FIFTY-ONE

AUGUST EAST

I slip inside the house as quietly as I can. Keller steps to the side so I can close the door. It clicks shut after the most annoying creaking sound.

"Love? Is that you?"

I let out a sigh, but it's Mom. She won't be mad about Keller coming inside.

I feel a renewed sense of hope sneaking into my life. I would try to stop it, but he's made it impossible. I glance at his ring that's now on my finger.

He gave it to me.

Me.

He must've gotten it early, because it's usually the junior classmen who get their rings, but he's Keller West. I don't get surprised when it concerns him. People bend over backward to please him, but he ignores the majority of it. I'm glad.

He could've easily ignored me. Moved along—but he didn't. He made it a point to talk to me. He didn't have to do that. But he did. It makes me feel so—I don't know—maybe *special* is the word.

Mom leans against the banister at the top of the staircase. She has a drink in hand. I thought she was going to try to do better? But who am I to judge her? I'm sure it's hard. I understand addiction. I have Keller.

She descends the staircase, careful to hold on to the railing. She's wearing her silky robe. It laps at her thick socks. She eyes Keller, then me.

Suddenly, she erupts with laughter. I'm left confused, but she's clearly been drinking.

"Did you hand out the invitations?" she asks.

I glance over at Keller. "He handed out most of them, but I'm sure the whole school will be here because of it."

"Good!" She nods with approval. Her drink sloshes in the clear glass. The firelight catches the amber hue. It's not her usual. It's something dad would drink. A hard liquor.

She steps up to Keller and pinches his cheek, he grimaces, rubbing it once she lets go. "You're so thin—we need to plump you up! Nice and delicious; I have so much candy for the party. I expect you to eat it all up."

We exchange a look.

"He was just in a coma, Mom."

She slaps her hand against the side of her head, "That's right! I do apologize. I've had so much going on—I don't mean to be callous."

Keller chimes in, "It's okay. I need to gain some weight back. It's harder to play football when I'm this light."

"I'm going to plump you right up! I made vegetable stew—it's in the kitchen. Be sure to help yourself."

"Thank you."

I narrow my eyes. "Where's Dad?" I ask.

She stops twirling and places the edge of the glass against her bottom lip and rolls it. "Your father," she straightens her spine, "decided it would be best if he went on ahead to Arizona."

"What?" My voice carries through the house.

"Oh, love," she steps closer, cupping my cheek, "he will call."

"Mom—my birthday is on Saturday," I grumble.

"I know my love, but, well, we had a terrible fight and I blame myself."

"I can't believe he left."

She sniffles, but produces no tears. I assume she did all her crying while I was at the Horror Festival.

"He left you that." She peers at the side table and there's a red box with a bow.

"I don't want it," I protest.

"Which is your right—but just know that this has nothing to do with you."

My chin lowers. Keller steps in closer. I feel his arm brush against mine.

"Okay, I'm going to wrap myself in a blanket and watch a movie in the living room—join me?" she asks.

I hesitate. "I—well, we watched three movies today, mom. I sort of just wanted to chill in my room and listen to music."

She gives Keller a once-over. "Very well, but leave the door open."

My cheeks redden. "Mom," I whine.

"We will." Keller agrees.

She grins. "Okay, have fun."

She waves the glass around and begins humming a tune to herself. Soon, she's out of sight and I feel this weight in my gut.

Keller picks up the gift as I hit the stairs running—following close behind.

CHAPTER FIFTY-TWO

KELLER WEST

I watch him pace the room. I hold the gift in my hands. He stops once or twice to glare at it.

"Can you believe he did this?"

I part my lips, but he isn't done.

"I mean the nerve—and leaving days before my birthday! I'm turning sixteen! It's a big deal, right? Sixteen is supposed to be special or something—I just—God! I'm so pissed!"

I place the gift on his side table and reach in, taking his hand and stopping him from wearing a groove on the wood floor.

"East, I know this sucks, and I honestly don't know what to say to make any of it better, but I know adults are a mess."

He chuckles. "Right? And they act like we're immature." He huffs.

"I think we all have our moments."

He leans into me. I try to hold him up and we nearly topple over.

He grabs my arm. "She is right. You need to eat."

"Hey." I push back.

"I can feel your ribs."

His hand slips along my side.

"Try to behave," I whisper.

"It's hard." He leans his forehead against mine and I sigh.

"I know," I whisper back.

He steps away and drops on his bed. He rolls on his side and presses the button on his boom box and music plays. It's Duran Duran, *The Chauffer*, one of my favorites.

He taps the bed, then pushes himself against the headboard. I'm stuck in place for a moment and he shakes his head, reaching for me. I can see my ring on his finger. It makes me happy.

"It's okay. She's probably asleep." He is encouraging me to join him.

I sit down and he grabs my hand and pulls me back so we're crammed shoulder to shoulder.

He leans into my side and I wrap my arm around his shoulder.

"I'm so mad at him."

"I get it," I agree, because I do.

341

"I would never do this to him—not in a million years."

He's nestled against my chest, so I rub the side of his arm with my fingers, letting out a sigh.

"I've spent my whole life hating my dad."

He glances up at me. "Really?"

"Yes, really. He pushed me into football and then continued to push and push, and I hated him for it. Then he started fighting with Mom and you know the rest. And now, he's home, like nothing happened and he's trying to talk to me about shit and I don't know what to say."

East lets out a sigh. "I'm so sorry. I hate that you feel like this, and it makes me realize that I've always loved my dad. We've always gotten along. He's super positive about everything—so it makes this really bad. I hate it—not him."

I rest my chin against the top of his head. "Adults suck."

He hides his face in the side of my shirt and muffles a laugh.

"And besides, I'll be here for your birthday."

"That's right." He peers up at me and I lean in and kiss his lips, but it's soft and sweet. Nothing more or less.

He settles back into my side and we sit in silence, listening to the music until he drifts off and I hold him, wishing this was where I could stay forever and a day.

My eyes feel heavy and I drift off, but then the telephone rings and we both jump like we're watching a scary movie.

East wipes his eyes and then reaches over to answer it on the third ring. He yawns, scratching the side of his head, "The Mill House."

I grin. It's funny he answers it that way.

His expression changes. "Yes, he is."

He hands me the phone. I reluctantly place the receiver to my ear. "Hello?" My heart jumps into my throat.

"Keller?"

"Yeah, Mom?"

"Good! I was worried, I called Shy, and she said you were probably with East."

I glance at the clock on his nightstand, "Oh crap! I'm sorry." It's nine-thirty. The Horror Festival ended at six. "We started listening to music and I lost track of time."

"Could you come home?"

My brow furrows. "Yeah—everything okay?"

She hesitates. "Of course, I was just worried."

"I'll head home now."

I wave at East as I drive away. I didn't want to leave him, but I had to.

I pull into the driveway and another car is sitting by the curb. I enter the house to elevated voices and round the corner to see my parents in the living room. Ty Miller's parents are sitting on the couch.

I nearly trip, not knowing why they're here. It's not that my parents don't know his parents—it's a smaller town, we all know each other, but they don't come here. In fact, they've never been here before. Not for one barbeque.

"Keller!" Ty's mom approaches me with open arms and hugs me. I'm confused.

She backs away. "You look thinner," she states.

I scowl. "Coma."

"That's right." Not showing any sympathy.

"I pulled through," I snap.

"Yes—yes. You boys are tough."

She returns to the couch. Ty's dad doesn't bother to get up and shake my hand. Funny that I notice things like that. I mean, Vincent shakes hands. So does East.

I'm tired of the mystery. "So—what's going on?"

Her eyes glass over. "Do you know where Tyler is?"

"What's happened?" I ask

His mom wipes her nose. "I was hoping you knew something."

I take a seat on the open chair. "I heard he was sick."

344

"No—he went on a date with that girl—Michelle."

His dad snickers; she isn't amused.

"Chuck," she whispers.

"What? The boy is wetting his whistle. That's all."

She rolls her eyes. "Stop being crude."

"Well! The girl is attractive and Ty is a ladies' man."

I'd love to argue with him because Ty is a douche-bag. He may attract girls, but they don't like him any-more than I do. I know it. It would be impossible to enjoy Ty Miller's company. He's an obnoxious idiot.

"Yeah." I hate agreeing with him.

"I mean, you know how it is, don't ya, boy?" he commands.

Everyone is waiting on me. "Yeah, sure." I feel sick saying it. I'm not like them. I never will be.

"He went on a date with her and never came home. Do you know where she lives?" his mom asks me.

"I—I'm sorry, I know it's out of town, but I don't know. I only met her once, at The Diamond, and she seemed cool."

"Cool?" his mother nearly shrieks.

"Seemed," I add.

She settles down.

"Well, if he calls or you hear anything, will you please let me know?" She rises, her husband along with her.

I nod. He passes me by, still not offering to shake my hand. I can see where Ty gets his manners. They leave without saying another word and I'm left wondering what the hell is going on with the people in Whynot.

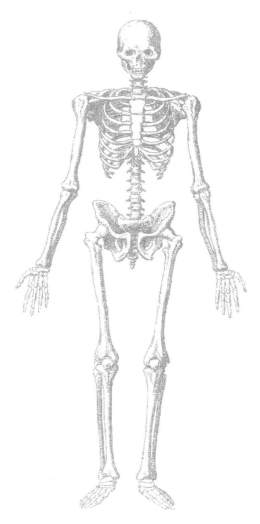

CHAPTER FIFTY-THREE

AUGUST EAST

I twist his ring on my finger, then hurriedly tuck it away when the bathroom door opens. I turn on the water and wash my hands, even though it isn't necessary.

"Dude, I heard he knocked her up."

The two boys wrestle before spotting me. They settle down and use the urinals. I finish rinsing the soap off my hands as they continue their conversation.

"His dad is going to kill him."

The dark-haired boy eyes me from the side, like I care about gossip, but I'm wondering who they're talking about.

"His dad? I'd worry more about his mom. She's the religious one."

My imagination gets the better of me until they finally say his name.

"Ty's an idiot; that girl might be hot, but no tail is worth knocking up."

I sigh, grabbing a paper towel and drying off my hands.

"What have you heard?"

I'm visibly shocked they've asked me. Most kids avoid me. Maybe being the son of a mortician, and living in the *scary house on the hill* isn't a curse after all.

I turn, feeling a little uncomfortable that they're both still finishing up. My eyes stay locked on his.

"About Ty Miller? Nothing."

"Huh, well, he took off."

"He did?" I ask.

"Yeah—where've you been, man?" The boy huffs like I'm an idiot for not knowing the latest gossip.

He zips his pants and they both walk out without washing their hands. I grimace. Most boys are disgusting. I have my days when my room is messy, but I always wash my hands. So gross.

I exit the bathroom and nearly run right into Keller. We do an awkward dance around each other. It's been like this all week. We've snuck in moments here and there, but he's still hiding how he feels in front of other people. But I'm not mad. I know he loves me. I reach into my pocket and fidget with his ring. His eyes lock onto my mouth. The heat rises in my stomach,

348

radiating out to my chest and arms. He has this power over me. I'm just glad the feeling is mutual.

"Hey—sorry," he says, like running into me would be a bad thing.

"It's cool." Kids pass us by. If we were alone, I would push him against the wall and kiss his full lips, forcing him to moan and beg me to stop. But I can't.

"Are you good?" he asks.

"Yeah." I glance at the bathroom door. "Two guys mentioned something about Ty Miller—I thought he had the mumps. I mean, that's the rumor," I admit, because I heard it from Evie and Vincent.

He rubs the side of his neck. It's a nervous tick he has, "His parents came to my house Saturday, I guess," he leans in closer, lowering his voice, "he ran off with his girlfriend, Michelle."

"Really?" I ask.

"Yeah," he confirms.

"Don't you think that's weird?" I ask.

He straightens. "Not really. Ty's an idiot."

I grin. He is, but it's still odd.

"So, how's it going?" he asks.

I snicker. He knows how I'm doing. We talk every single day on the phone when we're not together, and the rest—well, we sneak in make out sessions. I'm surprised my lips aren't chapped.

"Great," I reply. It's awkward—but humorous.

He thumbs behind him. I think he's blushing. I lick my bottom lip before biting it. He backs away, keeping his eyes on me for long as possible.

I sigh. The ring is sitting in my pocket. I'd love to pull it out and wear it, but the entire school would die—then die again from shock.

I'm sure every single girl knows what Keller West's class ring looks like. Every boy, too.

I just wish I could wear it outside of my house.

I turn, blinking with shock as Vincent and Evie are right up on me. They're both grinning like they've done something evil.

"What?" I ask, messing with the back of my hair.

Vincent nudges his chin and I shift my weight from one foot to the other.

"How are you?" he asks.

"Good, why?" My eyes narrow.

"It just seems like things are going pretty awesome," he admits.

Evie looks to him, then back to me.

My muscles tense and I pull out the ring and lean in, giving them a peek. Evie yelps, and Vincent's eyes go wide.

"Dude!"

Evie covers his mouth and mumbles behind her hand. I know he's sharing everything we can't discuss in school. Not here—not around these kids. But it makes me smile. I hide it away and Vincent stops talking behind Evie's grip. She removes her hand glaring at him.

"Stop," she insists.

I take a short breath and she wraps her arm around mine, pulling me along with her. We all make our way down the hallway.

"Honestly—can't believe you've been hiding this from me," she hisses. But I know she isn't mad at me. "How long?" she asks.

"A few days," I answer, eyeing the kids passing us by. We'll have to talk in code.

"Days?" Vincent exclaims.

"Shh," Evie warns.

"I got it at the Horror Festival."

"Man—that's cool," Vincent crows with support.

"Yeah," I admit.

"So, when's the wedding?" Evie whispers.

My cheeks redden.

She shakes me. "I'm kidding."

I don't respond.

"Wow, okay." She realizes I'm serious.

"I just—I love," I hesitate, "pumpkin pie."

Vincent grimaces. "Really?"

Evie leans forward. "Are you really that dumb?" she asks.

His eyes brighten. "Oh! Pumpkin pie."

"I think it's the best pie in the world." Evie nudges me.

"But seriously, pumpkin pie is all you could think—"

She shoots him a death stare and his lips snap shut.

"Pumpkin pie is amazing." She clears her throat, disgusted with his jab.

I nod, "It is the best pie—the only pie."

She shakes her head, hiding a grin.

"So—tomorrow," she coos.

"Tomorrow?"

"Um—Halloween party!" Vincent clarifies.

I blink through it. This is the first time I've forgotten about my birthday. Keller West has completely wrecked me. I can't think about anything else from morning to night.

"Yes! We have a pile of pumpkins. Mom had them delivered yesterday. I have to carve them up—with a sharp knife." I stab at the air, biting my tongue.

"Ahh—pumpkin pumpkins, right?" Vincent asks.

I roll my eyes. "Yes, the big orange round ones." I curve my hands. "Just come over after school, I'm sure she'll feed everyone. She keeps making big pots of stew every single day—like it's the only recipe she knows."

"Stew is delicious," Evie offers her support. I mean, she's right. I love soups and stews in Fall. It's my favorite.

352

"Deal!" he yells, while breaking off. Leaving me and Evie alone for a second. Kids are scattering. The second bell will ring soon.

"I am so happy for you," she offers.

"Thanks."

"No—I really am. I don't think I could've picked a better person for you."

"He is my person," I whisper.

"I can see that."

"Hey," I narrow my eyes, "do you know anything about Ty Miller?"

She sighs. "First it was the mumps, but now, I heard he got his girlfriend pregnant," she whispers, like it matters. The entire school is buzzing.

"And just took off?" I ask.

She bobs her head. "Yeah, I mean, Ty is an idiot."

"True but Michelle seems cool."

"Why?" she asks.

I hear the second bell. We have a minute to get to our last class of the day. "I—it's cool, I mean not for them because I wouldn't want a kid right now, but whatever makes them happy. Maybe it's what Ty needed."

She grimaces. "No one needs Ty as a dad—can you imagine?"

I narrow my eyes. "Yeah, true."

We split up, heading our separate ways.

KELLER WEST

I slide my hand over his. East is standing in front of me, leaning against the table. I press against him and hear a sigh escape his lips. He has a sharpened knife in his hand. I grab his hand and force the tip of the blade into the side of the ripe pumpkin. I have to push harder. My chest is pressed against his back. I'm vibrating with energy.

"Harder," I whisper next to his ear.

He nods, lips parted. His breathing is labored. We finally get it through. I'm relieved. It's the last eye on the pumpkin. We've carved a few while torturing each other.

"You're lucky my mom's here," he whispers.

"Don't tempt me." I growl.

"Ahh! You started without us?!"

I flinch, moving away faster than I planned, leaving East standing in front of me with the knife in hand.

"Only a few." East waves the knife around in the air.

Vincent's eyes widen. "Can I?" he asks.

East hands him the knife and looks at me, but I suddenly feel exposed. I hate that I feel this way. I try my best to show him I love him. I do, but even now, after everything, I can't seem to openly show it in front of other people. It makes me wonder how long I'll feel like this and what has to happen for it to change.

But it's not his fault—it's mine.

I have to find the courage.

"Twelve!" Vincent finishes counting. "Twelve pumpkins. That's a lot."

East grabs a towel and wipes his hands. "I told you my mom got a pile of them."

"We better get busy then—right?" I say.

Evie clicks the dial on the radio. Music fills the space and we all begin moving. Vincent is tapping his foot. Evie is swaying back and forth, and East is tapping his fingers against his thigh. I step forward and take his hand; he seems shocked at first, but I spin him once, offering a timid smile and he bumps against me while laughing. Evie grabs Vincent's hand. He rolls her out and back in. We end up dancing around each other, singing in unison at the top of our lungs.

Everybody wants to rule the world!

The laughter follows.

"I love Tears for Fears." Evie clasps her hands against her chest.

"You think they're cute?" Vincent quips.

"Um," she gives me a funny look, "who doesn't?"

I don't argue with her. They are cute, but not as cute as East. No boy is as cute as he is. I get caught up staring at him. He's perfect in every way. My perfect.

"It seems I missed all the fun!" East's mom has slipped into the kitchen undetected. We all look at her like we're in trouble. I know we're not. East's mom is one of the coolest adults I've ever met. But she seems tired and stressed. I don't blame her, with East's dad leaving and all.

I guess I didn't expect it from him. He seemed so nice, and I thought his parents were happy. It just goes to show you never really know what's going on with people. They can seem all put together on the outside while crumbling on the inside. I know this all too well. I've spent my entire life wearing a mask.

"Mmm." She strolls by and snatches up one of the knives. She lifts it like she is going to stab someone and then waves a hand. "I would be a terrible serial killer. I'd be giggling the whole time."

She swipes it in the air a couple of times and then stabs it into the top of one of the pumpkins. It sticks, swaying back and forth. We all stare at it. I didn't expect her to be so strong. I shouldn't judge, but she's a petite woman. Shorter than East. I'd guess she weighs
356

maybe a hundred and fifteen pounds, tops. I've gotten really good at guessing weight since I stare at guys barreling toward me on the football field.

"So, you're all coming tomorrow—yes?" she asks. Her face is tight with anticipation.

"Of course!" Vincent is the first to confirm.

She claps her hands. Maybe she is happier now. I mean, eventually they get happier. Mom did. I assumed she'd meet someone new but I woke up to my dad. I clench my jaw. He gives me headaches. I keep telling myself to ride it out. I know I can do it, but I don't want him here and it's wearing on me.

"You are all so thin—eat some stew. It's on the stove," she insists.

I grin when East eyes me. I'm not sure why he's exasperated.

Evie chimes in, "I'd love to have some—Vincent, too. He's always hungry, Mrs. East."

His mom seems to be frozen. I don't know if she's breathing. I watch her chest, I see nothing. Then she blinks out of it. "You can all call me Rosetta. Mrs. East seems so formal, don't you agree?"

I nod, I get it. East's dad isn't here, and she doesn't want the reminder. My mom was the same way, it's hard to see her like this. She always seemed happier— he stole that from her. It's one of the meanest things you can do to a person.

"Eat," she repeats. This time firmer.

Vincent rushes in and gets some stew—Evie follows. East has yet to move.

"Darling, eat something."

"I've been eating every single day."

"More," she insists.

Silence settles in.

She blinks.

A grin spreads across her face, "I'll leave you to murdering the pumpkins. Please put them out, along the drive, leading to the front doors. We'll light them tomorrow night for the party." And with that, she leaves.

Vincent is dipping his spoon in the bowl. Large chunks of meat and potatoes cling to it. I can smell it from here. I'm sure it's delicious. My stomach growls.

"She seems happy," Evie says between bites.

"She's not," East confirms.

"But she will be—eventually." I try to give him some hope.

"Yeah, well. I need to finish carving these up." He grabs a knife and holds it out to me, flipping it in the air with more skill than I expected, so I can take the handle. He grabs a second knife and we finish up the rest of them while Vincent and Evie enjoy the stew.

CHAPTER FIFTY-FIVE

AUGUST EAST

I stand in the driveway among the lit pumpkins. I peer out on the town.

It's my sixteenth birthday. This is supposed to be important. Special. A milestone. I sigh. Dad should be here. I can't believe he —

I have to stop.

This is my day.

I woke to blueberry pancakes. A pile of them with fresh cream. My favorite.

My mom spent the day making food. The entire house smells amazing. There are plenty of apples and a tub full of water. The pumpkins are lit. The house has a candle flickering in every window. She's strung cobwebs on the porch and inside the foyer, which actually matches the motif of the house. Maybe we should keep them. There are trays of finger sandwiches, and bowls with chips, pretzels and popcorn filling the kitchen table and countertops. She also has a large black bowl with skulls on it filled to the brim with what she's calling Witch's Brew, but it's just punch in a few flavors. I expect someone to spike it at some point. She went all out. There's a crystal ball by the fireplace on the side table and a Ouija board in the living room, resting on the coffee table. She has horror movies playing on the TV, and horror music on every radio throughout the rest of the house. She even decorated the garden and wrapped caution tape around the dead tree—not that I'd be messing with it anyway—and she placed poison signs throughout the garden.

She told me I'd get my gift from her tonight. I was born at exactly five minutes before midnight. Halloween almost got away from me. The present Dad left is still sitting in my room. I haven't bothered opening it. I don't know if I ever will. He still hasn't called, but she said he would tonight to wish me a happy birthday. I don't know if I care all that much. He could've called this week, but didn't bother.

I suddenly get a chill. I'm nervous. What if no one shows up? I mean, that isn't possible, is it? No. If nothing else, I know that Keller, Shy, Vincent and Evie will be here and, honestly, that's all that matters to me.

Or is it?

I guess I sort of want every kid from school to show up. I didn't know I'd feel this way, but I do.

I swallow hard. I didn't put any thought into a costume. Mom offered to do my makeup. She made me into a living skeleton. My eyes are sunken and black. My mouth is a white row of teeth. She pulled out one of dad's old tuxedos. It fits me. All except the coat with tails, so I skipped it and just have on a white button down with black suspenders. But I have a top hat and I'm gripping it—practically wringing it out as I wait to see if anyway is going to —

I hear voices. Then it gets louder and louder. I look out to see that every kid from school is gathering in front of the gates. My heart leaps into my throat.

They came. All of them. I have to thank Keller West for that. I would guess that him passing out the invites made this possible. It just further proves how much they respect him here in Whynot. He's their star—and mine—but for me, he lights up the night sky.

I rush toward the gate and hold out my hand, ushering them inside. I jiggle my top hat, offering a wicked smile.

"Welcome to The Mill House." I try to play the part. I recieve a few smiles and a some girls giggle, but I assume it's from nerves more than anything else. I know most of them never thought they'd step foot inside my house, yet here they are.

They keep coming and I feel silly for worrying. Of course, they wouldn't miss the opportunity to come here—they're not alone. This isn't a dare. It's a Halloween party not only to celebrate my favorite holiday, but my birthday, too. I don't even know if they know. But honestly, it doesn't matter. This is the first time I've had a party of any sort. It was usually just me, my mom, and dad with a cake and some ice cream. It never seemed to matter much because every kid goes out collecting candy on this day. They already did their trick or treating before they came here—I skipped it to help mom finish up preparing for the party.

The crowd thins, moving past me toward the front doors, and then, there he is. He's wearing one dangling earring, a white t-shirt with specks of red on it, a black jacket, jeans—tennis shoes, and a pair of sunglasses. I recognize him from the movie trailers. He's Michael from a new movie called *The Lost Boys*. It won't be out for a year or so, but everyone is already obsessed with it. Including me.

"You're a creature of the night, Michael," I quote as he approaches me, removing his sunglasses. He's given himself dark circles.

"I didn't expect anyone to know who I was," he jests.

"*The Lost Boys*? Vampires?" I tilt my head. "I can't wait until that movie comes out."

362

He grins. "We always get advanced screening reels at the theater. We can totally watch it early."

"Sweet!" I exclaim.

His eyes run the length of me.

My eyebrow arches. "I had no idea what to do, so mom did my makeup. I'm Death."

"I love it." He solidifies his support, turning beside me.

Shy comes walking up, and she's decked out in a black corset, a white tulle skirt, plenty of pearls and combat boots. A black leather jacket hugs her shoulders. Her hair's back to normal and she has an enormous bow wrapping it.

"Like a virgin," I blurt out.

She rolls her eyes.

"Sorry." I clear my throat, but she doesn't seem to be upset. I said it before thinking it might be inappropriate.

"Who are you supposed to be?" she asks.

"I didn't know what to do, so mom made me Death—or what she thinks he looks like."

"How do you know Death isn't a girl?"

I wrinkle my nose. "It would make more sense."

She slaps my arm and I laugh. "Kidding—sort of."

"Who are you?" she asks Keller.

He points at himself. "I'm Michael."

"Michael?" she asks.

"From *The Lost Boys*."

"That movie isn't even out yet."

He grins. "I know—but it looks cool."

She tilts her head. "True. I guess you are clever. Everyone, a year from now, will be like—remember when Keller was Michael at the Halloween party!?"

I snicker.

Vincent strolls up, with Evie by his side. He's wearing a white lab coat and carrying an oversized syringe with glowing green contents. He's also sporting a tie and wire-rimmed glasses.

"Reanimator?" I ask, and Vincent grins from ear to ear.

"Yes. Just let me know if anyone dies. I'll bring them back with a little bit of this." He wiggles the needle.

Evie is wearing a black wig that's braided and a black dress, tights, shoes and has a bag strapped to her.

"Who are you?" Shy asks.

She speaks in a monotone voice. "Wednesday Addams."

"That seems right," Keller adds.

We all nod in agreement.

I reach in my pocket and produce the small rubber duck she gave me. "Mom used this as inspiration when she did my makeup."

"How did you get Gothic Quacker?" Vincent asks, eyes wide.

Evie sighs. "I gave it to him, because I wanted to. He needed a pick me up."

I'm grateful and she knows it. I slip him back into my pocket.

"I guess we should go inside." I glance up at the house.

"Oh, wait! I have something for all of you."

Evie digs in her bag and pulls out a square piece of paper. It has four flaps on the front of it, each one with a different picture. One skull, one crystal ball, one moth and the last one is a spell book.

She slips her fingers in the slots on the bottom and squeezes. She holds it up to me. "You get to choose first, birthday boy."

I feel the heat flood my cheeks.

Her eyes sparkle. "Pick one—one of the pictures."

I stare at the paper in her hand. "Skull."

She pulls the folded origami square back and forth, whispering, "S-K-U-L-L," to count her moves.

She leans in. "Okay, pick a number."

I see one, two, five and six. "Um, I'll take number one."

She folds back the paper and reveals the words so I can see them.

I read it out loud, *Let your intuition guide you.*

"That's your fortune, and it's brilliant advice, don't you think?" she coos.

I swallow hard.

"Do me!" Vincent practically yells.

"Vincent—calm down," Evie growls while he tries to snatch it away from her.

We make our way toward the front door. But before we can reach it, Keller touches my arm and holds me back.

"I got you something. I thought I'd give it to you before we go inside and things get crazy."

"Crazy, here?" I laugh through it.

"Do you know the kids at school at all?" he asks.

I grimace.

He pulls out a plastic cassette case and hands it to me. I look down at it. He's written in marker on the outside.

Remember me

I narrow my eyes. "Remember you?" I whisper.

"As I am, right now."

"Are you planning on changing?"

He tilts his head. "We all change for the better. Right?"

I lick my lip and bite into it. It almost seems like an ominous warning, but I know he doesn't mean it that way. I expect him to be soft and romantic. This is his way of trying to show me how much he cares. I wish it didn't seem like a goodbye. I never want to say goodbye to him. I know that now. Even if he eventually changes and doesn't want to be with me anymore, I want to be around him—to see his face. Hear his voice. It saddens me. I sniffle.

He leans in. "Hey—you okay?" he asks.

"I love it. Thank you."

His worry lines fade. "Oh, good. I spent weeks collecting songs. I filled it, both sides." He proudly eyes the tape cassette, then me. "I didn't add a list. I want you to be surprised.

"It's perfect."

He stares at my lips and then clears his throat. "I guess we should—" He motions toward the front doors.

"Yeah," I agree as we make our way inside the house.

CHAPTER
FIFTY-SIX

KELLER WEST

We enter the house to Halloween music and chatter. Kids are scattered everywhere, in small groups. East's mom comes strolling down the stairs dressed in a sheer white dress with a white tank and leggings underneath. Her face is painted like a skull. She has a flower wreath on top of her head and she's barefoot.

She makes her way toward us and clasps her hands together. "Everyone came." Her eyes spark with excitement.

"Yeah—seems like it," East says.

She reaches in and takes my hand; her skin is hot to the touch, "I could never thank you enough for this."

I look at East then back to her. "I'd do anything for—" I pause.

She winks at me. "I know." She taps my hand, then lets it go.

She backs away and raises her hands. "Children! Children." She gets most of them to quiet down. "Welcome to The Mill House on this most blessed of days—Halloween!" A few claps break through. "And I know you might not be aware, but my darling son, East, will turn sixteen at five till midnight!"

That seems to liven things up. The chatter gets louder.

"No—there's plenty of food and drinks in the kitchen. Please eat and don't forget to drink! There's a whole bowl of Witches Brew. I expect it to be gone! I guarantee once you take a sip, you'll beg for more. I don't want any of it left—do you hear me?" She glides around the room, eyeing as many kids as she can.

I watch them make their way toward the kitchen like she's bewitched them. I stay behind with East, Evie, Shy and Vincent.

"Thirsty?" I ask, but no one seems to be interested in getting in line.

"I think I'll wait," Vincent says.

"I agree—besides, I can show off my new moves." He does a decent impression of a robot. The music seems to get louder and the song changes. Shy ends up dancing with Vincent while Evie messes with her recorder.

East eyes her. I lean into his side. "You know how she is."

"Oh, I know. It's fine," he claims, but I hope he's being truthful. I just want him to have a great birthday. I know how upset he is about his dad leaving. He grabs my hand and pulls me through the crowd. No one seems to notice. I follow him up the stairs and we end up in the hallway. He spins me, pinning me to the wall. I grin before he leans in. His mouth hovers an inch from mine. I can feel his breath on my face. I let out a sigh. He won't let me move or kiss him. It's torturous.

"East."

His eyebrow cocks. "It's my birthday, so I get to do what I want, right?"

I'm consumed with how sweet he'd taste if he'd only let me kiss him.

He backs up and pulls me off the wall. We end up in his room. He places his boombox on the bed and motions me to join him as he crawls on the other side of it. He rests on his knees, so I do the same on the opposite side, facing him. He reaches over and grabs two sets of headphones and plugs them in, handing me one set. I put them on as he shoves the tape in the cassette deck and presses play. We stare at each other as the first song comes on. It's "Crazy For You" by Madonna. We stare into each other's eyes as the words envelope us.

He reaches in and takes my hand. I move up on my knees and we end up facing each other while hovering over the boombox.

There are so many things I want to say and sometimes I can't find the words, so I hope this tape helps him understand how much he means to me and how grateful I am to have him in my life.

We lean in, our lips so close—I want him, even knowing every kid from school is downstairs and could sneak by at any moment.

But I don't care.

I love August East. I love him now, then and forever. I want the whole world to know. I lean in, letting my lips brush against his. I know the door's open. I still don't care. I think I could be standing in the middle of the room downstairs, surrounded by my classmates, and still be staring into his eyes.

I draw his hand in and place it against my heart. He glances at the door. I shake my head.

"I love you," I mouth the words to him.

His lips move, "I love you, too."

"Always," I add.

"Always."

The song ends and I narrow my eyes. I hear something. Then I feel a vibration in his bed. I scramble off the bed as he does. We both toss the headphones toward the boombox and it's then we realize what's going on.

Wailing.

I rush to the door and East stops me as we both stare at the painting across from my door. The faces are now skeletal and the child—the child is missing. I narrow my eyes.

"What the hell is going on?" I demand.

He shakes his head. "Come on." He rushes down the hallway and I follow. Fearful of what we'll find, but knowing we have to go.

CHAPTER
FIFTY-SEVEN

AUGUST EAST

I stop at the top of the staircase and hold up a finger to my lips as Keller steps up next to me. The foyer is empty, and it's dead silent, like no one is home. But where has everyone gone? It was full of kids when we went upstairs and we were only gone maybe a half hour, tops.

But something's changed. I move down the staircase and see the fire is nearly out, but it was new when we went to my bedroom. It takes longer than that to burn away the pile of wood.

I move across the foyer and peer into the living room. It's empty. My brow furrows.

"I don't understand," Keller whispers behind me.

I see a flash of light at the end of the hallway. The frosted door leading to the poison garden seems to be glowing in an amber hue. Like a flame.

I shake my head, moving past the kitchen and see cups lying everywhere. I crush one with my foot. It seems like everyone dropped their paper cups and left them. I take another step toward the end of the hallway, then feel a hard tug on my arm. I'm pulled into a closet. Keller gets shoved in right along with me. The light comes on and Evie, Vincent and Shy are standing there with terrified looks on their faces.

My eyes widen. "What are you guys doing?"

"Hiding," Shy answers before rubbing the sides of her arms.

"From what?" Keller asks.

Vincent shakes his head. "Where the hell have you guys been?"

Keller's eyebrow cocks, so I take charge. "We went upstairs, to my room to listen to the cassette tape he made for me—for my birthday."

"It's been hours," Vincent whispers. His voice is raspy, like he's been yelling.

Confusion wrinkles my brow. "Um, no. We just finished one song."

Evie shakes her head. "Listen—I know it sounds crazy, but you've both been gone for at least three hours."

"Bullshit," Keller says.

Shy sniffles. Her makeup is smeared from crying. I try to ignore it, but it makes my muscles tense. I don't
374

know what's happened, but whatever it was, it can't be good.

"It isn't—and you don't know what we've been going through. It wants to kill us," she adds.

My eyes narrow. "It?"

He points toward the door. "We just went up—"

Shy steps in and touches his arm. "Listen, Keller. You've been gone for hours—I know it doesn't seem possible, but it is, trust me. I wouldn't lie to you." She stares him down and his lips remain parted, but he's stopped arguing his point.

"Okay—say we have, what's been going on?" he asks.

"Man, where do I start?" Vincent rubs the side of his head.

"At the beginning." Keller steps into a tight circle as we all whisper to each other.

Evie raises a hand. "Okay, you both went upstairs and Vincent and Shy were dancing and I was trying to get my recorder to work, but it seemed like the batteries were dead. I popped the back off and they were more than dead, they were corroded. The acid had leaked out of them. I dropped one on the floor and leaned down to get it, and that's when it started."

I take a short breath. "What started?"

"The first kid fell, then the second, and their bodies moved, like something was dragging them away. I stayed low, and saw at least two more hit the ground before someone screamed, but by then they'd all drank it."

"Drank what, Evie?"

Shy steps in. "The Witches Brew—in the kitchen. It had to be in that bowl."

I shake my head, none of this makes sense. "My mom made that for the party."

Vincent leans in closer to me. "Dude—that's not your mom." His fingers are up and separated now. He may be in a full-blown panic.

I feel a chill rush through me, but I can't comprehend what he's saying. "Vincent, what the hell are you talking about? It's my mom, and where is she?"

A knock comes to the door, and we all stand frozen. We back away, pressing our backs against the wall. I can see a shadow move across the base of the door.

"Darling?"

It's my mom's voice. I part my lips, ready to answer her, but Evie slaps her hand over my mouth, preventing me from calling out to her.

"Come out and dance with me, please?" she asks.

A tear rolls down my cheek, but Evie holds on. I feel Keller's hand slip in mine.

"Please—my beautiful boy—I'm lonely." Her voice lowers. It doesn't sound like her. It's hollow. Evil.

I swallow hard before reaching for the doorknob, but Keller stops me. I back away. It's killing me.

Suddenly smoke trickles in. I cover my mouth, as does everyone else. Vincent feels along the wall, but there's no way out of here but forward. It intensifies. Whatever is out there has started a fire to force us out. I gasp—everyone else is fighting to breathe. I panic and we all spill out into the hallway, piled on top of each other, but there's no fire or smoke. I narrow my eyes when I hear cackling. We stand, helping each other up one by one. Then I catch something out of the corner of my eye crawling up the wall. I lean in. It's a woman in a white dress. She scurries onto the ceiling.

Vincent yells. "Nope!" and rushes across the hallway and into the kitchen, grasping Evie's hand. She's leaning back, trying to get a good look at what appears to be my mom but isn't. She yelps as Vincent jerks her out of the hallway and into the kitchen next to him. She slaps his arm, and he lifts his hands, grimacing at her.

I step forward, as the creature twists half its torso like it's made of taffy, and stares down on me. It smiles, showing off rows of rotted teeth.

"What the hell?" Keller spits out.

I shake my head. "I—oh shit!"

It comes rushing across the ceiling in our direction,

so we run into the kitchen, joining Evie and Vincent, but Shy is left there, frozen in fear.

Keller reaches out and grabs her, pushing her into the kitchen at me, but then a bony hand wraps his throat and lifts him off the ground. He yelps, kicking his feet as he's lifted off the ground. I rush out to see this thing carrying him along while he claws at the hand wrapping around his throat. He can't breathe. I panic, rush back into the kitchen and grab a butcher's knife. I run back out with it held out in front of me, but see his legs kicking before the door slams at the end of the hallway.

"For shit's sake!" I yell, chest rising and falling. I try to catch my breath. My hands try to steady the knife as it shakes in front of me.

"Dude, I tried to tell you!" Vincent exclaims.

"I just—okay." I try to collect myself. "We have to go in there." I point at the door to the garden with my knife.

Suddenly, I hear Keller cry out in pain.

I run down the hallway, heart pounding in my ears, knowing that whatever happens, I have to save him—even if I can't save myself.

CHAPTER FIFTY-EIGHT

KELLER WEST

East's mom stands before me, mouth agape with sharpened rows of teeth. She finally releases me and I drop to the ground, realizing that I'm not alone. Every kid is lying in this garden—eyes wide open, some piled on top of each other with what appears to be blackened vines wrapping their necks and other parts of their bodies.

I rub my throat, sucking in a good amount of air to fill my lungs. It burns as I kick away from her, then peer up to see that I'm beneath the tree. The one East has always hated. I'm getting it now. I hate it too.

The tree is moist with sap—red and oozing down the side of the trunk. It appears to be bleeding, but that isn't possible, is it? I feel a vibration beneath me and more blackened vines break through the cobblestone and begin wrapping my ankle. It twists up my leg. I feel it tighten as it creeps its way up my body, finding my neck. I claw at it, but refuse to cry out in pain. I won't give this thing, whatever it is, the pleasure of watching me suffer.

She tilts her head. Her face is still covered in make-up, making her look like a skull. She's matched East's make up.

Her darkened eyes search mine. "He'll come for you," she hisses.

I shake my head, "No—he won't. I'll tell him to run." I fight to speak. The vine loosens as she jumps forward and slams her hand against my right leg. Her fingers dig into my jeans, breaking through the fabric, and her sharpened nails cut into my flesh. I fight as long as I can, but then cry out from the pain. She leans back, folding her back in two, and opens her mouth toward the glass ceiling. She lets out a shriek of approval before removing her hand and tearing away more of my flesh. I jolt forward, gripping my leg. The blood is pooling.

The door flies open, and East rushes in with a butcher's knife in his hand. His eyes search for me. I grit my teeth, trying to stop the bleeding. His expression changes from fear to anger—then sadness when he realizes I've been wounded.

"Get away from him!" he warns, crying out like a Viking going to war.

His mom turns and laughs, "I told you he'd come for you—did I not, Keller West?"

East moves closer, holding the knife out in front of him. Vincent, Evie and Shy rush in behind him and they form a line, East heading them up.

The woman lifts her hand and flicks her fingers. Black vines shoot out of the ground and grab Vincent, Evie and Shy by the ankles and lift them into the air, slinging them around like rag dolls before slamming them to the ground. All three moan, but they're still alive.

Vincent struggles to break free. "I can't believe I thought you were hot!"

"Vincent!" Evie yells. "Not now!"

I feel the vine tighten around my neck as my leg continues to bleed, then the blood moves away from me and toward the tree. It inches up the side of the trunk, mingling with the moisture.

The vines drag Evie, Shy, and Vincent toward the tree. They claw at the cobblestone, fighting to break free. It must need blood to become stronger.

"Hey!" East screams at her. She turns, spreading her bony fingers and shrieking at him. He draws back and throws the knife as hard as he can. It slams into her forehead and the woman tilts backward. I can hear bones cracking up her spine. The knife is embedded in her forehead and black ooze seeps from the fresh wound. Her arms twist at her side and she lets out a terrible sound, like an animal being slaughtered.

The vines loosen around my neck, but my leg is still bleeding. I'm feeling lightheaded. I know I've lost too much blood, but all I care about are my friends, and East, getting out of here alive. I don't have time to rationalize what's happening. It's do or die.

East rushes toward me, taking a knee and eyeing my leg. He grimaces. "It's going to be okay. I promise, Keller. I won't let anything happen to you."

I'm amazed at how level-headed he seems to be amid all of this chaos. Anyone else would crumble, but not him.

"Are you okay?"

He nods.

I point behind him. "I mean, you just stabbed your mom in the forehead with a butcher's knife."

His lips purse. "It's not my mom."

He pulls out his shirt and tears off a piece along the bottom of it and ties it above the cut on my leg. He reaches down and grabs a stick and places it in the knotted cloth and begins twisting it until the bleeding ceases. His hands are wet with my blood and I can't feel my leg, but at least I'm no longer bleeding to death. He leans in and cups my face. His tears streak his makeup. "Everything will be okay—just stay with me—please?" he begs.

"Always," I say with the last bits of strength that I have.

I hear groaning and see Vincent moving—then Evie. Shy shakes her head. They're all alive. All of them.

I have no idea what this thing is. All I know is everything I believed before I stepped in this house has changed. I think the only one of us who knew there was something more was Evie, and we played it off like she was just infatuated with ghost stories. But this was more than that. Much more.

East leans in, pressing his forehead against mine, but then he gasps. Falling back and pushing himself onto his feet, he reaches down and removes the butcher's knife that's been buried in his side. He hisses, dropping it to the floor and turns to face his mom, who's now back on her feet. The hole in her forehead is still oozing like the maple tree behind me.

"That wasn't very nice of you," she spits out at him.

"Maybe don't show up and ruin Halloween," he snaps.

"It's my favorite time of the year—it's a powerful night, you know? The veil between the living and dead is at its thinnest."

"Thanks for the history lesson, now what the hell do you want?"

She catches movement out of the corner of her eye and lifts a finger, wagging it back and forth. "Nuh uh uh." The blackened vines wrap Vincent's arms and legs and start pulling him apart.

"Seriously?" he yelps.

"Hey." East snaps his fingers, and he has the knife in his hand once again. This time, he stabs her in the side of the head. It digs in deep—going about three inches. He stumbles back and his mom hisses like a snake.

"Would you stop doing that?"

She grabs the handle and pulls it out of her temple, bringing a little bit of brain with it. She wipes it off the end and promptly eats it like a snack.

East stands tight-lipped. I grimace. Vincent rolls over and starts gagging.

She sneers at him. "I can't believe you like horror movies."

He lifts his hands. "Movies being the key word! Not whatever you are!"

She takes one step toward him and East distracts her. "What are you?"

The woman tilts her head. "Your mommy."

He shakes his head. "You're not my mom."

"Oh—that's a shame. I like you, East, I always have. We've had so much fun together during the fire in your hometown—which we started, by the way—and
384

now, in Whynot. They're like pigs to slaughter—you know. These humans. Easy to lure in with a pretty face and a little leg." She lifts the bottom of her dress higher and higher. But East refuses to look.

She rolls her eyes. "Boring."

East presses his hand against his side. I can see the blood covering his fingers. The woman's eyes lower. "Oh dear, did I go too deep?" she asks.

"Where are my parents?"

The woman grins, her blackened teeth exposed, "Mmm, well, I guess it's no matter if you know the truth now, is it? In these final moments. You'll be sixteen soon, and all mine." She claps her hands like an excited child.

I fight to hold the tourniquet on my leg. My fingers are covered in blood. I know if I let go, then I'll bleed to death, but I can't let him do this alone. I know I only have one choice—and it will mean the end for me. But dying for someone I love is worth it.

Memories float through my mind's eyes. Every moment I've spent with him. From the last life to this one. I see his smiling face—feel his kiss. Draw his body close to mine. I hear his whispers in my ear and feel his breath on my neck. I understand now that Maggie was right. It was all true. I've loved August East for more than one lifetime. He has always been a part of me.

The best part.

The only part that mattered.

I adjust myself, pushing myself up onto the bench and holding the stick tight. I think about the years I've had in football and appreciate them more. Maybe my dad was a blessing and not a curse after all.

CHAPTER FIFTY-NINE

AUGUST EAST

I stand before what resembles my mom as she's changed—shedding the sharpened, rotting teeth and black veins running across her arms and legs. Now she's trying to appeal to me as someone I've loved my entire life, making it harder as I grip my side and try to stop the bleeding. I refuse to fall. I can't move out of the way. Keller is behind me. She can't have him, now or ever.

"I guess you should know what I am." Her voice sounds like many, but she clears her throat and continues to talk, sounding like my mom now, which makes it even harder. I adjust my weight. The bleeding won't stop and the pain is intensifying.

Her eyes lower. "I could fix that, you know." She snaps her fingers.

I swallow hard. "Tell me what happened."

"You had the answers all along. You see, Charles was a curious creature. He was obsessed with eternal life. That's why he grew this garden." She waves her and my eyes follow. I see the hemlock and nightshade mixed in with the roses. "He would sip poisoned tea—little by little, adding more to it. Over time, he built up a tolerance, but it came at a cost. His body weakened, but his mind—oh, it sharpened like the edge of a knife." She lifts the butcher's knife, dripping with my blood, and runs it across her tongue. She makes a sipping noise. I grimace. Her tongue is now split in two, like a snake. She wags it at me, but regains her composure.

"And?" I ask.

She tilts her head, lowering the knife in her hand and lets it fall to the ground, the blade makes a clinking sound against the stone. But I guess she doesn't need it now.

"And, well, it caught up with him—this morbid obsession with life and death. He began trying to summon dark things. Things like me, to do his bidding, but what he doesn't understand is a demon doesn't have a master—we just require a host—a puppet, as you will." She does a little twirl, lifting her bloodied hands above her head like a ballerina.

"Tell me," I demand. I'm trying so hard to stay upright. My pant leg is now moist with blood. She points to my wound and grins. "I guess I should hurry up!"

I scowl at her.

"Anyway," she rolls her hand, "his only child was a curious thing, like him, but with a little nudging," she pushes her hands out, "I got it to try some of these delicious plants in the garden." She grins—it's unnatural and sends a chill up my spine. "But it didn't go very well. The child died right over there." She points at the tree and makes a face with her tongue hanging out. "Then Charles' wife found the small thing and decided to follow along. I'd been talking to her too. Whispering in her ear while Charles tooled away on his selfish little project, ya know? So, it wasn't that hard, but then Charles—I did mention he was selfish, correct? Anyway, he fell to his knees all dramatic, in despair," she falls down before me, clutching her chest, "and drew it out, right here. The incantation he needed to summon me—and oh, did I come." She closes her eyes and sways on her knees. "The tree became a portal fed by their souls. I entered the child and brought that creature to life, but it was hard to be good. Eventually, I grew tired of Charles; although I loved him, I had to be free. He had me trapped here with those pesky pentagrams. And then—oh, he did the unthinkable. He tried to bury me alive! In that mausoleum in the cemetery out back. Along with him—can you believe it? But I escaped, as all things eventually do, when I crawled inside of his body. I almost made it out, too, but he was a tricky one and painted that pentagram in the living room. Then took enough poison to finally kill off his rotting corpse."

She pauses, like she's uncomfortable with the memory.

"I was beginning to think that I would be stuck in this house forever, in that damned wretched tree. But all they have to do is taste me, you see? First, it was Paul—who was able to gain your trust, and then, once done with him," she flicks her fingers and the bark of the tree peels back and it ejects Paul's body. He slides across the cobblestone. I gasp, but she isn't done, "it only took one lonely night for me to pass from him to your mother."

I grit my teeth. "Fuck you," I hiss.

Her eyebrow cocks. "Language."

I fight to stand as the blood continues to seep through my fingers. I know I don't have that much time left before I pass out.

"Everything would've been fine except for the meddling." She flicks her hand, and the tree ejects another body. I see Brian James on the floor. He's covered in red sap, just like Paul. I can't tell if they're dead or not. Another body comes flying out from the thick trunk of the tree and hits the ground. This time it's Ty Miller. "But, truth be told. I needed them. I just chose the most annoying of the bunch. You see, the tree is a gateway that Charles opened for me, but it needs souls and blood—and it finally had enough."

My heart leaps into my throat.

"What happened to my dad?"

Her evil laughter rolls in the back of her throat.

"What did you do?" I cry out before my gaze lands on the tree in horror. I can see my dad's pale face inside the tree.

I turn to face her, fist clenched, fighting back the tears.

"You are so special, East. You have a darkness inside of you. Together we can do such amazing things. I'll give you everlasting life this time—if you'll just allow me."

"This time?"

"You don't believe in reincarnation? Oh dear. Well, I've been chasing you from one life to the next. I need you. You need me. I can take away all of that self-doubt and misery. Make you feel like you belong. Give you strength. A home. A place you belong. I can stop that terrible feeling of loss. You know the one. The guilt that churns inside your gut and eats away at you like a belly full of worms? It's the way you never feel like you can keep anything good. I know how you feel. I know you want to be with him—with Keller. You've always wanted that and I'm the only one who can make that happen. I can give you that gift. I can give you love. But you can't have it without me. You have a curse in your blood. Something Charles passed down to you—and to your mother. When he summoned me, he cursed you all."

I close my eyes. Her words are like a siren's song. I've always felt lost. Out of place. Awkward when I shouldn't. She's trying to seduce me with the deepest longings I have. She's chipping away at my fears. I have always felt guilty. Like I'm the reason bad things keep happening. I've never felt worthy of having love. Especially something as special as what I have with Keller. I've tried to sabotage it all along by denying him—denying us—being with Shy. I've made it nearly impossible for him to want me, and yet he still does. He's forgiven me and accepts me as I am.

"And him—you can have him—forever, I will stop taking him away from you if you just let me in." She taps my chest. I know she wants my body. She needs me to surrender.

I turn to Keller, but his face is taut with disbelief. He shakes his head as I search his eyes for understanding. All I've ever wanted was to be with him. I know this now.

"Besides, I'm tired of watching you whine every time he dies. It's exhausting."

I look down at my side. Keller shakes his head.

"I love you," I whisper, while turning back to face her. Maybe I can control this thing—this demon that

Charles summoned? Maybe I can save everyone this time? I can save all of my friends.

Maybe this is the only choice I have.

"How do I know you're telling the truth?" I hiss, tasting the iron on my tongue.

"Come." She grabs my hand. I wince as she drags me out the side door and into the cemetery. She lets go and begins tearing away thick vines to reveal a tombstone. I step forward and my eyes widen. I see Keller's name. She does the same to the next one, and again—his name is etched on each stone. Again and again, the stones have my name or his. I look toward the sky. The sun is gone, and the moon has risen.

"Yes—you know this is the only way," she whispers.

I nearly stumble. The bleeding hasn't stopped. I'm sure this cut to my side is her insurance plan. Even if I say no, she'll tell me I'll die anyway, and for nothing, leaving everyone I have left in danger.

"Will my mom still be here?" I swallow some blood.

She looks down the front of her body. "I may be able to piece this thing back together."

"Will I know her?" I plead.

She tilts her head. "You will know everything. From the beginning to the end, my dearest, if you just allow me to slip inside."

I take a slow breath. "What do I have to do?"

She steps in and removes my hand. I gasp. A thick black sludge oozes from the side of her mouth. It smells like death.

She opens her mouth, leaning in like she's going to kiss me. I close my eyes. Afraid of what will come next, but knowing this is the only way out.

CHAPTER SIXTY

KELLER WEST

I fight to stand, holding onto the stick as tightly as I can. My leg is numb, but I've regained feeling in the other one. I know what this thing did to my leg has ended my football career, but I don't care. In some ways, it feels like a blessing.

I spot the knife and rush over to cut through the decaying vines that are continuing to wrap around Shy's body. I cry out as I fight to set her free. Finally, I succeed and she sits up and wraps her arms around my neck. I have to pry her fingers from me. I rush over to Vincent, then Evie—they both fight for air.

"Go get help!"

The woman, who claims to be a demon summoned by Charles Porter, has dragged East out of the garden. I stumble forward and feel a hand on my arm. Vincent helps me stand; Evie joins him. She has a gash across her cheek that matches the one on his forehead.

"I have to get outside."

"Not alone you don't. This is a team," Evie says proudly.

We make our way out the door and deeper into the cemetery. I can hear voices and we come to a stop close enough for me to see the woman is removing East's hand from his side. She cups his face. "It's just one little kiss and it'll be all over," she hisses.

I rush in, knocking him out of the way, and press my lips against hers. I feel a numbness sweep through me as the woman struggles to break free, but I won't let her go. Finally, every bit of the black ooze seeping from her mouth has entered mine. I choke, grasping at my throat. I stumble backward. I feel a fire churning in the pit of my stomach, but then I fall to my knees and grind my teeth. Every muscle feels like it's tearing from my bones. I fall back and East catches me in his arms. I gasp for air as the bubbling ooze lingers in my throat. I cough and some of it spills out onto my cheeks.

I can barely breathe. I'm drowning in whatever this is. I can feel my body dying. I reach up with a trembling hand and touch East's face.

"What have you done?" He fights through the tears.

"I promised. I'll always protect you."

He shakes his head. My vision blurs and then I'm blinded.

"East—are you there?" I call out. "I can't see you! Where are you?"

I can hear someone crying. I think it's Evie.

I tilt my head. "It's okay, Evie—it's okay. Everything will be okay." I arch my back as the pain sweeps through me. My heart skips a beat and then another. I groan. My hand twitches. I'm losing control of myself. This demon is tearing me to shreds from the inside out. It doesn't want to be inside of me, but I'll fight to keep it right here. I'd rather die than see it go free and cause any more harm.

"Mom—Mom? Wake up, Mom—please?" East can barely speak, he's grief stricken. I know the demon has killed her. I can't see her body, but I know it's there. East trembles against me.

I move my lips, desperate to console him, but nothing comes out. I want so badly to tell him I love him one last time. That everything will be okay. To bury my body deep and keep it there. To use the books Charles left behind and find a way to make sure this thing never hurts anyone again.

East rocks me in his lap. "I've loved you for so long, I don't remember where I begin and you end, Keller West."

I feel a hand against my cheek. It's warm and comforting, but the icy chill is rushing through my veins. My heart skips another beat and I fight to get in one last breath. My body shakes. My lips quiver. Death has come for me, but what kind of death will it be? Will I know this thing is inside of me? Will it torment me forever in my dreams?

And then I feel it—his lips crashing into mine.

My body warms, blood rushes through my veins. My heartbeat strengthens as he holds onto me, taking every bit of the poison that's consumed me. I moan, struggling to break free, and finally I'm strong enough to push him away, but it's too late. August has allowed the demon to pass from my body to his. He cries out in pain. Pressing his hand against his stomach. I know how he feels. It kills me to watch him suffer. He stumbles to his feet. Vincent and Evie move toward him. Shy comes rushing out and shrieks when she sees the black ooze trickling from the edge of his mouth.

He reaches up and touches it. His trembling hand lifts. His eyes nearly roll back in his head.

He takes a haggard breath and looks down at me. His eyes are changing color. What was once green and hazel is now darkening, nearly black.

He tilts his head.

"I don't know if I can hold it back," he warns.

I push myself up, limping toward him. My leg is

no longer bleeding, but the injury remains bone deep.

"East—what have you done?" I beg him to explain.

"I'm the only one who can survive it," he admits.

He looks at all of us and then turns, making his way to the mausoleum. He climbs the steps and turns back to face us. He pulls out a small bit of hemlock and stares at it in his hand. "I grabbed something to help me sleep. I'm going to take this demon with me."

"East, wait. Please wait—don't do this," I beg.

His eyes lock onto mine. "It won't let me die. I know that now. But I will go to sleep forever. Just promise me that you'll visit from time to time. Okay? Live a long and happy life. Find love and hang onto it. I'm sorry it couldn't be me."

He shoves the piece of hemlock in his mouth and pushes on the door.

I narrow my eyes, rushing forward as he slams the door shut, locking it from the inside.

I fall against it, beating my fists against the door, fighting to breathe through the grief.

"East— Why— Why— No, why! Please come back to me! Please!" I cry out like a wounded animal.

CHAPTER SIXTY-ONE

KELLER WEST

I put the car in park and stare up at the house. It's been fifteen years since everything happened on that Halloween night.

I wouldn't let the town tear The Mill House down; instead, I contacted the historical society, and, with Evie's help, we were able to protect it. Making it a protected relic. No one understood why, except a select few.

I eventually bought it, when I could afford to, and even though I don't live here, I check on it from time to time. As I promised. I have a woman who keeps it clean and preps it when I return for an occasional weekend here and there.

She doesn't believe in ghosts and is the only one who agreed to take the job. I'm glad she doesn't spook easily. I needed a guardian to watch over the house while I was away.

I step out and draw my coat in around my neck. It's October 31st. His birthday. He'd be 31 now. I'm 32 but I feel much older. The years have worn on me, but I've kept my hope locked away inside my heart.

Only East has the key. He took it with him when he sacrificed himself for us.

For me.

I take a step, and the limp is still there. It gets worse in the Fall, when the cold air sinks into my bones. I usually grab my cane, but I left it behind. Maybe I'm a fool. I don't know. The injury the demon inflicted on my leg ended my football career once and for all, and I slipped back into a normal existence. As normal as it could be after what happened here.

I sigh.

The house still looks the same. I didn't change a thing. I wanted everything as it was. Even his room sits dormant. The boombox and abandoned headphones lie on the bed. The posters are still on the walls. It's like it's frozen in time, and in many ways, so am I. I've never been able to move forward from him.

Refusing to love. Refusing to allow anyone close to me. I walled up my heart and have no regrets. None.

"Keller?"

I turn to see Shy running toward me. Vincent isn't far behind. She wraps her arms around my waist and holds on tight. I hold her against me—remembering how she always felt so safe. In a lot of ways, Shylo Martin was home for me before East came along. I still love her as much as I did then, but we don't talk as much as we used to. My work doesn't allow for much socializing; in many ways, also a blessing.

I want to be the best at what I do and I finally, after years of trying, feel like I am. I guess that's why I've come home—to stay, I hope.

I study Shylo's face. She's aged, but she's more beautiful now. Vincent got a haircut. It's not as unruly as it was throughout high school. I came back to watch his speech as valedictorian. He was clever. It made me laugh. Shy tucks her hair behind her ear. It's longer now, but she kept those beautiful curls and it makes me smile. Her wedding band catches what little light is left in the day. Vincent steps up and shakes my hand and then wraps his arm around her shoulder.

"How's the little one?" I ask.

Shy looks up at Vincent and grins. "Just like his dad and not so little now. He's five and wears a helmet when he's doing anything."

I chuckle.

They got married before finishing college. I was glad to see Shy ended up with someone who treats her right. Vincent always loved her and always will. Shy is much like me. We may seem confident, but I don't think we ever felt quite worthy of the status we had, or still have, in Whynot.

"Hey!" I turn to see Evie getting out of a cab. She reaches back in and grabs her oversized bag, fighting to get it out of the backseat. I run in to help her, but she wrestles it free. She turns to grin up at me. She's also aged—but in a good way. Her hair is long now and pulled up into a messy bun atop her head. She has a pencil shoved through it.

"Hey you." The cab pulls away. She drops her bag on the street and hugs me. I moan.

"Sorry," she backs away, "I just missed you. Talking on the phone isn't the same, ya know?"

"How was the tour?" I ask.

She sighs. "Exhausting and good. It's a double-edged sword."

"I see the books are going great. I checked them out online. Number one best seller, huh?" I want to celebrate her wins. Evie never believed she'd have so many people who love her, but they do. It took her a few years to embrace it, but now she does a book tour every year to talk to her fans and sign her books. She's written five so far, all about ghosts, demons and possessions. People love them. I do, too. She's a brilliant writer.

She pulls her latest novel out of her bag and hands it to me, "I signed it."

I stare at the cover and read the title.

'*The End of August*' is staring back at me.

I grin, clutching it to my chest. "Thanks."

"I want to thank you for being cool about me writing and releasing this book. We all know it's a true story, but the world thinks I took liberties with what happened here."

"I trusted you'd do it right."

Her gaze softens, "Of course. He's a hero, ya know?"

We all form a straight line and stare up at the house.

"Are you ready?" she asks.

"Yeah—I am."

I unlock the gate, and the chain falls away. No one will come here now after all that happened that night. I appreciate that because I don't want them here. The reporters said it was a case of a woman losing her mind when her husband left her and then tried to kill all the kids in the town at the Halloween party. Then she killed herself and her son. But the kids in town didn't die. East's mom didn't put enough poison in the punch to kill them. I often wonder if there was enough left of Rosetta in there that ruined the demon's plans. I think I'm right. A mother's love is a bond you can rarely break. She loved East and I think she also saved the kids by not putting enough poison in the punch. It was her last gift to everyone before the demon killed her while moving out of her body and into mine.

The kids woke up dazed and confused. They didn't remember a thing, but once the police got involved, everything came to light. Mr. Rider, Brian James, Ty Miller, Steven East and Rosetta all lost their lives here, and that will never be forgotten.

Evie tilts her head, "I still don't agree with the story we gave them about East—I mean, his mom put him in the food?"

Vincent grimaces. "I'm sorry! It was all I could think of. I mean, we couldn't say, *hey, a demon crawled out of his mom and into him in some black ooze.*"

"Technically, it crawled out of me and into him," I correct him.

Shy clears her throat. I don't speak about him. It's too painful. I guess I could've buried that night and moved away for good, but I could never do that knowing he's back there—locked away in a deep sleep.

"Okay. I guess we should go inside." I resign to the idea of standing on the street forever.

I can't linger on these memories. They'll wreck me.

I climb the steps and unlock the door. I enter the house and it's like stepping back in time. Nothing's changed. The fire's even lit.

The woman I hired to keep this place clean steps

out of the kitchen and waves. She's always so cheerful. Her smile reminds me of Steven.

"Mr. West! You've come home."

"Yes, finally," I say.

"The food is stocked in the refrigerator. I went to the grocery store for you. I bought milk, coffee, everything you need. I even made a nice chunky stew."

Everyone grimaces but me. I don't want to hurt her feelings. She's been amazing. I don't plan on letting her go. I'd like for her stay on with me. I know I'll need her help.

I place a hand on her shoulder. "Thank you—go home. Enjoy the holidays. I'll see you in January."

"Thank you."

She gives everyone a quick glance before slipping her coat on and then pauses at the front door. Her bright eyes land on me. "This house needed you, Mr. West."

I take a slow breath and she slips out, closing the door behind her.

"Anyone hungry?" I ask.

They all speak in unison. "No."

I chuckle under my breath. I'm sure no one wants anything to do with stew, now or ever. East's mom had the refrigerator full with it. Even the freezer was packed to the brim. It's just one more reason why I think she was fighting as hard as she could. It's heartbreaking that she didn't make it. But I know she can rest easy knowing all those kids didn't die like the demon planned.

We walk down the hallway, past the closet we all hid in together, and then out into the garden. The tree is now gone and a beautiful fountain sits in its place. The water is bubbling. The sound is nice and peaceful. It's of a woman with a small child sitting on her lap. She's holding an open book, and the child is smiling. I thought it was appropriate. I commissioned it. In many ways, I feel like it's a fitting tribute to East and his mom—as well as Charles' wife and their child. It was here that they all met their fates. But I feel differently about life and death now. Everything has changed for me. I'm at peace with who I am.

I pick some roses from the garden and hand one to each of my friends. We exit the side door and walk through the cemetery. We follow the winding path past the tombstones that have been covered up with fresh ivy. I planted it here to hide our names on the stones. It was just one less thing I wanted to explain to the detective. I spent a few days with him. We all did, answering questions about what happened.

Evie, Shy and Vincent all told him they drank the punch and fell asleep with the rest of the kids from school. I had to explain how East's mom attacked me with a knife and cut my leg. I also told him she

407

admitted to killing her husband and the rest of them—including East. I had to agree with Vincent, who told him East's body would never be found because his mom put him in the food she served at the party. We got rid of all of it, just to be safe.

We end up at the end of the pathway.

I tilt my head, cracking my neck.

I approach the mausoleum and place the rose on the steps. They all follow me, doing the same.

Vincent cracks his fingers and Shy digs her heel into the ground.

"Are you sure you can do this?" Vincent asks me.

I take a short breath and release it. "I know I can."

"So, we go in—kick this demon's ass, bring East back, then what?" Vincent asks.

Evie rolls her eyes. "We'll worry about that after we get him, Vincent."

"I just wanted to know what the plan is." he whines.

"It's okay. Everything will be fine," I assure him.

I unbutton my coat and drop it to the ground.

Shy touches my arm.

I look at her. "It's time."

I approach the door and place my hand against it. It's always warm, no matter what time of the year it is. I pause for a moment. I know I can do this.

I reach into my pocket and retrieve what I need.

408

"He's going to be pissed at you," Vincent says while laughing.

Evie leans forward. "Vincent—shut up!"

"Do you have the ax?" I ask him.

"Yes," he replies.

I turn with a bible in one hand and holy water in the other. My white collar is now strapped against my neck. The corner of my lip curls.

"He'll just have to get over it."

Thank you so much for taking this journey with me! Please remember to review this book online. Even a few lines will do.

And you never know, we may return to Whynot someday, just to see what they're doing now.

Xoxo,
Rue

DON'T FORGET TO REVIEW THIS BOOK!

Rue Volley is a USA Today Bestselling Author and award-winning screenwriter who is best known for creating compelling storylines with a multitude of twists and turns that leave her readers virtually speechless.

She specializes in paranormal romances that include otherworldly characters who, regardless of their supernatural abilities, feel oddly familiar, or in other words, human. This, coupled with her easy reading style, a wicked sense of humor, and excellent world-building skills, has garnered her a fiercely loyal fan base over the past decade who support her regardless of what genre she chooses to write in.

Connect with Rue on Facebook, TikTok, Instagram, and Bookbub.

Don't forget to follow her on Amazon so you'll know when she releases her new books!

Made in the USA
Monee, IL
10 October 2022